STONE OF LEGENDS

Forged of Bone

Supernatural Institute

Fated by Starlight

Born by Moonlight

Hunted by Firelight

Kissed by Shadowlight

Supernatural Community

Magic in Light

Power in Darkness

Dragons in Fire

Angel in Embers

Supernatural Standalones

Beast of Shadows

Links to all of Krista's books may be found on her website.

www.kristastreet.com

N
S
NELIVE SEA
THE
SILTEN
CONTINENT

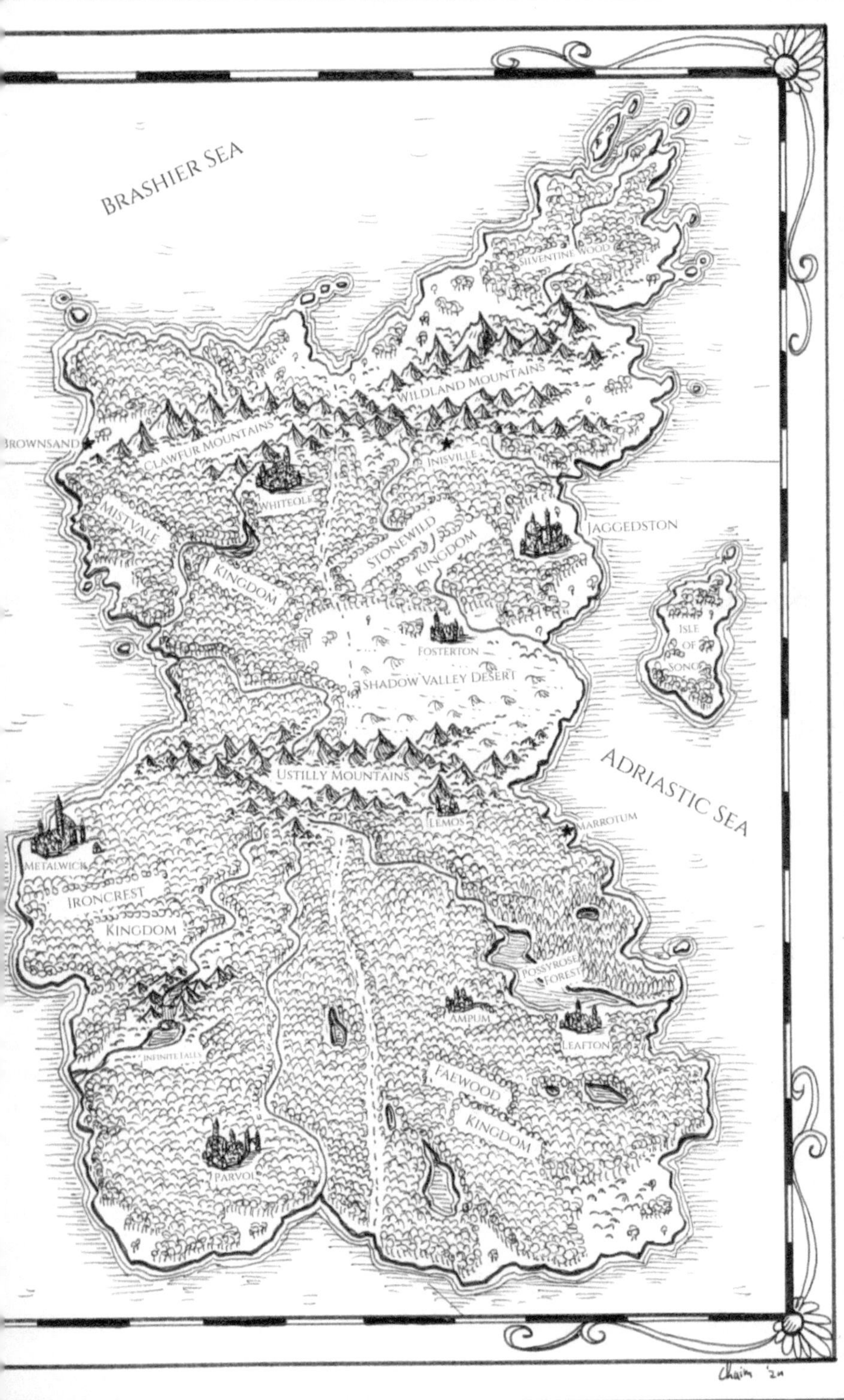

BRASHIER SEA
SILVENTINE WOOD
WILDLAND MOUNTAINS
CLAWFUR MOUNTAINS
BROWNSANDS
INISVILLE
WHITEOLF
JAGGEDSTON
MISTVALE
KINGDOM
STONEWILD
KINGDOM
ISLE
OF
SONG
FOSTERTON
SHADOW VALLEY DESERT
ADRIASTIC SEA
USTILLY MOUNTAINS
LEMOS
MARROTUM
METALWICK
IRONCREST
KINGDOM
POSSYROSE
FOREST
AMPUM
INFINITE FALLS
LEAFTON
FAEWOOD
KINGDOM
PARVOL
Chaim '20

GLOSSARY

<u>Kingdoms of the Silten Continent</u>

Faewood – southeast kingdom, colors are turquoise, white, and dark brown. Magic is elemental.

Ironcrest – southwest kingdom, colors are silver, magenta, and dark orange. Magic is sensory.

Mistvale – northwest kingdom, colors are bright yellow, dark purple, and deep red. Magic is mental.

Stonewild – northeast kingdom, colors are forest green, gold, and sapphire blue. Magic is shifting.

Seas of the fae lands

Adriastic Sea – the ocean to the east of the Silten continent and to the west of the Nolus continent.

Brashier Sea – the most northern ocean in the fae lands, large icebergs often present.

Nelive Sea – the ocean to the west of the Silten continent.

Tala Sea – the ocean to the south of the Solis continent.

———————————✦

Fae races

Nolus fae – the Nolus fae reside on the central continent. They often have various shades of colorful hair, pointy teeth, glowing skin, and otherworldly strength. They typically live two to three hundred years, but royal Nolus fae live for thousands of years.

Lochen fae – the Lochen fae reside on a southern continent, islands, and in the seas throughout the fae lands. They can morph into fish-like creatures, similar to mermaids, but they can also walk on two legs and live on land. There are subspecies of Lochen fae who live in fresh-water rivers, lakes, and ponds. The Lochen fae typically have green eyes, sharp canines, and varying skin shades and hair colors.

Silten fae – the Silten fae reside on a continent surrounded by oceans. Silten fae have numerous subspecies. The Silten species that is considered the most powerful are the *siltenites*. Siltenites have bodies like humans, pointed ears, and varying skin and hair shades. The other Silten fae subspecies are called *wildlings*. Wildlings have primitive Old Wood magic, which connects them to aspects in nature. Wildlings typically have animalistic features: horns, scales, hooves, and tails, yet many are as intelligent as siltenites. Wildlings that don't reside in cities, usually live in underground dens, hollow logs, or wooded forests. Silten fae ages vary based upon their subspecies, but siltenites live thousands of years.

Solis fae – the Solis fae reside on the icy, most northern continent of the fae lands planet. Solis fae have silvery white hair, crystalline blue eyes, and wings. They typically live for thousands of years.

PRONUNCIATION GUIDE

<u>Names</u>

Primelle Hollaran – Prim-elle Hall-are-enn

Kole – Coal

Gwenery – Gwen-err-ee

Timith – Tim-ith

Vissy – Viss-ee

Harrietta – Hair-ee-ett-uh

Siam – See-um

Opalin – Ope-uh-lin

Roosep – Rooh-sepp

Bennif – Ben-iff

Abel – Abe-elle

Master Fistideeous – Fiss-stid-ee-us

Nivinity – Nih-vin-it-ee

Nym – Nim

Jessip – Jess-ipp

Felix – Fee-lix

Fae Races

Lochen – Lock-uhn

Nolus – Naw-luss

Silten – Sill-tun

Solis – Saw-liss

Places

Whiteolf – White-ole-ff

Clawfur Mountains – Claw-fur

Coswell District – Coss-well

Armoth District – Are-moth

Eucaladas – You-kuh-la-duss

Daphnis – Daff-niss

Jaggedston – Jag-edd-stun

Inisville – Inn-iss-ville

Marrotum – Mare-uh-tum

Ustilly Mountains – Oo-stilly

Cliffs of Sarum – Sarr-um

Silventine Wood – Silv-enn-teen

PREFACE

Stone of Legends is book one in the *Fae of Legends & Lore* trilogy, which is a slow-burn, fae fantasy romance that takes place in Krista Street's *Supernatural World*.

This trilogy is the sixth series that Krista has written in her *Supernatural World*, but while all of Krista's fantasy and paranormal romance books take place in the same setting and have similar world-building references, each series is entirely separate so may be read in any order.

STONE
OF
LEGENDS

CHAPTER ONE

"He's going to die, Prim. Do you really want to risk leaving and not being at his side when he passes?"

My aunt's words pierced my concentration, and my movements stilled. Outside, the capital was awakening, the start of a new day filtering into the windows from the busy street below.

Before me, my entire bed was covered with various supplies. I'd been reaching for a second pair of boots, but my hands fell to my sides, my boots forgotten.

"He's not going to die," I replied, the normal cheer absent from my voice as her words glued themselves to my consciousness. "I'm going to save him. You'll see."

But despite my firm reassurances to her, my stomach flipped, and sweat moistened my palms. The worry pummeling me from my aunt's anxious aura wasn't helping.

Hands shaking, I resumed packing, but my Aunt Gwenery continued to stare at me as if I somehow had a magical response that would alleviate her fears at what I was choosing to do.

Her gaze practically burned a hole into the side of my head, and I knew she wanted me to stay, instead of insisting that I follow through with my plan, but I *couldn't* stay. Staying ensured Uncle Timith died.

So, I inhaled sharply and finished so I could leave.

My aunt released a breath. Arms crossed, she began to drum her fingers against her biceps, but I ignored that too.

"Will you pass me that book?" I asked and nodded toward one of my favorites. It was a collection of the flora and fauna of our realm, my particular expertise, and could come in handy on my journey.

Gwenery released an audible sigh but did as I asked.

I stuffed it into my sack, then surveyed what remained. Most of my big items—boxes of food, my bedding, and camping supplies—were already downstairs and ready to go.

But before me were my most precious things, the ones I'd decided not to pack until this morning since I was still researching things until late last night.

My gaze alighted on the *seekerill*, the magical device my uncle had created. It was of upmost importance that I not lose it, and I prayed to all of the gods and goddesses that it would be my saving grace in the end.

Aunt Gwenery stopped tapping her fingers and stepped forward to lay a hand on my arm. "Prim, just remember, if you do fail and you don't find the Stone, his death won't be your fault."

Her gentle words, in such contradiction to the constant arguing we'd been partaking in this morning and throughout the previous week, had the tenseness in my shoulders loosening. It was the first supportive comment she'd made to me all day. Or rather, ever since the Wishing Stone had appeared in the night sky and my plan had begun to form.

I smiled genuinely and leaned into her touch. "Thank you for that."

My aunt nodded and smoothed a strand of hair back that had fluttered onto her cheek. Her normally coifed lilac hair—the color a trace of her Nolus fae lineage—was in disarray this morning. Wispy strands flew around her nape. Nowadays, she threw her hair into a haphazard bun on a whim, as if not even aware of what she was doing. Weeks of sleepless nights would do that to anyone.

My own simple woven braid kept my long brown hair tethered and free of my face. It was the fastest hairstyle for me, so it was one I'd chosen regularly since Uncle Timith had fallen ill. The plain style also matched my drab neutral-colored attire. Both would be needed if I wanted to avoid drawing attention or being targeted during my journey.

My aunt, on the other hand, wore a vibrant heavy gown. And while most females in the kingdom chose dresses or gowns to wear each day, gowns wouldn't do for my upcoming journey, although the billowy skirts would have made hiding blades easier.

Regardless, I'd managed to conceal a weapon within my boot and one at my thigh. But blades weren't my greatest defense. My mind was.

I offered my aunt what I hoped was a reassuring smile, then stuffed the last of my items into my sack. Once done, I mentally ran through my list to ensure I hadn't forgotten anything.

My book from the Isle of Song – check.

Uncle Timith's seekerill – check.

A lock of hair from Goddess Nuleef – check.

I'd placed the lock of hair in a side pocket so I would have easy access to it, and I wondered anew if it was real. The color was certainly unique since its fine golden strands shone as bright as metal in the sunlight, but I truly didn't know if it was authentic.

I'd purchased it from a merchant two evenings prior, and even though the merchant insisted it was genuine, nobody could know for certain if the hair had once graced a goddess's head. But according to the ancient texts, Goddess Nuleef had once walked this land thousands of summers ago, and if carrying a lock of her hair helped—real or not—then I would do it.

Because I would need luck due to my simple yet risky plan. If the Isle of Song book was wrong, or if the seekerill malfunctioned, then I would have failed before I'd even started, and only luck would carry me through.

But if my book was right and my device didn't malfunction . . . then my gamble would pay off.

Hope surged inside me because then my uncle would live.

"Primelle, is there anything else you need?" Verin's soft question snagged my attention to her. The servant stood by the door, a plate in her hands. A steaming biscuit slathered with butter and drizzled with honey waited upon it. "Or perhaps your favorite snack? I thought you may want to eat before you left." She lifted the plate, offering it.

"No, Verin, I'm fine. Thank you, though."

"Are you sure? You haven't eaten today." She thrust the plate forward more, yet her gaze was glued to my feet. I couldn't remember the last time she looked anyone in the eye.

"Again, thank you, but I don't need food. I'm not hungry." *Because how can I possibly eat at a time like this?*

"Are you sure?" Her brows pinched together, and the tips of her fae ears turned pink.

I sighed, and a flare of irritation wafted through me. I knew the servant meant well, but she was always trying to feed me. But eating was hard, ever since my uncle . . .

I tempered my frustration and forced a smile. Verin didn't deserve the brunt of our misfortune. After all, nourishment was required to survive, and she was just trying to help. But given the state of our household, that'd been challenging during the previous weeks.

"Actually, Verin, if you want to start taking everything

outside that I've already packed, that would be helpful. My boxes are in the entryway, but if anything's too heavy for you, I can use my telekinetic magic to lift it."

"I shall manage." She dipped into a curtsy and scurried from the room, taking the aroma from the honey-drizzled biscuit with her.

I was about to cinch my sack closed, but another book on my nightstand caught my attention. It was a romance novel, hardly relevant for what lay ahead, but I snatched it up anyway and thrust it into my bag. A distraction might be needed at some point. It wouldn't hurt to bring it along.

"That should be everything." I eyed the window. Morning sunlight streamed into the room. Any minute now, the bells would toll seven in the morning. I faced my aunt and tried to ignore her brow pinched with worry. "I should go. They predicted the Wishing Stone would have landed within the last hour. I imagine many fae have already left by now."

"You're truly doing this, aren't you?"

"Yes, I am, so please stop making me feel guilty about it."

My aunt sighed, the sound long and heavy. "Come here, Primelle." She pulled me into a hug, and I instantly clung to her.

Tears formed in my eyes at her tight squeeze, and it all of a sudden hit me at what I was about to do. "I'll save him, Gwen," I said, my words thick. "You'll see."

She chuffed lightly and squeezed me harder. "Do you know how many fae are going to be after the Stone?"

"A few?" I joked.

She laughed lightly, and a rush of relief filled me that she seemed as determined as me not to part on bad terms. "The problem with the Wishing Stone is that *everyone* knows it's coming."

"True." I shrugged and pulled back. "But that doesn't mean *I* can't find it before anyone else."

Her look turned tender. "Always so optimistic."

"My most endearing trait, as you constantly say." I batted my eyelashes playfully. "But you just wait. I'll find it even though the entire realm knows it's arrived. Because remember, I have a unique plan. A plan nobody else could possibly have since Uncle Timith only made one seekerill, and if it works, he'll be saved."

"I know, I know." She sighed again and brushed a lock of hair from my forehead. "If only nobody else knew of its arrival, I'd feel much better."

"If wishes were fishes, we'd all cast nets."

She shook her head at my light tone, but a chuckle still escaped her. Yet, despite me trying to make her feel better, I could understand her trepidation. Unlike a number of celestial events our realm experienced, she was right. *Everyone* had known the Wishing Stone was coming.

Given the Wishing Stone's magic, it'd bypassed the Dark Night—an area in our solar system that was cloaked in magic and made all light appear black. And because the Wishing Stone had been visible for so many days, millions of fae knew it was coming, which meant many others likely had prepared as well.

I had no idea how many fae would be hunting the Stone, but it was imperative that I found it before any other could claim it, because the Wishing Stone's magic allowed its finder one wish, *any* wish, such as a wish that would cure a fairy of a mysterious, terminal illness. A wish that would save a fairy's life.

I lifted my pack and slung one of the straps over my shoulder. Just as fast, my aunt squeezed my hand. "Please be careful."

"I will be."

"And if someone accosts or attacks you—"

"They won't. My magic's strong. The fact that I possess telekinetic magic and the ability to link consciousnesses with others, as well as magic from two *other* kingdoms, will keep me safe, and if it doesn't, there's always my *other* magic. No harm will come to me. I promise."

Her breath sucked in. "Prim, you *can't* use your *other* magic. You know that."

I huffed. "I know, and it's not like I actually will. I was just trying to reassure you that if it's a life-or-death situation, I'll be okay. But honestly, Aunty, in the previous millennia, most fae gave up hunting the Stone after a few days. In all likelihood, I'll be by myself in the Wood for the next week or two. I'll probably only encounter wildlings and local siltenites in the cities I pass through, and I won't have to worry about anything dangerous." I elbowed her good-naturedly. "Calm down. I'll be fine."

"May the Goddess help me," she muttered under her breath, but her love for me still swelled in her aura. "You always did think any obstacle could be overcome."

I smiled impishly. "That's because it can be, and remember, the celestial scholars were all predicting the Stone would land on our continent. That in itself gives me an advantage since I don't have to cross any seas or oceans. It's like the gods want me to find it."

"Do you really think the seekerill and your book are the key to locating it?"

I shrugged. "If I didn't, I wouldn't be hedging all of my bets on that or leaving you and Timith at a time like this." And I meant that. The rare book I'd acquired from the Isle of Song had specific instructions on how to find the Stone, something most fae didn't have. Of course, there was no guarantee the book was correct, but at least it was a solid lead to follow.

I began to walk toward the door, and my aunt followed.

"Just promise me one thing, Prim. If Timith's end is near, come home, even if you don't have the Stone. He won't want to take his last breath with you hundreds, or even thousands, of miles away from here." Her voice caught. "Not seeing you at the end would break his heart. He'll want to say goodbye."

My throat bobbed, and despite trying to stuff my emotions down, my chest tightened. "I'll be at his side if it comes to that. I won't let him die with me gone."

Despite my optimism and determination to see this through, her dire reminder of my uncle's state sank in. After all, the palace healers had given my uncle only weeks to live, and there was no guarantee that course would hold. Nobody understood his sickness. For all we knew, he could die tomorrow.

My chest tightened even more as I thought of the male who had been like a father to me. Timith had gone from a robust, healthy male entirely full of life to a severely ill, emaciated, shell of a fairy. All in only a few weeks' time. It was terrifying how quickly his illness had progressed, which meant I had to find the Stone. Death called to my uncle. At this point, finding the Stone was the only chance we had to save him.

I headed out of my childhood bedchambers into the hall. Until my uncle had fallen ill, I hadn't lived in my aunt and uncle's home for many full seasons. But I'd moved back the other week, after it became apparent my uncle's mysterious ailment wasn't a passing matter.

My own home, a small dwelling on the other side of Whiteolf, was closer to the Whiteolf Academic Library, my previous means of employment before I'd taken leave, but lately my home had merely become a storage apartment for my things. I hadn't been back there since I'd left it.

A moment of nostalgia hit me when I remembered the day I'd been hired by the library. It'd only been six months ago, and I'd been so excited that they offered me the position that I ran to the palace, which was only several blocks from the library, to tell my uncle that I'd gotten the job. Even though my aunt and uncle had always been adamant that I not bother my uncle while he was working, I hadn't been able to help myself. But instead of scolding me for venturing to the royal palace and interrupting his day, Timith had been ecstatic for me, nearly as excited as I'd been that I'd gotten the job. He always cheered for me, even when I'd broken the rules, but now, he was dying, no longer able to cheer for anyone at all.

Aunt Gwen followed me down the long hall of their large three-story home in the heart of the Coswell District. Downstairs, banging sounds came from the front door, and I figured Verin was nearly done taking my things outside.

I passed a few windows on my hurried stride toward the stairwell. Outside, fae were already hard at work. This area of the capital was mostly inhabited by artists, many without the funds my aunt and uncle had, but considering my uncle had the creative ability to invent nearly any device he sought to forge, he fit right in despite his wealth.

The stairs loomed, but before I reached them, I stopped at my aunt and uncle's bedchambers' door.

No light shone beneath the closed door. Most days, my uncle preferred the curtains shut. Bright sunlight bothered him, and it was only one more thing to add to the growing list of symptoms that pained him.

I curled my fingers around the doorknob, and the door opened silently on well-greased hinges. Darkness greeted me, then the quiet rattle of my uncle's breath.

But he's still breathing. He's not dead yet.

Quietly, I crept into the room, my aunt right behind me. Together, we padded to my uncle's bedside.

The outline of Timith's skeletal frame appeared in the dim lighting. My heart clenched when I gazed down at the male who'd once stood strong and tall. When I was young, he'd carried me on his shoulders, taught me how to control my magic, and helped me understand the importance of respecting another's free will.

He'd also shown me all of the ways one could create magical wonders if one only allowed their imagination to fly. Every day, he'd allowed me into his workshop to observe his creative inventions, and he'd never minded my numerous questions, or even the odd times I'd accidentally broken something when I'd dropped it as a wee child. His patience was endless. His love brilliant. And his devotion infinite.

I loved him fiercely, and I clung to the hope that we would find a way back to the happy family we'd once been. Because he was so young, only six hundred summers. Much too young to die.

Emotion clogged my throat, but at least we had the palace healers on our side. Given my uncle's occupation being so important to the crown, the royals in Mistvale Kingdom had allowed their personal healers to tend to him. Every morning they'd come by, right at sunrise, when the universe bathed our realm in fresh magic. Gratitude filled me at the king and queen's sweet gesture, but it wasn't like it hadn't been deserved. Timith Hollaran had served the royal family for over half a millennium. He'd earned his right to their care.

A shuddering breath filled my lungs because even with all of the wealth of a Silten continent's kingdom at his disposal, it hadn't been enough to cure my uncle. None of the healers could explain what had happened to him, but they were still trying to save him. They would likely try until the end.

My aunt crouched down and took my uncle's hand. "She's going now, Timith. Prim's going to retrieve the Wishing Stone. You just need to hold on until she comes back."

I waited. Waited for his eyes to open, then crinkle in the corners when he saw me. Waited for his boisterous laugh that had once infected this home like a constant breeze. Waited for his hand to reach for mine and give me a strong squeeze to indicate that he'd heard her.

But instead of his usual responses, my aunt's words only elicited a slight nod from him. His eyelids didn't even crack.

My heart clenched, and I was about to turn away, but then he rasped, "I love you, Little Primmy."

I froze, and tears threatened to choke me right there. He hadn't called me that in so many summers, but when I'd been growing up, it'd been his favorite moniker for me.

Somehow, I managed to swallow my response, but I fell to the floor on my knees and clutched his bony hand. Despite trying to maintain my composure, my voice grew thick. "I love you too, and I'll be back soon. You'll be on your feet again and back to normal before you know it."

I pressed a kiss to his hand. Hot, dry skin greeted me, but the hint of a smile ghosted his lips.

Tears threatened to overwhelm me anew. Hastily, I stood again and blinked away the moisture that stubbornly refused to abate.

I cleared my throat and gave him a buoyant smile that captured all of the fierce optimism swirling through me. "I'll be off then, Uncle, but I'll see you soon, and next time you see me, I'll have the Stone with me."

CHAPTER TWO

My aunt followed me outside, both of us jogging down the steps leading up to their home. Commotion from the streets filled the air. Fae either walked by in rapid strides, rode astride *domals*, traveled in hired carriages, or flew by on enchanted carpets. The activity caused the narrow lane to feel congested and busy.

Artists were hard at work too. Already, several fae who lived in our neighborhood were lined up at their open-market stands that they often employed until lunchtime.

Most of the artists were painting, sculpting, or weaving. It was a common sight as many of the local creators took advantage of our realm's magic, which was replenished each morning at sunrise.

Vissy, just two homes over from ours, sat on her stool as the tangy scent of her telekinetic magic swirled in the air and tingled the breeze that hit my cheeks. Long black hair fell down her back. She had a painting half constructed and already infused with her magic. The idyllic rendition of the Clawfur Mountains had nymphs dancing near a waterfall. The painting had come to life. Quite literally. The small creatures twirled among the trees she'd created, swinging from branch to branch or hanging from vines while laughing. It would make a beautiful addition to anyone's home.

Vissy must have felt me watching her because she glanced my way, and her full lips lifted in a sad smile. She called over the street's commotion, "How is he this morning, Prim?"

I opened my mouth, but Aunt Gwen beat me to answering. "The same, perhaps a little worse."

Vissy bobbed her head, and her painting hand fell to her lap. "I'm sorry to hear it. I pray to the gods and goddesses every night that they'll find a cure."

"Thanks, Vissy." I dipped my head. "Please continue doing so."

She blew me a kiss, then lifted her brush again and returned her attention to her canvas.

Other neighbors walking by also murmured greetings and words of condolences. After the third fairy we knew uttered his sympathy, my smile grew strained. They were already talking as if Uncle Timith was dead.

Behind us, the door to my aunt and uncle's home banged closed, and Verin raced down the stairs with the last of my supplies. She'd already placed most of my things near the lane's cobblestones.

I shaded my eyes and glanced up the street, looking for Ree. My best friend had said she was going to see me off this morning, but there was still no sign of her.

"Do you see Ree?" I asked my aunt.

Gwen also craned her neck. "No, but perhaps Siam was fussy again this morning, and Harrietta's running late. You know how it is with little ones."

My shoulders sagged, but she was right. Life for Ree had drastically changed since she'd become a mother.

"But Opalin and Roosep are definitely coming to see you off," my aunt added. "They wouldn't miss saying goodbye."

Remembering that our dear family friends would also be here buoyed my spirits, and I ducked into the small storage compartment beneath the steps leading to my aunt and uncle's home to grab my new enchanted carpet. Its heavy weight and thick fibers made carrying it difficult, but once I had it on the lane and had made enough room to unfurl it, its magic activated.

Lifting, it hovered over the busy street, a hand's length above the cobblestones. Using my telekinetic magic, I transported all of my supplies at once and set them on the carpet. Once everything was in place, I whispered another command, and invisible magical bands wrapped around my belongings. *Good.* I would need that magic to keep everything locked together because I planned to travel fast.

"Will that be all you need, my lady?" Verin asked, her gaze on my toes.

"Yes, thank you for your help."

She thrust a bottle forward. "I packed this for you to drink along the way, in case you get thirsty."

The opaque bottle concealed its contents, so it could have been anything from water to wine, but I appreciated the gesture. "Thank you, Verin."

I set the bottle on the carpet, and she bobbed her head and hurried back inside.

Aunt Gwen's mouth puckered, and she peered down the street again. "Opalin and Roosep should be here any minute. They knew you wanted to leave at seven."

Before I could search for them, a flash of magic puffed at my feet, and a *dillemsill* appeared.

"Primelle Hollaran, you have a message," it chirped.

I leaned down and picked up the tiny messenger bird with purple feathers and a long yellow furry tail. "Yes?"

The dillemsill squeaked through its small beak, "Harrietta would like you to know that she won't make it to your residence this morning as she'd hoped. She's heartbroken she won't see you, and she requests you connect with her as soon as you're able, and to also send her regular updates during your travels."

I smiled sadly. I wasn't surprised by the message. Not only did my friend have a young infant, but she was also newly married and was already back to work even though Siam was so young. But Ree had married at a *very* young age, and she and Bennif needed rulibs, even more so now that they had an additional mouth to feed.

Of course, Ree and Bennif hadn't expected to conceive so soon. Miraculously, Ree had fallen pregnant the first month they'd begun trying for a family. And even though it normally took females decades, if not centuries, to conceive, Ree had fallen pregnant immediately and had subsequently become quite overwhelmed.

My aunt patted my shoulder. "It was as we guessed."

"Indeed." I sighed. "Oh well. She has a lot on her plate without me adding to her burdens."

I brought the bird closer to my mouth so it could hear my message clearly. "Please inform her that I'll miss her as well, and I'll see her soon. And, of course, I'll check in as often as I can."

"Is that all, miss?" the bird chirped.

"Yes." I set it down, being careful to avoid putting the small bird anywhere a domal's hooves could tramp on it in the road.

The dillemsill began to spin. Its wings flapped and twirled around its body as the small creature's magic grew. It spun so fast it became a blur, and then in a wink of magic, it disappeared.

I ran a hand down my braid and eyed the street again. "I should really get going. Perhaps Opalin and Roosep got waylaid too, and—"

"Are you off hunting as well, Prim?" a boisterous male called from down the lane.

My spine stiffened, and the hairs on the back of my neck tingled. I was so tempted not to turn around. *So* tempted, but if Abel was also after the Wishing Stone, there would be no avoiding him. No matter how quickly I planned to traverse the land, he was bound to catch me.

Stars Above. Just my luck.

I swung around, my smile brittle. Sure enough, Abel was also packing supplies onto a carpet. I sighed. "I am, and from the looks of it, so are you?"

My aunt muttered something under her breath. I didn't catch it, but I doubted it was flattering.

Abel stood tall, his broad shoulders and meaty build making him dwarf those around him. "Aye, every night that I've seen the Stone in the sky, I've felt it pulling me. It wants me to find it."

I rolled my eyes, not even caring if he saw it. "I'm sure it does," I replied sarcastically, and then added, "It probably wants to be found by you as much as I want to marry you."

His eyebrows slammed together. "What was that last bit you just said?"

"Nothing." I knew there was no point in repeating it. It wouldn't deter him.

He began walking toward me, the usual swagger in his step. "Perhaps we could travel together?" His words dipped suggestively. "Side by side? I could watch out for you, especially when you're sleeping. You know how the Wood can be at night when—"

"That's what wards are for, Abel, so I'll pass, but good luck to you." Before he could say another word, I swirled back around, but I still caught Vissy's grin.

"When are you going to give up, Abe?" she called good-naturedly. "Prim's made it abundantly clear she's not interested."

A grunt came, then the puff of Abel's aura, swelling with irritation, beat against my back. "Some females play hard to get. Everyone knows that. Doesn't mean she doesn't actually want me."

"Actually, it does," I remarked.

Abel just grunted.

I sighed and gave my aunt a side-eye.

"Don't provoke him," she said under her breath. "And please, do your best to avoid him."

"Oh, believe me. I will."

I glanced down the street one last time and decided I couldn't wait any longer. But just as I was about to give up on seeing any other loved ones before I left, a female called over the crowd, "Primelle!"

Aunt Opalin frantically waved upon a swiftly moving carpet, her flapping arms barely visible above the street's congestion.

A grin bloomed across my face, and I waved as well, then

laughed at how exuberant she appeared. "You made it, Aunt Opalin, and not a moment too soon!"

She finally came into clear view, and her smile broadened. Even though she wasn't technically my aunt, only a dear family friend, she still seemed to enjoy that I'd taken to calling her that.

Finally reaching us, Opalin jumped off her carpet and said in a breathless rush, "Oh, Prim, I'm so glad I got here in time." She pulled me into a fierce hug, and my magic immediately recognized her unique essence. Rose buds, sparkly illusion magic, and thyme. It all was so *Aunt Opalin*, and I hugged her tightly in return.

"Me too. Ree had to cancel, but I'm glad you could be here." I glanced behind her. "Where's Roosep?"

She blew a strand of blond hair from her face. "I'm so sorry, Prim. He wishes he could have been here too, but he couldn't get off work." Opalin's brow pinched, and worry filled her green eyes.

I nodded understandably. "It's all right." Like my uncle, Roosep also worked for the royals. "I know his job keeps him busy, but thank you for coming, and tell Roosep I completely understand that he couldn't be here." I squeezed her hand. "I hope it wasn't too much of a nuisance for you to travel all the way over here at this hour?"

"Of course not." Opalin swished her fingers through the air. "I wouldn't have missed it for the realm."

I glanced toward the street and its busy traffic, then gave

her an apologetic smile. "I know you just got here, but I really should get moving."

Opalin pulled me into another hug. "I knew you'd be on your way soon, so don't fret."

Gwen hugged us too, her thin arms locking around me and Opalin, causing Opalin to laugh. "May the stars, moon, and galaxy bless you, Prim."

Opalin sobered, and Gwen's formal goodbye had my throat tightening. All thoughts about the irksome male down our lane, not seeing Ree, and missing Roosep too, vanished. With Gwen and Opalin's love clouding around me, it was enough to infuse me with joyous purpose.

I hugged them back just as hard. "Thank you." I pulled away and gripped each of their hands. "I love you both."

Gwen nodded resolutely, but Opalin had tears in her eyes.

"We love you too, Prim," Opalin replied.

"Safe travels," my aunt added, "and don't forget to check in every night."

"I won't. I promise." I sat on my carpet and whispered a command to it. The enchanted carpet lifted higher beneath my crossed legs, just waiting for my next instruction.

Above, the pale green sky shone even brighter in the early morning sun, and I shielded my eyes to see the street better. I needed a break in the congestion to take off.

Aunt Gwen and Opalin moved back from the curb. Gwenery stood with her chin high, yet her hands were clenched so tightly together that her knuckles turned white.

I double checked the magic around my supplies, spotted an opening in the busy street, then lifted a hand. "Bye."

My aunt and Opalin lifted their hands in farewell, and with a whispered command, I was off.

I FLEW through the Coswell District, dipping and weaving around those who were traveling slower. I moved progressively east, flying in the direction of the Wishing Stone. When it'd streaked across the sky during the early hours of the morning, just before sunrise, it'd been headed toward the eastern horizon. It wasn't much to go off of, but once I reached the Wood and night fell, I would consult my constellation map. With any luck, what my book from the Isle of Song told me would prove true. And if not . . . then I would be traveling blind just like everyone else.

Wind streamed across my cheeks, and my enchanted carpet zoomed around everything in its path. I was flying as high as allowed, which meant I could easily fly over the slower-moving traffic on the streets beneath me, but I wasn't allowed to crest the buildings. That privilege was only reserved for royalty.

When I passed the stone bridge leading to the Valehill Market—where Ree worked—I looked for a flash of red hair on the other side. My shoulders slumped. My carpet was moving too quickly, and I was unable to find my best friend in the long lane that led all the way to the capital's center. Already, hundreds of fae were present, buying supplies and goods for the day. When the market and bridge disappeared behind me, a twinge of regret filled me.

Even though we exchanged dillemsills, I should tell her goodbye mentally.

I knew Ree would appreciate the gesture, especially since she'd asked me to connect with her as soon as possible. She was likely feeling guilty that she hadn't been able to see me in the flesh.

Linking consciousnesses with another fairy had taken me many summers to master. Mental projection was a rare skill that few fae with Mistvale magic held, even though my *other* hidden magic was even rarer.

I tried not to be reminded that my uncle had ultimately been the one to help me perfect my unique abilities during my maturing summers. Instead, I tugged on a stream of magic and wove the thread that would link me to Ree. The connection clicked immediately since I was so practiced in contacting her.

Ree, are you there? I asked quietly.

A slight scratch filled my mind as my magic brushed against her distant consciousness. Magic streamed out of me, passing the distance between us as if we were only a stone's throw away. But even though I could force my magic into a fairy's mind, I never did so with Ree. Instead, I waited just on the precipice, asking her for entry.

Seconds ticked by. Morning was always the busiest time

for her, and even though I longed to touch base with her before Whiteolf became a distant speck behind me, I also didn't want to disturb her if she was making a large sale.

But, not surprisingly, an answering pulse tingled in my mind, and our connection linked completely. The familiar aura of my best friend filled my mind, then her voice sounded within me.

Stars, Prim, I'm so glad you were able to connect so soon! Have you already left? I was hoping to see you off, but Siam was quite fussy this morning, and he's been clinging to me nonstop. When I tried to pass him off to Bennif, he was having none of it. But at least my dillemsill reached you. I just got your return message.

A smile split my lips. *I'm glad the dillemsill already found you, and yes, I've already left. I just passed the bridge to the market. I tried to spot you, but I have my carpet moving too fast. And please don't worry. I kind of figured Siam might be the reason you were unable to visit this morning. Did he keep you up most of the night again?*

Her sigh was as clear as her voice in my mind. *He did. I managed to get a few hours of rest, but you know how it is when babies are teething.*

I laughed softly. *I don't, but I'll take your word for it.*

Her laughter joined mine, and a sense of peace settled within me. Sobering, I added, *I'm sorry I've been so absent lately. I promise that after I find the Stone and cure my uncle,*

I'll be around more. And please give my apologies to Siam. I know I've been an awful galaxy-mother lately.

Ree's mirth filled our connection. *I'll be sure to let my six-month-old know that his galaxy-mother sends her regrets, but don't you dare say you're sorry for not being around. I know it's been crazy for you. The fact that you're caring for your uncle, and that you traveled to the Isle of Song by yourself last week, would occupy all of anyone's time.*

My guilt lessened at her fierce response. *Do you think Siam will forget me while I'm gone?*

Doubtful. An edge of worry crept into her tone. *You won't be gone that long, will you? I thought you said it would only be a few weeks.*

No, you're right. My plans haven't changed. I promised Aunt Gwen I would be back in time if— My throat thickened, and I couldn't continue.

Ree's mood dimmed, strumming to me along our connection. *I'm so sorry, Prim. I still can't believe this has happened to Timith. Just take care out there. Be smart and stay away from any fae you get a bad feeling from. You know what the legend warns of about fae hunting the Stone, so make sure you come back in one piece.*

I laughed softly. *You're starting to sound like Gwen.*

She laughed too. *It must be because I'm a mother now. It's aging me.*

My amusement grew. *You're only thirty-three summers.*

I feel more like three hundred and thirty-three summers.

I giggled again, and felt thankful for our typical banter. It could always make my darkest days brighter.

Prim, hang on. A customer is here. A moment of silence came from Ree, and I waited patiently and returned my attention to what lay ahead.

My carpet careened through the last of the busy streets. Not too far down the lane, rows of thatched-roof homes waited. The quaint houses in the Armoth District were some of my favorite pieces of architecture. The houses weren't big or grand—not as the kingdom's ten Houses were north of the city—but bright colors infused their siding and the Wood had been welcomed into this fold of the capital, even more so than the others. Vines dipped around the home's corners. Tree branches wove through some windows. Even wildlings had been welcomed, some scampering in and out of the abodes.

I'm back. Ree's voice abruptly filled my mind again. *How's Timith today?*

I snapped my attention away from the streets. *The same. Maybe a little worse, but not by much.*

I felt her nod even though the movement made no sound. *I know I likely can't do anything for you while you're gone, but I'm planning to bring over another meal for your aunt tomorrow. And if you think of anything more I can do to help, just reach out. Okay?*

I will, but don't worry, she still has Verin to help her, and we both know how exhausting your life is right now with Siam, so please don't stress over it.

She sighed. *It's the least I can do, even if I don't get much sleep these days, because servants and friends are two different things.*

My throat grew thick again. Ree's kindness and constant thought for others were two of the reasons I loved her so much. She'd always been that way, even when she was only nine summers old and we'd met for the first time. As soon as she'd seen me—the new girl in primary school who'd acted so awkwardly since I'd never met other children before—she'd marched right up to me and told me we were going to be the best of friends.

And she hadn't been lying. I still acutely remembered the intense relief I'd felt when she'd declared that. It was as though she was daring anyone in the classroom to treat me badly, and if they tried, they'd have to deal with her too.

I'd counted her as my best friend ever since even though it'd been so many summers since Ree and I had met. But she'd wormed her way into our family, just like Opalin and Roosep had done. In a way, Ree was the sister I'd never had, and she was like another daughter to my aunt.

Thank you for everything, Ree.

I felt her nod again, and then she added, *I'm always here for you all, you know that. And I mean it, Prim. Stay safe, and may the gods, moons, and galaxy bless you on your search.*

I mentally blew her a kiss. *Give my best to Siam and Bennif. I'll be in touch when I can.*

We murmured a quick goodbye, and I closed our connection.

The second I was alone in my head, I sent thanks to the gods and goddesses for imbuing me with such strong magic that allowed me to link mentally with others. And remembering how strong and capable I was caused a smile to spread across my lips.

Optimism flared through me anew. I could do this. I *would* find the Stone.

I settled back in for the remainder of the ride out of the capital. I itched to get to the open Wood so I could move faster. Already, signs of the impending forest were visible. The Armoth District was falling behind me, and even more vines and leaves wove around the upcoming streets and architecture.

When I spotted a family of *spillins* peering out at me from a hollow in a *babbo* tree, my smile grew even wider. The mother wildling blinked at me, and I raised a hand in greeting, but then a male fairy called from behind me, "Prim! Why the hurry?"

And just like that . . . my smile disappeared.

CHAPTER THREE

When Abel pulled up his carpet beside mine, I pressed my lips into a tight line. His carpet hovered only inches away since we flew at the same altitude. And of course, he flew so closely that we nearly brushed into each other. The only option I had to ditch him was to dive into the slower-moving traffic below and hope he wouldn't follow. Not ideal.

Dammit. I'd been too caught up in chatting with Ree that I'd been oblivious as Abel snuck up on me.

Obviously, my plan to outrun him in the capital wasn't happening. To make matters worse, once we got to the Wood, it would be even harder to lose him. Since fae weren't allowed to fly above the trees, I had to travel on the Wood's road. I sighed. All in all, I didn't have many options to avoid him unless I wanted to choose a slower path, and that was still no guarantee he would leave me alone. He might just follow me there too.

"Didn't you hear me calling you earlier? You didn't reply." Abel inclined his head toward me, and his amber eyes flashed. "Prim? Hello?"

I kept my attention straight ahead. "No, I didn't hear you, but I can tell you if I had, I still would have ignored you. What can I do for you, Abel?" Out of the corner of my eye, I caught a sly grin spreading across his lips.

"So formal. Really, Prim, why the sour mood? As I mentioned earlier, I thought two heads together were better than one."

I snorted. "Using that logic, the more that accompany us, the better. In that case, why not ask Lexer to join us too?" I was pretty sure I'd heard a rumor that another neighbor of ours was planning to hunt the Stone.

Abel's brows snapped together. "Lexer? You want Lexer with you?" Jealousy clouded his aura, thick and menacing.

His aura brushed against my Shield—the magical barrier fae could erect to protect themselves against others' magic— and the feel of him made me want to recoil. But I forced myself not to show any outward reaction.

"No, Abe, I don't want you or Lexer to travel with me. I thought I'd made that abundantly clear." I eyed the meager supplies on Abel's carpet. He would be lucky if he packed enough food to last him a few days, and he didn't seem to have any bedding. Perhaps he planned to stay at inns each night.

Or . . .

I narrowed my eyes. "Were you hoping to mooch off my supplies? Is that why you raced to catch up with me?"

His expression flattened, and his tone turned growly. "Of course not. You know how I feel about you. I don't know why you keep fighting it. Besides, we'll work better together as a team, even if you packed more than me."

I arched an eyebrow. "Work better together for whom? You? Or me?"

"Both of us."

"No thanks."

"I wasn't asking."

Irritation prickled my skin. "That's the problem, Abel. You never ask. You just force. And no matter how many times I tell you that I'm not interested in you, you refuse to give up."

"Males like a chase. Don't you know that? And I know a huge part of your refusals are because you enjoy playing hard to get."

I gritted my teeth. We'd had this exact conversation so many times over the past two summers. He would never see reason, and I really needed to learn that I was wasting my breath every time I argued with him.

I flew around another street corner and replied icily, "It doesn't matter if you were asking or not. I'm not interested. Leave me alone, Abe. I mean it."

A flare of darkness wafted in his aura, roiling around him like a demon and completely overpowering his earlier jealousy. "There's no reason for you to act like a witch to me."

"A *witch*. Did you seriously just call me that?"

He scoffed. "Well, you're acting like one."

Magic heated inside me. It was so tempting to put him in his place once and for all. *So* tempting. But then my uncle's teachings from my childhood reared up. The teachings he and Gwenery had infused into me over and over until it became so automatic that I sometimes forgot I even possessed the extraordinary magic that I'd been born with.

"You must never control another, Prim. Never. Free will is every fairy's right. You must respect that and subdue your temper. Always."

I took another deep breath and released my ire, then said in a calm tone, "Go away, Abel. I don't know how much clearer I can be. Leave me alone."

I commanded my carpet to veer right. I shot into an alleyway so abruptly that the beverage Verin had packed for me tumbled right off the carpet. Abel's curse carried through the air, but I didn't slow to collect the bottle. I needed to lose my neighbor.

But my swift maneuver didn't deter the soddy bastard. I'd only just reached the next street when his shout came.

"Goddess Above! Stop, Prim!"

I clenched my teeth together and commanded my carpet to go faster.

I shot forward. Wind flew over my cheeks. Yells from fae I passed along the busy streets rang through my ears. I would have called out apologies to them, since I was speeding and going much too fast for city streets, but that would only distract me from getting away.

Shoulders hunched forward, I zoomed around corners, soared close to rooftops, and veered down each new lane I encountered. I was determined to lose Abel once and for all, and if speed was needed to do that, then so be it.

Yet, each time I glanced over my shoulder, eyes watering in the fierce wind, it was only to see a distant Abel valiantly trying to catch up.

Muttering beneath my breath, I pulled on a stream of my telekinetic magic. Using one's magic on others was illegal, but if I didn't use my magic on him directly and instead used it on objects . . .

Behind me, boxes stacked in the street toppled into Abel's path, and flags hanging from homes and shops reached out to try and snare him.

"Prim! You . . ." Abel roared.

But I didn't stop, and I drowned out his reply since he was likely calling me a witch again.

Luckily, my new attempts began to work, and Abel fell farther and farther behind me.

A smile bloomed across my face. "Thank the stars."

I zoomed around another corner, wanting to put a few more streets between Abel and me before I slowed to a normal pace. Behind me, my supplies heaved, shifting beneath the carpet's magical bands and groaning when they rubbed into one another. But I didn't slow.

Keeping up my dangerous pace, I dared a final glance over my shoulder.

Abel was nowhere to be seen.

Grinning, I turned back around and began to whisper a slowing command to my carpet, but my stomach shot into my throat.

A male was standing directly in my path, and I was less than a second away from hitting him.

Even though my carpet would have done something to avoid the collision—since its magic didn't allow them—the carpet's magic didn't fully protect me.

Like Verin's bottle, I'd made the fatal error of not securing myself to the carpet as diligently as I'd done with my supplies, so when my carpet came to a jolting stop, I didn't.

I flew through the air, limbs twisting, eyes wide. The wall of a house neared.

Oh shite.

I squeezed my eyes shut and braced myself for a bone-crunching impact.

A whip of air elemental magic abruptly flared.

Before I could hit the wall, the elemental magic wrapped around me. My airborne tumble slowed, my momentum disintegrating.

In my next breath, I plummeted downward, and then two hard arms curled around me.

I blinked.

"What . . . how . . ." My chest heaved. I gulped and tried to process everything. The very male I'd nearly hit held me. We were crouched only an arm's length from the house I'd almost smashed into, and his air element had miraculously saved my neck from being broken.

A low discontented rumble vibrated the male's chest, but his words were calm when he said, "Might I suggest securing yourself better next time you decide to fly at an illegal rate through the capital?"

His voice was deep and smooth. A tingle radiated down my spine. "I'm . . . I'm sorry."

I peered upward and was rewarded with a glimpse of piercing blue eyes. Dark hair upon his head ruffled in the breeze, and the hilt of a sword stood up from his back. Rugged features that were smooth and devoid of any real expression snagged my attention. But unlike his veiled demeanor, my eyes widened in surprise as I took in his features.

Gods . . .

He was likely the most handsome male I'd ever seen.

For a moment, all I could do was stare at him, then I finally found my voice again. "I . . . I'm *so* sorry. I didn't see you, or rather, I *did*, but not until the last moment. I completely apologize, but I was trying to—"

A rush of wind, indicating another carpet had just stopped near us, blew over my face.

"Why are you touching her?" Abel's terse tone cut off my thoughts. "Let her go. Immediately!"

My entire body tensed, and my spirits plummeted.

Abel hovered above us, standing indignantly on his carpet as hatred flashed in his eyes while he gazed upon the stranger who held me.

I sighed in exasperation. Apparently, I hadn't lost my neighbor after all.

"Who are you?" the stranger asked calmly, his tone and expression giving away nothing.

Abel sneered. "I'm her betrothed."

I huffed and glared at Abel. "*No*, you are most definitely *not* my betrothed."

"Well, I will be. It's just a matter of time." Abel glared at the stranger again. "Unhand her. Now!"

The stranger's arms tightened, and his gaze shot upward. The angle gave me a clear view of his square jaw and the strong lines of his throat. "She said you're not her betrothed." His tone dipped, a low warning in it.

Something gleamed in Abel's eyes as he and the stranger stared off. Something I'd never seen before. And my neighbor's aura felt positively insane.

That was new, and a moment of unease slithered through me, especially since the Stone's legend said things like this could happen. Fae who were hunting the Stone could change. Become dangerous. Become *unhinged*.

Heart rate ticking up, I replied as calmly as I could, "Abel, you've never been my betrothed. You need to stop with these delusional beliefs."

Abel's lips pulled back, making him look more wolf than fae. "I *am*. You just won't accept—"

"No, you're *not*," I nearly shouted.

The stranger's attention drifted back to me, and perhaps it was the chaos of the morning or the worry that I would never find the Stone due to Abel's behavior, but I did the first thing I could think of to deter my irrational and potentially dangerous neighbor. Especially since this stranger looked like someone nobody would want to mess with.

"In fact, Abel, this male is my betrothed. Isn't that right?" I asked the stranger.

Before I could decipher the stranger's widening eyes or contemplate the wisdom of my decision, I pressed both of my palms to his cheeks and slammed my lips to his.

The stranger stiffened.

Abel gasped.

I closed my eyes, mortified at what I was doing, but committed to seeing this through since I was desperate enough to do *anything* to get Abel off my back.

So I kissed the male, moving my lips under his, then slanting my mouth to get a better angle. The stranger smelled of pine, cedar, and the sea, and he tasted of mint and fresh air. Goddess, he tasted *good*. No, not good . . . *intoxicating*. His scent wrapped around me. Just as fast, his aura spiked.

Even though I should have been pulling back, I deepened our kiss.

But amazingly, the stranger did too.

A low growl filled his throat, humming right through me and causing goosebumps to rise along my flesh. His arms curled me tighter in his embrace, holding me in an entirely new way as his mouth moved with mine.

Stars Above.

The stranger's tongue darted out, running along my lower lip, and something flashed on his wrist, but I didn't pay it any attention. I opened my mouth beneath his. His tongue caressed my own, and then, all I felt was *him*.

A hard chest. Caressing hands. An aching need. Tongues and taste and absolute *want*.

A low moan left me.

Time stopped.

The streets of the capital vanished.

My belly flooded with desire, and I tangled my fingers in his hair, then kissed him even more.

"*Fuck*," he whispered low and hard. "You're—"

Another flare of magic came from his wrist, but he stopped talking and wrapped me even tighter in his embrace, and then he *devoured* me.

Our kiss turned frantic. Raw. Another moan left me. I wanted him. Needed him. Goddess Above, more, more, more. I wanted *more*.

I wanted to straddle him, ride him, climb him like a tree.

Lust hit me so suddenly that I could barely breathe.

A snarl tore through the streets.

A rush of air hit me, and my arse fell to the cobblestones. Coldness suddenly greeted me.

My eyes flashed open, but the stranger was gone.

Fury emanated from Abel, and my barely coherent mind struggled to comprehend what appeared in front of me.

A knife.

Abel had the stranger pressed against the back of the house, his arm lodged under his throat, with a *knife* threatening to slice the stranger's neck open.

My jaw dropped.

"Abel!" I pushed to a stand and struggled to uncloud my thoughts. "Abel!" I screamed again, but my psychotic neighbor didn't release him. I scanned the area, but there weren't any fae around, or if there had been, they'd scattered.

I whipped back to face him, but Abel hadn't relented. If anything, he pushed the knife even more into the stranger.

I blinked stupidly and assessed the situation as quickly as I could. Strong shoulders filled out the stranger's tunic. Black leggings clung to his muscular thighs, and his hands—that were still held up in surrender—were so large that I questioned the wisdom of Abel's decision. Those hands looked as though they could crush stone, yet the stranger appeared reluctant to act.

Maybe I'd been wrong. Perhaps he was a gentle soul despite his size, and the huge sword he carried was just for show. He might not know how to fight or get out of this situation.

A situation *I'd* put him in.

My eyes flashed wide. I would have to save him. Perhaps my fire element. *No, he could get burned in the process.* Or maybe, I could use my telekinetic magic and wrestle the knife from Abel's hand. *No, the stranger's throat could get sliced accidentally in the process.*

Oh Gods, maybe I would have to use my *hidden* magic, because if it was the only option . . . *No, I just need to call the kingsfae.*

Trying to maintain a level head, I assessed the situation more. Abel hadn't advanced with his knife. He was simply holding the stranger, and the stranger wasn't fighting or provoking my crazy neighbor further.

Right. I need to call the kingsfae. If I did, Abel would be arrested, and perhaps this innocent stranger would be spared, and nobody would need to learn my secret.

I whipped around, searching for help, but there was no one nearby. Whoever owned this house didn't appear to be home, and this far into the outskirts of the capital was quieter. Trees were everywhere, and even the houses were farther apart.

I was on my own.

Shite. Whirling back around, I said in as calm a voice as I could muster, "Abel, put the knife down. Don't hurt him. He's done nothing wrong."

"He *kissed* you," Abel hissed.

I gulped and took a hesitant step closer to them.

Abel pressed the knife more into the male's throat. The blade sank into his skin, threatening to tear it open.

"Abel! Abel, no. *Stop.*" I held my hands up and took another step cautiously forward.

Abel seethed, his lips curling back.

The stranger still didn't move. He didn't even blink.

"Abel, this is ridiculous, even for you." Despite my words, I was careful to keep my voice low and gentle. "You are *not* my betrothed. You never have been, and I'm not bound to you in any way. Who I choose to marry is not of your concern, and I've chosen to marry this male, even if it was unbeknownst to you. Now, please, release him. He's done nothing wrong. *Please*, Abel."

But Abel's hand tightened so much around the knife that his knuckles turned white. "How long have you been with her?" His focus stayed on the stranger, as though my words had fallen on deaf ears, and the earlier flare of jealousy that had wrapped around his aura when we'd spoken of Lexer increased a hundred-fold.

The stranger's attention slid my way for the merest second. When our gazes locked, something flashed across his expression, the first break in his composure. A look of heat, fire, and *want* burned so quickly, but it was fleeting and gone so fast that I wondered if I'd imagined it.

"Nearly a month," he replied calmly, then eyed Abel again. "And as she said, I'm her betrothed. She's *mine*. It's best that you remember that."

A shiver struck me at his possessive tone. *Mine.* Every fae male knew what that declaration meant, but then I remembered that this male was merely playing along, doing me a solid favor considering how psychotic my neighbor was acting.

"Abel?" I said softly, trying again. "Let him go. Please."

Abel's nostrils flared, and he glanced my way. "You are meant for *me*, Prim. Sooner or later, you'll accept that and—"

A blur of movement and a surprised shout of pain came from him. Then, Abel was on the ground, face-first, both hands held behind him by the stranger.

I blinked.

Blinked again.

What just happened?

"How—" I couldn't manage to ask more.

The stranger shoved his knee into Abel's spine, and the huge sword at his back gleamed in the sunlight.

My neighbor struggled and thrashed beneath him, but it did no good. Whatever the stranger had done had pinned Abel completely. And on top of that, he'd also dislodged Abel's knife and had flicked it down the alleyway to clatter harmlessly to the ground.

"You just . . ." My gaze met his, and I realized that he likely *did* know how to use that sword strapped to his back. "But how? How did you do that so fast?"

The stranger's tone was no different than it'd been a moment ago. Calm and smooth. As though females nearly ramming him with their enchanted carpet, or forcing a realm-shattering kiss upon him, or having an unhinged neighborly dispute brought to his feet were no different to him than having a cup of morning tea.

It also wasn't lost on me that he ignored my question completely and merely said, "Do us a favor and call the kingsfae."

CHAPTER FOUR

I tapped my foot impatiently on the street. Before me, a young kingsfae held a crystal ball beneath my palm. The crystal's magic siphoned my testimony onto a piece of parchment he held, effectively writing down everything I'd recalled happening with Abel. It only took a few minutes, and once the magic signaled that the events had been recorded, the kingsfae pocketed his crystal ball.

I smiled pleasantly up at him, even though the sun was already high in the sky. "Is that all you need?"

His throat bobbed, and his gaze traveled over my face. The tips of his ears turned pink, and he hastily glanced down at his parchment. "I, uh . . . let me read through this."

He began to scan his document. Smile straining, I tapped my foot even more.

Hours. I was *hours* behind schedule, all because my stupid neighbor had turned into a complete lunatic this morning.

I glanced in Abel's direction, but he was too far away to appreciate my annoyance.

The stranger was still in the alleyway too, and like me, he was also being questioned, but he was farther down the lane, nearly out of earshot. Regardless, my stomach flipped the second I beheld him again. The stranger was *so* masculine. Physically, everything about him was enticing.

The kiss we'd shared still blazed through my mind. I'd never reacted like that to anyone before. My response had been so intense and visceral.

My core clenched, and I hastily turned my attention away. Goddess, maybe the Stone was affecting me too. It was the only thing that could explain the all-consuming lust I felt for someone I'd just met.

Finally, the young kingsfae finished re-reading my statement, then carefully folded the parchment and slid it into his pocket beside the crystal ball.

Once his supplies were stowed away, he gave me a shy smile and cleared his throat, bobbing it in the process. "Try to stay safe out there, Miss Hollaran. Unfortunately, as you experienced this morning, the Stone's arrival is causing some fae to act rather badly." He glanced toward Abel, who was at last being hauled away in magic-suppressing glowing blue cuffs by two other kingsfae.

"Tell me about it. But thank you for your help." I beamed, relief surging through me that I could finally leave. "You've been very kind. Am I free to go now?"

The guard blinked as I peered up at him. For a moment, all he did was stare at me.

A breeze flowed down the street, and a few strands of hair fluttered around my cheeks. I tucked the stray strands behind the tip of my ear, and his throat bobbed again as his attention drifted to my fingers.

Out of the corner of my eye, I saw the stranger's focus shift toward us. It was subtle, the barest movement of his chin, but his aura wafted through the air, and it felt as though he drifted it covertly toward us. As if assessing the situation.

My spine stiffened. It was baffling how the stranger's every move had captured my attention since this entire debacle had started. Even more baffling was that I'd kissed him, or rather, forced myself on him.

Now that I'd had a moment to think about it, I'd realized that was exactly what'd happened. I'd *forced* him to kiss me, even if the stranger had returned it. But for all I knew, I'd caught him off guard, and he'd kissed me in return automatically, not even realizing what he was doing.

Goddess, maybe the legends are right, and the Stone can make anyone hunting it turn crazy. Even me.

"Sir, am I free to go?" I asked the guard again, since he just stood there, not responding.

The young guard shook himself, his cheeks pinkening slightly. "Yes, yes, of course. Good day to you, Miss Hollaran. And best of luck, but like I said, be careful out there while you're hunting the Stone. This is likely going to be the first of many unreasonable fae you'll encounter." He inclined his head toward Abel again, then a flash of worry crossed his features. "Speaking of which, are you sure it's wise for you to continue? This morning's encounter could have ended tragically."

I laughed lightly. "You sound like my aunt."

His blush turned scarlet, but I didn't regret my cheeky reply. My entire life, fae had underestimated me. When most looked at me, they saw a young female of average height with a soft build and, consequently, assumed her magic was as weak as her biceps. But I wasn't weak. I was anything but weak if I allowed myself to use the full extent of my power.

Still, I patted the guard's arm reassuringly, if a little condescendingly. "Please don't worry. I'll be careful. Of that, you can be certain."

The guard's attention shot toward where I touched him. His cheeks flamed, and a hint of red trickled down his neck.

"Right, um, of course. Apologies for my concern, Miss Hollaran." He awkwardly tipped his head, then scurried away to join the other kingsfae.

As soon as he did, one of his fellow law-enforcers whispered something, then elbowed the young guard and glanced toward me. I could have sworn the young guard's blush grew even fiercer.

Not able to help myself, I winked and gave them a wave.

Farther down the street, the stranger's eyes narrowed, but he also dipped his head in farewell to the male who'd been questioning him. His kingsfae took a step back, his aura bursting with eagerness, then he bowed at the stranger. Actually *bowed*.

I cocked my head. *Well, that's odd.*

Not for the first time, I wondered who the stranger was, and not just because of my physical response to him. I still didn't know his name, since before taking our statements, the kingsfae had immediately split us up.

But now that I was finally free to go, I needed to thank him. He'd saved me from potential future weeks of Abel's pestering behaviors.

I glanced at my enchanted carpet, which lay motionless on the street since I'd deactivated its magic. All of my supplies were still sturdily secured to it. Another blessing. Amazingly, I hadn't lost anything, except for Verin's bottle.

I breathed a sigh of relief, and my earlier annoyance with Abel and concern that I was hours behind schedule began to melt away. Optimism surged through me anew, because this delay was proving to be just fine after all, even lucky if I thought about it. It'd entirely gotten Abel off my back.

I walked toward the stranger, approaching him from behind. Since he had his back to me, that impressive sword running the length of it, I couldn't help but notice the width of his shoulders. *So broad.*

A tingle shot through me, but before I could say anything or reach out to touch his arm and catch his attention, he turned to face me.

His movements were slow. Steady. It was as if his every

move was calculated, and I was reminded of the efficiency in which he'd taken down Abel in one fluid move.

I gulped and thought of what this stranger had been put through.

What a morning.

When only an arm's length separated us, I stopped, but I had to tilt my chin up to meet his eyes. Another breeze drifted down the quiet street, bringing the heady scent of the Wood. I entwined my fingers together and gave him what I hoped was a thankful yet apologetic smile.

"I'm so sorry for everything this morning, truly, but I can't thank you enough for your help."

He stared at me, his eyes so vivid and sparkling. Seriously, how was it possible for them to be so blue? Vain females would kill to have eyes like his.

"And I'm very sorry about forcing myself, I mean . . . kissing you," I added in a rush. "Truly, I acted rashly, and I can't apologize enough, but thank you so much for playing along."

His expression still didn't falter. He was that *still.* But his gaze had fixated on my mouth.

"So—" I thrust my arm forward for a formal handshake. "Thank you . . ." I let my words hang since I still didn't know his name.

He glanced at my arm, and it felt like centuries passed as I stood there. But just when I thought for certain he was going to leave me hanging, he reached out and wrapped his hand around my forearm.

Our fingers encircled one another, and I became acutely aware of the feel of his forearm. It was hard and corded. Thick veins were palpable beneath my grip, and Stars Above, once again tingles shot up my arm, a shiver following. I pumped our arms a few times just to do something normal.

I could have sworn that his nostrils flared, ever so slightly, as if he was scenting something, and the longer we stayed in contact, the more my magic vibrated inside me.

It felt as though something in my chest cracked. Yawned. Stoked. *Grew.*

Head spinning, I abruptly let go of him and stepped back. He took a step forward, as though he was going to close the distance between us, but stopped himself just as a whip of magic came from his wrist.

Chest heaving, I cleared my throat and gave him what I hoped was a radiant smile. But honestly, at this point, any smile would do. Something was seriously wrong with me, considering how I was reacting. *Goddess, the legends were right about the Stone.*

"Thank you again," I said, relieved that my voice sounded normal and even.

His gaze was transfixed on my face, but he didn't respond.

"May I ask your name before I leave?" I said, then wondered why I bothered to ask. It wasn't like I would ever see him again.

Another moment of silence passed.

And then another.

My heart began to beat like a steady drum.

Like the handshake, I was certain he was going to leave me hanging, but then he said, "Kole." His deep, smooth voice rumbled all the way through me, coating my insides and making me want to melt like butter at his feet. "Kole Sword-wielder."

Swordwielder.

Before I could process what his last name implied, the stranger gave me his back, then strode around the alley's corner and disappeared into the bustle of Whiteolf.

He was gone before he could see my mouth drop to the ground.

Swordwielder. His name was Kole *Swordwielder.*

No wonder the guard had bowed to him.

CHAPTER FIVE

Despite my shock at *who* had saved me from my delusional neighbor, along with my heightened response to him and potentially impending insanity thanks to the Stone's arrival, I didn't have time to contemplate any of those minor hiccups. However, if the Stone truly was going to turn me into a fairy as deranged as Abel—with or without Kole Swordwielder's presence—I had best go about finding it immediately, so its effects would stop.

The second Kole disappeared from view, I picked my jaw up off the ground and leaped back onto my carpet. It wasn't long until I was journeying steadily eastward again, and the capital fell behind me.

The Wood's abundant trees and plants flew past my peripheral vision. Vibrant swathes of color filled the land. When a burst of magenta and sapphire vines, a common species of *ploramix*, brushed against my shoulder, I ducked my head to the right and kept my carpet going at its max pace.

And with every mile that passed beneath me, my head cleared more, but that only made my heart thrum. Because while my mind no longer felt muddled—hopefully, it would stay that way—it wasn't free of my uncle's impending doom.

I couldn't fail. I *had* to find the Stone.

My anxiety on the cusp of blooming, I used the Wood to keep me grounded. Rich scents from its soil and abundant plant life helped keep me focused, so I concentrated on that, and I began to catalogue each plant I recognized in my dashing flight across the land.

Diafill, a beautiful flower that only blooms at the cusp of nightfall. Useful for temporary magical beauty enhancements when crushed, and relieves sore feet when boiled.

Meer, a deadly herb that can be mistaken for thyme, and has killed more fae than any herb combined.

Avose, my favorite plant in all of the Wood, known for its lightly scented petals that make a lovely addition to salads if served whole, but if crushed, dried, and placed toward the sun at the cusp of dawn, it will become infused with magic that is the perfect cure for horrendous hangovers.

The fact that I knew the recipe for a hangover cure had made me very popular in my university days before I'd begun my job at the library.

Hours passed as I flew steadily eastward. I stopped several times to consult wildlings, but they all told me the same thing.

Hundreds of fae had already flown through the Wood ahead of me, also heading east toward wherever the Stone had landed. Because of Abel, I was behind all of them, but it'd resulted in another unexpected patch of good luck.

There hadn't been any fae on the road who had bothered me.

I'd passed a few who were traveling in slower-moving carriages, but they'd ignored me, so I'd spent the day almost entirely on my own. Perhaps the lock of Goddess Nuleef's hair was working after all.

Evening neared, and the chatter from wildlings in a nearby tree filled the air, distracting me momentarily. At dusk, the Wood always came alive in a new way as nocturnal animals and the Wood's sleeping wildling fae awakened.

I activated my sight sensory ability, courtesy of my Iron-crest magic, and catalogued the dozens of wildlings that appeared perched on branches, rummaging through the Wood's floor, or flying from tree to tree. With my eyesight enhanced, it was so easy to see them in their shadowy burrows or pick them out despite their camouflaged coats.

Above, the pale green sky grew darker. I couldn't see the horizon—it was impossible considering how dense the Wood was—but if I'd been able to glimpse it, it would have undoubt-edly been a myriad of blazing colors.

In other words, nighttime would be here before I knew it, and that only meant one thing.

I would soon know if what my book from the Isle of Song proclaimed was true.

A burst of nerves flipped my stomach. *Please be true. Please be true.*

Nerves alight with hope, I bit my lip and searched my surroundings for where I could camp for the night. I would need to be careful not to disturb any of the local wildling fae. Their homes were often in underground dens, hollow trees, burrows on the Wood's floor, or nests in the tree branches.

Wildlings weren't like *siltenites*, my kind, who were entirely magical. But wildlings did harbor Old Wood magic, which was usually primitive, and varied in strength depending upon their wildling subspecies, but even though the wildlings weren't siltenites, they were still fae, despite that many siltenites considered the wildling fae lesser.

Yet I had learned over the seasons, during my many visits to the Wood in my university days, that even though wildlings often looked more animal than fae, they were anything but. Many were intelligent. Most were kind. They also made very good allies given their innate understanding of the Wood, and throughout the coming weeks, the wildlings would inevitably make my journey less lonely since many of them were capable of language despite their animalistic forms.

My thoughts drifted to Kole. I wondered if he ever spoke to wildlings or if he felt, as so many other siltenites did, that they were beneath him. I hoped not. It would be disappointing if he did.

Abruptly, I snapped my shoulders back. "Gah, seriously, Prim? You're thinking of him again?"

I harrumphed. It wasn't the first time my thoughts had meandered his way. It didn't help that I had no idea who he was, other than *what* he was, given his last name. The mystery of him only added to my curiosity. To have one of his kind randomly roaming Whiteolf's streets was rare, and I doubted he was hunting the Stone.

Or perhaps he was. Perhaps he had been tasked to find it by the Imperial Council, in which case, he would be a very worthy opponent.

"Even if he is after the Stone, it doesn't matter. Just forget him." I huffed and berated myself anew because it was crazy— truly *crazy*—that he still managed to creep into my thoughts hours after meeting him. "Maybe the Stone *is* making me go insane. Actually, it probably already has. You are currently talking out loud to yourself, Primelle. That is *not* a good sign."

I snapped my mouth closed and concentrated on what I needed to do. I needed to find a place to rest and eat, and I should check in with my aunt. After that, once it was dark enough for the stars to appear, I would consult my book and map.

And then . . . I would *know*.

I MADE camp by a small stream. A cluster of *femeral* bushes surrounded me, which usually deterred a number of wildlings. The femeral's pungent scent was particularly bothersome to wildlings with stronger senses of smell, which decreased my chances of unwittingly camping across an underground burrow. And while the plant's aroma wasn't exactly pleasant, I wouldn't be around it long enough for it to bother me.

While making camp, I connected with my aunt, and I tried to take some reassurance from that. My mental call to her had been short, but she'd promised me that Uncle Timith was much the same as he'd been that morning.

In other words, I still had time.

Planting my hands on my hips, I surveyed what my telekinetic magic had unpacked. Around me, my supplies were neatly stacked since I'd only taken out what was needed for the night. I hadn't bothered with my tent. The sky was clear, no rain in sight, and come dawn, I'd once again be off, so the less I unpacked, the better.

I finished munching on the meat and cheese sandwich I'd prepared for dinner and peered upward. Through the Wood's canopy, a star appeared.

Darkness was *finally* upon me.

Hope bursting through me, I grabbed my constellation scroll and my book from the Isle of Song, then jumped back onto my carpet.

"Here goes nothing."

I whispered a command, and the carpet began to levitate up and up. I kept it moving vertically, and the treetop neared.

I briefly contemplated how smart this move was. Technically, I wasn't breaking any laws by commanding my carpet to do such a feat, but I wouldn't be able to move across the trees once I crested them since that was forbidden, yet I figured since I planned to stay stationary, I had an excuse for my actions on the unlikely chance anyone saw me and reported me to the kingsfae.

Leaves rustled against my face, their smooth texture like *cottonum* on my skin. It took a moment of wrestling awkwardly through a few vines and branches to break free, but eventually, my carpet pushed entirely through the last of the canopy.

The second the full night sky appeared, a gasp escaped me. Stars. Everywhere. *So many* of them littered the night sky.

Planets were visible too. The distant pulses of Eucaladas and Daphnis shone near the horizon, their auras throbbing lightly. And far, far off in the distance, Whiteolf was only a speck, barely visible near the western horizon.

I briefly admired the ribbon of the glowing galaxy that stretched from horizon to horizon, emitting colorful clouds and flaring magical auras, then turned my attention eastward, to the last remaining proof of the Wishing Stone's arrival.

Its hazy tail still streaked across the sky, hinting at where it'd landed.

Or where it'd supposedly landed . . .

My heart pumped steadily, thrumming in my chest as more anxious nerves brewed in my stomach. Brows furrowed, I picked my book up with shaking fingers. I knew most fae were heading entirely in the direction of the Stone's remaining tail, and that seemed logical, but if my book was correct, that wasn't its true path.

I carefully set my book on the carpet, then unfurled my constellation map, my fingers slipping once since I was so nervous. When I finally had the map spread out before me, I picked up the book that one of the gargoyles on the Isle of Song had loaned me. I ran my fingers carefully over the leather-bound cover. *Legends of Our Realm.*

In the previous weeks, ever since the Stone had first been spotted, I'd been preparing. Capturing the Stone could end all of the misery my family was facing, and I'd dove into discovering *everything* I could about it.

Thankfully, my job had been my saving grace. Loolee, my boss at the Whiteolf Academic Library, hadn't been happy when I'd taken an unexpected, extended leave to stay at my uncle's side, but she'd still been instrumental in helping me with my research. It was upon her advice that I spent an entire week traveling to and from the Isle of Song, where the most prestigious university and library of our land waited.

It'd been an arduous journey, given that the isle was on the opposite side of the continent, but I'd sailed on a ship around the northern coast, paying more rulibs than I wanted to remember, to get there. But that cost had been worth it. I'd been able to travel there and back at an expedited rate thanks to four fae with elemental air magic, and two fae with elemental water magic, who had propelled the ship to travel at ungodly speeds. If not for them, I would have still been traveling the great distance to that island.

And it was at the Isle of Song's library that Master Fistideeous, a very helpful gargoyle scholar, had placed *Legends of Our Realm* in my hands. If not for my employment at a library, I would have never been allowed to take the book off the island, but thank the stars that I had librarian status because I'd been referencing the book ever since.

Carefully, I opened it, being mindful not to bend the page too drastically or crease the spine. Preserving magic had been used to save the old book from decay over the seasons, but that didn't mean it was indestructible, and the thought of any precious book being ruined made my heart break.

The scent of anise and thyme—the telltale sign of parchment preservation magic—rose from the pages, and I stopped at the third chapter titled *The Wishing Stone—Elusive Gem and Coveted Relic.*

I'd read the fifty-page chapter several times over in the previous week, and one of the verses had actual directions on how to find the Stone. I had no idea if it was true, but I'd bet everything on the hope that it was.

I thumbed to the correct page, my fingers shaking again. Only one moon was full, and it barely illuminated the words. I called upon my Ironcrest magic, and my eyesight sharpened.

The verse appeared, as visible as though it were midday, and I began to read.

Upon the first night of the Wishing Stone's arrival, its hazy tail will remain in the sky. This can only be seen once the sun has fully set. The tail will be present for three nights total, dimming more each day until it entirely disappears. Many will be fooled by this, thinking the tail leads directly to the Stone, but the tail is only a guide. The stars are what will lead one to the Stone if the Stone deems you worthy.

On the eve of the first night, take note of the tail's tip. The brightest star closest to the tip should be most respected. If the star pulses and shines briefly with color, you've been given a gift. Follow that star. It will be your guiding light as you search for the Stone.

I closed the book and glanced at the Wishing Stone's remaining hazy tail, then at my map. The stars around the Stone's tail were on the map, and I studied each one, taking note of where the tail was in relation to them.

Eyes narrowing, I focused on the tail's tip more. My eyes popped. One star, just as the book claimed, was directly around the tip.

I quickly searched for that star on my map.

My jaw dropped.

It wasn't there.

"But how can that be . . ." I glanced at the star again, wondering if I was seeing things. Perhaps desperation was making me hallucinate. Maybe what I was witnessing wasn't even there. Maybe my sensory magic was going haywire.

I squeezed my eyes shut and counted to ten, but when I opened them, the star remained.

My breathing increased, and I again recalled what the chapter had taught me. The legend stated those who sought the Stone for unselfish purposes were more likely to find it.

I focused on the star anew, my stomach twisting into knots.

I was just about to blink when the star twinkled, then turned bright pink. It shone as richly as decadent candy.

Spine snapping upright, I stared at that star, and my breaths became so fast I got lightheaded. Eyes watering, I blinked, and when I focused on that star again, the color was gone.

I willed the pink hue to return. My sensory magic strained, and my pulse leaped, but I didn't dare shut my eyes again.

"Come on, come on," I whispered. "Show me again. Show me that I didn't just imagine you."

But the star kept twinkling, no different than any of the other millions of stars in our galaxy. But it was still a star that didn't fall on *any* constellation map.

It was only when my eyes began to burn that I finally allowed them to close and my sensory magic to calm. I huffed a breath.

"Did I really see it?" Despite my worry, a grin spread

across my face. "Yes, I did. It turned pink. I *know* it did. I wasn't hallucinating. And it's not on the map. Therefore, it must be a sign from the gods and goddesses. They've deemed me worthy of finding the Stone."

I gave a silent prayer of thanks to them, curled my map once more, then withdrew the seekerill from my pocket.

I set the device on my carpet and aligned it perfectly with the magical star that had flared pink. It was imperative I got this part right, so I checked its direction, then checked it again.

When I was certain the seekerill was aligned correctly, I pressed the button on its side. The device chimed, then hummed and vibrated slightly. Only a moment passed, and then a clap of magic emitted from it as the device registered the direction the elusive star pointed at.

"Don't fail me now. I'm counting on you to lead me straight to the Stone," I whispered to the device.

Turning it every which way, I checked its magic. But no matter which direction I positioned my body, the seekerill's needle spun to track the star's direction.

Heart pounding at how lucky I felt to have seen that star and have a unique device like the seekerill, I tucked it carefully back into my pocket. But despite the fortuitous turn of events, I couldn't stop the slight ache that filled my chest. The seekerill was just one of many inventions my uncle had created over the seasons for the king and queen.

"Thank you, Timith," I whispered. "Just stay alive. I'll find the Stone, and then I'll save you." Tears moistened my eyes, but I quickly brushed them away. "Now, time to sleep, and then I'll set out early in the morning."

I was about to descend back to camp, but a screech rose from the Wood. A horribly ugly sound that twisted my insides.

I paused and looked around.

The night breeze brushed my cheeks, and the top of the Wood's canopy stretched for hundreds of miles. I activated my sight sensory magic again and scanned the area, but the only thing unusual was smoke from a few small fires curling above the trees' canopy. Those fires were likely from other fae hunting the Stone, who were also camping in the Wood. Other than that, nothing seemed amiss.

"How odd." Brushing off that chilling sound, I was about to descend, but the noise came again.

Screeching. No . . .

Screaming.

I whipped around, trying to decipher which direction the screams were coming from. Out of nowhere, a loud expletive came from a male siltenite.

"What in the realm?" I whispered.

With a frantic command, I zoomed my carpet toward the commotion, making a beeline above the trees in the direction of the screaming that had turned ear-piercing. The noises grew, along with curses from the male. No wait, there were *two* males yelling and at least one screaming wildling.

Raucous laughter followed, and then the shrillness of the wildling's screams came again.

My heart was racing just as a rustle in a tree's leaves alerted me to their exact location. I stopped my carpet above it and peered below. More laughter filtered up from the males, then a pitiful wail rose from a wildling.

I stretched my mental magic out, assessing the situation more. Two streams of siltenite consciousnesses answered my magic's questioning pulse. Then another that was smaller, less complex. It was the kind of consciousness I would expect from a being with a mind not as advanced as our kind.

"Look at it. It actually thinks we'll let it live," one of the males sneered.

I bristled at the male's taunting words. Just as fast, a small dozen pulses of other consciousnesses, so tiny and barely formed that I'd almost missed them, strummed toward me. Fear bled from them.

My jaw dropped. *Babies.*

It hit me all at once what was happening. A dozen baby wildlings of a species I couldn't determine were below, and their mother wildling was defending them against two siltenite males who no doubt decided to either torment them or simply kill them for fun.

"Bastards." I clenched my teeth and carefully stepped off my carpet onto the tree's tallest and sturdiest branch. It sagged beneath my weight but held.

I glanced at my belongings to ensure my map was still safely stowed on the carpet. Thankfully, it hadn't budged despite my stepping off.

I returned my attention to the tree and crawled carefully along it. The branch was thick, but it still swayed, making me grip it tighter, but I climbed slowly and carefully downward. The males below continued their sadistic tormenting, none the wiser to my presence.

"Cut its ear off," one said. "That'll really make it scream."

The other laughed. "After we're done with the mother, we should carve up the babies."

The first snickered. "I love how sick you are."

My stomach heaved just as they both laughed again, and another painful cry rose from the wildling mother. Her chin tilted upward, tears shimmering in her eyes, and through the leaves, we made eye contact.

Her expression pleaded with me to help, and the scent of her blood drifted in the air. Another one of the males had just cut her anew.

My pulse thrummed with fury, and I quickly nodded that I was on my way, but then the male slashed her again, and she screamed in pain.

"Screw this," I whispered. I was about to leap off the last branch and blast them both with psychic magic, paralyzing their minds and capturing their essences, when a third male's voice droned through the trees. "Enjoying yourselves, I see?"

My hands nearly slipped.

That voice. I'd heard that voice before.

I peered through the remaining branches and leaves, trying to get a better view of the newcomer, but even with my sight sensory magic activated, too much foliage obscured my view. Not even my magic could see through objects.

Cursing, I climbed down another few feet, just as one of the bastard males replied, "Who in the realm are you?"

"Someone passing through. I couldn't help but hear this wildling's calls of distress."

The second male growled just as my feet touched the last branch closest to the forest floor. I quickly dropped onto it, my movements silent, then lay flat.

Rough bark met my palms, and the tree's rich scent flooded my nose. I clung tightly to the branch and peered around its thick width. A clear view of what was unfolding appeared before me, and my breath sucked in.

I was right. It was *him*.

A small clearing revealed a terrified and bleeding wildling mother standing defiant before her den hollowed out in the tree's base. Quivering babies huddled behind her, and two siltenite males flanked her.

But across the clearing, another male had appeared.

Kole Swordwielder.

His stance was casual yet his attention stayed focused.

The same large sword that he'd worn earlier was strapped to his back. He hadn't reached for it, but energy thrummed around him.

Neither of the bastard males, nor Kole, showed any aware-ness of my presence, which wasn't surprising since I kept my breathing silent and even, and the foliage still hid me.

"Leave now and torment no more wildlings along your journey, and I'll let you go." Kole's voice came out calm and smooth. As he'd been earlier today, his face was entirely devoid of emotion, yet a steady pulse of power emitted from him, like a cloak of menace just waiting to be unleashed.

The first male I'd heard torturing the wildling scoffed. "Perhaps we should be saying the same to you. I'm not sure if you've noticed, but there's two of us and only one of you."

Both males stepped forward, hands going to their waists where blades waited to be unsheathed.

The first continued. "You know, you should be more careful. Way out here, nobody will hear your yells. Too many fae are hunting the Stone, and the kingsfae have their hands full."

Kole's expression didn't falter, and his voice was just as even when he replied, "Which I suppose made you two imbeciles think you could get away with murder tonight."

The second male laughed. "It's only a wildling. What's it to you?"

"Wildlings are still fae."

Both males sneered. "So you're one of *those*, a siltenite who thinks wildlings have rights."

Kole's voice remained steady. "They do have rights. Perhaps not as many as you or me, but murdering an innocent wildling is still breaking the law."

"Only if you're caught," the first replied.

Kole's composure didn't break. "I won't say it a third time.

Leave now. Do not harm any more wildlings along your journey, and I'll let you go."

Both males laughed again, and before I could blink, they lunged at the same time, giving way to the fact that they'd done this before. Practiced maneuvers had them in Kole's space in less than a second. I barely had time to inhale before they were on Kole, knives gleaming, and arms swinging to strike.

Kole's sword appeared in his hand, his movement so fast it was a blur.

Blade met blade, the sound of clashing steel ringing through the Wood.

The wildling mother grabbed her babies and fled, the dozen youngsters clinging to her back in her haste to escape.

Grunts and groans came from the fighting males. Despite the two seeming to be common criminals, their fighting stances were far from a novice's.

But Kole's sword met them blow by blow, his expression steady, his movements precise.

Yet the males were right about one thing. It was two against one.

When one leaped behind Kole, his lips peeling back in a gleeful smile just as his knife thrust upward, my eyes widened.

"No!" I screamed and dropped to the forest floor.

Kole's narrowed eyes glanced my way just as a huge rush of magic shot out of me, ensnaring both males' minds as their knives twisted to impale Kole.

Both males seized mid-movement.

One jerked, his entire body twitching. The other turned as stiff as a board.

Magic rushed out of me, capturing them completely and halting their attack.

I was breathing so hard my rough pants filled the Wood, which had suddenly turned quiet. Wind brushed over my cheeks, and the night air chilled my skin.

Kole focused on me, not even a flicker of surprise on his face, and the males tipped over, still lost to the magic I had encased them with.

Bodies twitching, eyes vacant, knives still clutched in their grips but entirely useless, they stared upward unseeing.

Calmly, Kole sheathed his sword, the sound of it sliding into place with deafening precision ringing through the Wood.

The Imperial Council Warrior and I stared at one another, and then he said so calmly that it made me shiver, "What in the galaxy do you think you're doing?"

CHAPTER SIX

Kole's cool tone registered just as he crouched and pulled two sets of cuffs from the back of his waistband. Blue glowing magic flared around them, their energy crackling. Kole secured the cuffs around the males' wrists, and a satisfying spark emitted from them when he locked them closed, but neither male gave any indication to the fact that their magic had just been suppressed or their limbs restricted. They still stared unseeing, my magic rendering them unconscious.

Frozen in place, I struggled to understand what was happening and what I'd just done.

As before, Kole moved quietly and purposefully until he was towering over me, his shoulders so broad they blocked the moonlight that filtered through the canopy. Dark hair ruffled in the breeze, one lock slipping down to brush his eyebrow.

All I could do was stare at him.

"Why did you intervene?" His gaze was penetrating.

Unnerving. "You put yourself at risk by doing so, and things could have ended very differently because of it."

"I . . . I didn't risk myself."

"No? And what if one of those males had turned on you?"

Some of the shock of the situation faded, and I stood up straighter. "Well, I handled it, didn't I? Even if one had turned on me, that wouldn't have changed the outcome."

"But that still doesn't answer my question. *Why* did you do it?" He continued to stare at me intensely, and when a breeze kicked up, his scent wafted around me.

I tried not to inhale. Tried not to notice the alluring aroma clouding around me, of cedar, pine, and the sea. The scent was uniquely him, and it was impossible to ignore. Gods and Goddesses, but Kole smelled *so* good. Amazingly so.

But even though I wanted to soak up his scent like parched soil in a desert, his unrelenting stare took precedence. Once again, just like this morning, he watched me in a way that was unnerving.

I fiddled with my fingers even though I was trying not to fidget. "Because you . . ." My mouth opened and closed as I struggled to fully answer his question. "Because one jumped behind you, and it looked like he was going to sink his blade into your back. I thought you were about to be—" I stopped mid-sentence and realized how ridiculous I sounded.

I could have sworn his lips twitched. "You were concerned for my well-being?"

I ducked my head, my cheeks flaming. "I don't know. I just acted. I suppose I didn't bother to think why."

I glanced upward, expecting to see Kole's annoyance. Most fae males took pride in their strength, especially those trained in combat. Having a fae female, half his size nonetheless, jump to his rescue was likely to wound whatever ego he possessed.

But the sour look I expected to find was absent. And his earlier humor had vanished too. Once again, his expression was like reading a blank page.

A moment passed, only the breeze whispering through my ears.

Finally, Kole canted his head. "Do you really think I've never fought two males at the same time before? That I don't know how to handle myself?"

His question was asked blandly, as if he truly was curious to hear if I thought him so weak, and that even if I did, his self-confidence was robust enough not to care.

"Well, now that you mention it . . ." I offered a wavering smile, hoping to lighten the mood or at least get a smile from him. "I suppose you're probably capable of such a feat. Otherwise, you likely wouldn't have your job."

He tilted his head more. "And what job is that?"

"I'm assuming you're a warrior for the Imperial Council, since the kingsfae back in Whiteolf bowed to you, and you know, your last name is Swordwielder, and you're carrying that"—I gestured to the sword at his back—"huge monstrosity, along with those blue cuffs you just slapped on those two."

He shrugged, neither confirming nor denying my suspicions of his employment. But he *had* to work for the Imperial Council. It was well known that their warriors had been assigned surnames that suited their task. If one heard a name such as Swordwielder, Bladeslicer, Flamethrower, and so forth, it was a pretty good indication that their employer ran the covert group of warriors that were sent throughout the continent as needed to subdue conflict.

Those conflicts were often political in nature and arose in such a manner that no king or queen wished to claim responsibility for them. When such an event occurred, and a ruling monarch called upon the Imperial Council for assistance in a matter that required a warrior's skill, the Imperial Council Warriors were dispatched.

The warriors would be sent to whatever skirmishes had arisen. The matters were taken care of swiftly and quietly before they could escalate into an all-out battle. As a result, conflicts were smoothed, wars were avoided, and deaths were drastically reduced.

Of course, such a practice was only effective if it was done in the early days of a conflict or the beginning of an uprising. If an army was already marching, or if civilians had gathered in large numbers to form a militia, the monarch hoping for help was out of luck. But otherwise, the warriors were said to be quite effective.

One thing I did know was they were a secretive bunch. If the Imperial Warriors were involved, most fae were none the wiser that any violence had occurred at all. The warriors were rumored to be that efficient, that quiet, which only further flamed my belief that Kole was one of them. It definitely explained his ability to mask everything he was thinking or feeling, even if his Shield couldn't keep me out.

I eyed Kole again, taking in his impressive build and steady composure. He hadn't even flinched while fighting those two males. And as an Imperial Council Warrior, he could have easily bested them. He probably could have taken on three, four, five, or perhaps even ten fae at once. And surprisingly, he'd done everything with only physical skill. I hadn't felt the traces of rising magic that indicated he was using intrinsic power. It'd been the same when he'd taken down Abel.

All in all, everything I'd seen so far strengthened my belief in *what* he was, but it was also a reminder that I'd been entirely foolish to intervene.

Trying to cover up my embarrassment, I beamed.

Kole's attention dipped to my mouth, but he quickly looked away. "Where did you come from anyway?"

I pointed behind us. "That tree."

His brow furrowed. "Right, I noticed you appeared from a tree, but *how* did you get there?" For the first time since meeting him, a genuine trace of emotion flitted across his face. He looked perplexed, and I had the ridiculous urge to laugh.

Me, Primelle Hollaran, had stumped an unflappable Imperial Council Warrior.

I cackled inwardly at that thought, but suppressed the

giggle that wanted to rise. No need to start laughing like some unhinged buffoon. The stars knew this warrior already thought me entirely daft, given the circumstances in which we'd met. First, I'd kissed him unabashedly. And now, I'd appeared out of a tree only to "save" him from sure death.

Daft indeed.

Kole cocked his head, waiting for me to reply.

"Oh, I, um . . ." The second I realized I would have to explain my actions, all traces of humor left me. I swallowed and wondered if I was about to get a set of blue cuffs slapped onto my wrists too. "I was nearby and heard the commotion. I came to investigate."

"From the top of a tree?"

I smiled again, grinning so broadly my cheeks hurt. "Traveling by treetop is underrated. You should try it sometime if you've never done it."

He side-eyed me, then glanced upward to peer through the trees. "Traveling by treetop, you say?"

"Oh yes, swinging from vine to vine. Jumping from branch to branch. Truly, you should give it a go. It's quite freeing."

"Is that so?" He stepped closer to the tree, then placed his hands on his hips.

He glanced upward, and I gulped.

My hovering carpet was clearly visible above the Wood's canopy.

His attention dropped back to me. "That's very interesting *treetop traveling* you're engaging in. Funny how you failed to mention that swinging upon vines, or jumping from branch to branch, also required an enchanted carpet."

My stomach bottomed out, and my mouth opened and closed in silence. I finally blurted out, "I wasn't trying to break the law. I swear on the galaxy, but I heard the wildling's screams, and I couldn't just let them kill her."

He eyed one of the unconscious males. "And what would you have done if I hadn't been here, and it was just you against these piles of domal dung?"

"It would have depended upon the situation. Upon what they did."

"They're murderers."

"I agree, although some wouldn't see it that way. Some believe there's nothing wrong with killing wildlings."

"I happen not to agree with that, and the law doesn't either."

"No, it doesn't, and I'm of the same mind as you. These bastards are murderers through and through."

"Which makes it all the more dangerous for untrained fae, such as yourself, to take them on."

I smiled broadly again and lightened my tone. "Yet I still came out unscathed."

His focus drifted to my lips once more, his eyes hooding slightly, but then he blinked and looked away. I couldn't have deciphered his expression if I'd tried.

I huffed. "You're very good at that," I stated, before I thought better of it.

He cocked his head. "Good at what?"

"Not revealing what you're thinking."

He grunted, and I wasn't sure if that meant he was offended or complimented.

I grinned again, not sure what else to do. It was the typical fallback on my part. Smile. Laugh. Find humor. See the positive side. For full seasons, it was how I'd dealt with my problems. Usually, it worked, and no matter how difficult a conundrum was or how awkward a situation appeared, my sheer determination to see the bright side shone through, and those around me began to share in my good nature.

But Kole didn't even crack a smile, and I had the most ridiculous urge to begin babbling. Unfortunately, that was exactly what I did.

"Are you going to cuff me too and let the kingsfae pick me up?" As soon as I said that, I wanted to smack myself. Kole hadn't made any further conversation about my illegal use of travel to this area, and while Imperial Council Warriors weren't known to deal with petty crimes and so forth—the kingsfae had that pleasure—it didn't mean that he couldn't if he chose to.

I held my breath, my stomach suddenly heaving. I'd ridden my carpet over the Wood's canopy after all, even if the distance had been short. But because of that, if Kole chose to enact the law that forbade non-royal fae from flying haphazardly above the tree line, he could have me arrested, and then I wouldn't be able to hunt the Stone and save my uncle. None of my preparation would amount to anything, and all because of my stupid need to—

"It's fine," he replied. "I won't arrest you or report you."

"You won't?"

"Like you said, you were trying to help. In situations like this, I tend to look the other way."

My heartbeat calmed a little. "Thank you," I breathed.

"You're welcome."

At my feet, one of the males suddenly twitched. Kole glanced downward, a lock of dark hair falling across his forehead. He toed the male, who still showed no signs of regaining consciousness despite his involuntary jerks. "How did your magic do this?"

His question was asked calmly, but it struck me that I'd been so caught up in the past few minutes of speaking with Kole that I'd forgotten to release the would-be murderers from my hold.

I immediately sucked all of my psychic magic back inside me, then slammed my Shield down hard and fast, just as a new fear began to grow. Granted, I hadn't completely taken control of the would-be murderers' minds. I hadn't turned them into catatonic puppets ready to do my bidding, but still . . .

I avoided the urge to twist my hands together.

"Um . . . I . . ." I stalled, trying to figure out what to say because nobody else could do what I could, not that I knew of at least. Sure, plenty of fae in my kingdom had psychic magic. Some even had similar magic to mine that allowed fae to control others with verbal commands. Mistvale was the land of mental powers after all, but the depth of my magic, the utter *strength* of it and how it operated so covertly, with no words being spoken, and the other fairy not even being aware of what I was doing, was entirely unheard of.

Little did Kole know that if I wanted to, at this very instant, I could shred through his Shield, wrap my magic around his mind, and completely overtake his free will. All while just standing docilely in front of him.

Just the tiniest flick of my magic would have this warrior, this feared male of the Imperial Council, be a slave to my bidding. If I'd wanted to, I could have had him killing fae left and right, or had him trailing dutifully after me as my personal bodyguard and companion. I could totally and *completely* overtake him if I chose to.

And it wasn't just him that I could do that to. It was *everyone*. I had yet to meet anyone whose Shields repelled me. Even scarier, I could overtake dozens of others at once. Perhaps even hundreds at once. Maybe even thousands. I didn't know because I'd never fully tested it, but my magic felt bottomless.

And that kind of power terrified fae.

Only my aunt and uncle knew that I possessed such strength because power as strong as mine only created terror and doubt in others. And if fae began whispering that I had aspirations to use my magic to control the realm, I could be subjected to potent potions that subdued my strength, dulled my senses, and essentially turned me into a mindless, drooling imbecile. Just a shell of the fairy that I'd been.

So I hid my magic, never using it to its full capabilities, and truthfully, I had no desire to anyway. I'd never once had aspirations to use my magic to hurt others. Just the thought had my smile wiping clean.

Yet other fae didn't know that. History had shown that magic as strong as mine had always been viewed as a threat, not an asset.

I swallowed the thickness in my throat and reminded myself that Kole hadn't seen the extent of what I could do, just a snippet.

The warrior looked at me intently, his gaze as weighted as a mountain. "What did you do with your magic for this to happen?"

I reminded myself that acting insecure would only heighten his interest, so I shrugged nonchalantly. "I stopped their minds from communicating with their limbs."

"And you must have made their minds sleep too if they fell unconscious like this."

"Well, yes, that too, I suppose. It all rolls together."

He continued watching me. "How do you classify your magic?"

Dangerous. Impossible. A galaxy of might.

I again avoided the urge to fidget. Mistvale fae had such a wide variety of mental magic, but the majority fell into several categories: creating illusions, getting glimpses into the future, causing hallucinations in others, moving objects telepathically, manipulating another's emotions, projecting oneself psychically a small distance from one's body, linking consciousnesses, and performing other mental tricks.

But none were like me.

I smiled blandly and lied through my teeth. "My tutors always said my mental magic was like a switch being shut on and off. I can activate or deactivate a fairy's mind, which is why these two passed out." I shrugged again, and it took everything in me to continue standing there acting like the portrait of innocence. "Overall, it's not that impressive, but it's obviously handy if someone's attacking me."

"You would have to get through their Shields, though, to do that."

Shields don't work on me. "Yes, true. Luckily, these two didn't have strong Shields in place."

"They felt fairly strong to me."

I scrunched my nose up. "Did they?"

But he ignored that perplexed reply and said, "Is that all your magic can do?" He stared at me anew. All knowing. All seeing. As though he *knew* I was lying.

My eyes widened ever so slightly, but I quickly reminded myself there was no way Kole could know the full extent of what I was capable of. No possible way, so I smiled again. "Pretty much."

"What about magic from other kingdoms. Do you possess any of those?"

Yes, I also have elemental and sensory magic, but I can't shift. I don't have magic from all four kingdoms.

"Just the one." I smiled brightly. "What about you? Which kingdom are you from?" I had a fairly good idea that he was from Faewood, since he'd used air elemental magic on me back in Whiteolf, but I wasn't certain.

A breeze rushed through the trees above, jostling branches and swaying vines, but instead of answering me, all Kole said was, "I see."

A shiver rolled down my spine, and I wondered how much he truly did *see*.

But even though my own curiosity was burning to have him answer *my* question, I took a step back and forced another guileless smile. "Anyway, if you're not going to report me or arrest me, then I should probably get back to my camp."

He watched me, his eyes once again hooded. "Are you going to fly your carpet illegally again in order to return to your camp?"

His question had my hand stopping mid-reach for the tree branch.

I dropped my arms to my sides. "Oh, um, no. No, of course not. But I do need to retrieve my carpet. It's still, you know—" I waved upward and again resisted the urge to fidget.

"It's all right." He gestured to my carpet. "You may return to your carpet and camp, traveling back the way you came, but you're only allowed that short journey."

I swallowed. "Yes, sir."

I wasn't even sure what made me respond in such a formal way, but at least I managed to stop the salute I'd seen the kingsfae give to one another. I wasn't sure what it was about this male, but Kole had a way about him. A way that demanded those around him submit, and damned if I could stop my ridiculous, if slightly cheeky, response.

But I'd gotten myself in enough trouble for one day. I didn't need to press my luck further.

"Goodnight then!" Before Kole could change his mind, I jumped and grasped the tree's branch, then scampered upward, thankful once again that I was wearing pants and not a heavy gown.

My braid swayed behind me, but my feet were quick and my movements sure. Ree and I had spent enough of our childhood climbing trees that it came back to me like second nature.

But even though I was in a hurry to flee, my magic still registered Kole's presence. Even without meaning to, I caught how he watched me on my entire climb upward, and stranger still, that his attention followed me after I'd leaped onto my carpet and zoomed away as fast as I could.

And it was only when I was back at my camp, my map and seekerill safely stowed away, that I lay on my sleeping mat and gazed upward while realizing that I'd never asked him the question that was now burning inside me.

Just why was an Imperial Council Warrior in Whiteolf, and now in the Wood, all alone and far away from any fighting or true conflict in our realm?

CHAPTER SEVEN

A tingle of magic roused me during the night. Subtle pulses of flaring magic emitted against my skin, alerting me to the presence of something outside of my warded barrier.

Somehow, I managed to keep my breathing even as I groggily tried to assess my surroundings more.

A creature was waiting just outside of my ward.

My heart abruptly galloped. I moved my hand subtly beneath my blanket until I felt the blade sheathed at my thigh. Fingers curling tightly around it, I listened to my ward's magic.

It only took a second to realize that whatever was watching me sleep wasn't large. It was quite tiny in fact, and it definitely wasn't a siltenite or feared predator of the Wood.

Relaxing, I released the blade and blinked my eyes open. My lips parted in surprise.

The wildling mother that Kole and I had saved only hours

ago was watching me. The second we made eye contact, she ducked her head sheepishly.

"It's all right," I said sleepily, then peered around her.

Twelve babies waited just behind her, peering around her bushy tail.

All of them were outside of the magical ward I'd erected around myself to stop any would-be assassins in the night. Not that any existed at the moment, but I had a feeling in the coming weeks, if I managed to get close enough to actually find the Stone, assassins might be something I would have to worry about.

"Are you okay?" I whispered quietly.

She nodded despite the blood that had congealed around her torn ear. Several cuts also littered her body, but I was relieved to see that nothing those two bastards had done to her would result in permanent injury.

The wildling mother gestured to something outside of my barrier, near my hip, and it was then I saw the pile of fresh berries waiting on the Wood's floor.

My eyes opened more. "Did you bring that for me?"

She nodded, and a small smile spread across her lips.

"That was very kind of you. Is that a thank-you gift?"

She nodded again.

I smiled sleepily. "How thoughtful of you, but it's all right. There's no need to thank me. I'm glad you're all safe and that the warrior captured those two males. They won't be bothering you again."

Her nose twitched, her babies' noses doing the same. Since they were *zilee* wildlings, they weren't capable of language, but they were more intelligent than most siltenites gave them credit for, and I knew she understood me.

"I have a salve for your injuries. I made it myself, using *errgone root*." I sat up more. "It'll help your cuts heal faster." I was about to reach for my pack, but she turned her bushy tail and leaped back into the Wood, her babies quickly following.

I lay down, and sighed happily. In other words, no salve needed or wanted. She'd come simply to thank me for intervening.

I eyed the pile of berries again and then called quietly into the Wood, "You're welcome, and you take care, my friend." Content, I rolled back on my side and drifted off to sleep.

———————*

THE NEXT MORNING, I didn't waste any time getting ready. The second I was dressed and packed, I pulled out the seekerill. The needle spun and eventually settled in a northeast direction.

"Northeast it is." I snapped the seekerill closed and tucked it deep within my pocket.

I sailed back to the Wood's road, and soon, I was speeding along. The early morning wind chilled my skin as the sun steadily rose.

Potent magic bathed our realm as the sun crested the horizon. I closed my eyes, savoring it, as the magic in our galaxy called to my own.

Cross-legged, I allowed myself a moment to enjoy this unique time of day, but just as fast, I wondered if the palace healers were currently at my aunt and uncle's residence. They came by most mornings at sunrise, hoping the new day's magic would aid them in curing my uncle. But of course, nothing they'd tried had worked yet.

I munched absentmindedly on cubed cheese and the juicy berries the wildling mother had left for me during the night. Determined not to ruminate on my uncle's illness, I tried to concentrate on the simple luxury of a nice meal. The berries were fat and sweet. They were difficult berries to find too, since they only hung from *rathers*, a vine known for growing high in the tree's canopy. That meant the wildling mother, despite her injuries, had likely climbed to the top of numerous trees to find such a bounty. It touched me that she'd spent time picking the best berries the Wood had to offer, even while injured and probably hurting.

Her thoughtfulness had my soul settling. There was so much good in our realm. So much, and soon, I would find the Stone, and my uncle would be saved.

Smiling anew, I briefly wondered if the mother had also collected a pile of berries for Kole. But who knew if she'd been able to find him. In all likelihood, he'd had to drag those two males back to Fillow, the small village I'd passed yesterday evening. There was a small kingsfae post there, so unless Kole planned to take them all the way to the courts himself, he would have had to leave them there.

I bit into another berry. Its decadent flavor coated my tongue, but once again, my attention returned to the warrior. A flash of his lips crossed my mind. The way he'd kissed me. The delicious way he'd smelled.

But I shoved those memories off as quickly as they came and instead focused on *why* I'd met him at all. It made no sense that Kole was this deep into the Wood when no unrest was occurring.

But I quickly brushed that thought off, too, and finished eating. My concentration needed to be on traveling as fast as I could. *The Stone. Find the Stone.* That was what mattered. Not Kole Swordwielder.

I CROSSED into Stonewild Kingdom in the late afternoon. Since Whiteolf wasn't overly far from the border, it hadn't taken as long as I'd feared it would to reach it.

And the second I crossed the border, long before any signs appeared noting the new kingdom, magic alerted me. Heady power filled the invisible barrier that separated Mistvale from Stonewild. Land that had once bred mental powers now birthed shifters.

I tried not to feel uneasy about traveling into a new kingdom, and I reminded myself of the promise I'd made to my aunt. Stay safe. Be smart. Don't alert others to my arrival. And I intended to make good on that promise. Given that Stonewild wasn't overly welcoming to fae from other kingdoms, it was best that I did so.

I traveled steadily for the entire day and did my best to stay obscure, but twice in the afternoon, I witnessed several altercations between other fae, and in the early evening I was positive that two males were following me.

Once I realized that, I zoomed along the road as fast as I could, then crashed into a *hideabims*, using the illusionary plant to hide.

Thankfully, that worked, and the two creeps passed by.

I kept up my swift pace for three full days, and other than the two bastards that had tried to kill the wildling mother and the two creepy fae who'd been following me, the worst thing I'd had to deal with was a nasty rash that had sprouted on my skin thanks to the hideabims bush I'd hidden in. But at least the two creepy males were long gone.

I rubbed the lock of Goddess Nuleef's hair as early morning moonlight illuminated the road in front of me on the morning of my fourth day. Sleepiness made my eyes heavy, but my fingers moved over her hair in a rhythmic pattern. It'd become a habit to caress it. For whatever reason, I found the action soothing.

I settled in for another long day of traveling, and felt thankful that my rash had finally cleared which made sitting cross-legged tolerable again. But abruptly, goosebumps sprouted on my skin. Just as fast, a low growl rose from the Wood.

My carpet continued on its course, but I grew stock still.

The growl was distant, not at the road's edge, but my magic instantly went on high alert. Even more so when I realized that was the *only* sound I'd heard. The Wood had gone entirely silent.

Not good.

Automatically, my hand slipped into my boot, and I pulled out my dagger. Using my magic, I stretched my senses out around me to assess the area more.

Dozens of consciousnesses strummed back to me. Wildling fae and animals were everywhere, some sleeping, others awake, but all of them were *silent*.

Another growl came, but it was quieter than the first, as if whatever had made that sound, had moved farther away.

I stretched my magic more, and the second I did, I alighted on a complex consciousness that was clearly siltenite and . . . familiar.

My brows scrunched together as Kole Swordwielder's magic pulsed faintly toward me. He was out there, right now, deep in the Wood. And from the feel of it, he was moving steadily away.

"What in the realm?" I whispered.

Apparently, the warrior hadn't retreated to another area of the kingdom after all. Instead, he was still in the Wood, still near where I traveled.

I recalled how he affected me when we first met. My response to him had been so heightened, so *visceral*. I'd been certain the Stone had begun to affect me adversely, as it'd done to Abel, but since that time I'd returned to acting normally. My thoughts had cleared, my responses had been what they'd always been, but now . . .

My breath caught in my throat, and my magic tracked him, memorizing his signature flavor that made following his location easier, but when he moved over a mile away, I stopped my curious stalking.

He was obviously doing something. What, I had no idea, but just as fast, I realized that the sound of the Wood had awoken again. Wildlings chattered. Birds tweeted. Animals snuffled and moved along the forest floor.

The sun crested the horizon, and I finally calmed my magic completely.

Still, I was stumped and slightly concerned at my vivid interest in the warrior. I needed to keep my thoughts clear if I was to save my uncle.

Frowning, I hurried away and continued my travel north, knowing that Kole Swordwielder was falling farther behind me, and I tried as hard as I could not to wonder what the Imperial Warrior was up to now.

ON THE EVE of my fifth day traveling, a bitterly cold wind descended from the north. I'd been steadily following the seekerill's direction and could only hope I was on the right path, because one thing had become entirely apparent. The seekerill wanted me to go north. Far north, it would seem. Which meant cold and snow.

However, the one saving grace was that most fae weren't searching where I was. I'd inquired with several wildlings the previous evening to learn what they knew, and among their far-reaching chatter, I'd learned that most siltenites were scouring the eastern shores for the Stone.

But that didn't mean my hunt would be easy. I shivered, thinking what was in store for me. At the very tip of Stonewild Kingdom, the Brashier Sea waited, the iciest and coldest sea in the fae lands. I could only hope the Stone hadn't landed *there*.

Since I'd entered Stonewild from its western border, I was already north of Stonewild's capital, Jaggedston, and well beyond the heat of the Shadow Valley Desert. The Wildland Mountains loomed, and not for the first time since departing Whiteolf, a moment of trepidation hit me.

The farther north one traveled in Stonewild, the wilder the terrain became. Fierce creatures were said to roam the Wood there, and I hadn't even seen half of what was to come. Silventine Wood was on the very tip of Stonewild Kingdom, and I prayed the Stone hadn't landed there either. If it had, I would be lucky if I made it back to Whiteolf alive.

Nerves tumbling anew, I tried to concentrate on staying

warm. I had a small fire burning around me by using my elemental magic, and I'd kept it alight all day as I'd flown down the road. I'd also used my magic to heat my blood, but that was rather tiring, so I'd stopped doing that mid-afternoon and only used the warmth my outward fire produced. But elemental magic was my weakest magic, so by evening time, my fire was flickering.

My only consolation was that I'd continued to move fast, but by the evening, even my speed didn't provide comfort despite the fact that I was making good progress.

A storm was brewing. Above, swirling navy and indigo clouds blanketed the pale green sky, the sun hidden entirely. It would be a true gale from the looks of it.

I tried not to worry over what was to come, but I was tired, achy, and my fingertips were numb despite my fire.

It didn't help that I hadn't had anything warm to eat since leaving Whiteolf, and the newly formed cold brought that fact back with icy clarity. The thought of a hot cup of tea and a steaming plate of roasted *ustorill* and herbed potatoes had my mouth watering and my stomach cramping, so when I came upon a small village south of the mountains, I paused.

Dusk was nearly upon me, and the scent of impending snow filled the air. I hovered silently on my carpet, taking in the small village that, according to a sign, was called Inisville.

Inisville wasn't large, and I guessed no more than a few hundred fae lived there, but there was a *salopas* ringing with lively song down the main lane. Lights also burned in houses, and several shops were still open.

The village was so tiny it didn't fall on any of my maps, but like most Silten villages, the Wood had been welcomed into its fold versus trying to deter it. Branches wove around siding, leaves sprouted from rooftops, and the scent of the Wood permeated the air. A few fae were walking through the streets, locals most likely given their casual and unhurried strides.

I bit my lip, contemplating what to do. A village promised a night of shelter. It also promised a hot meal.

But staying here could attract attention. Unwanted attention.

Who knew what other travelers were here or what they would try to do if they knew I was hunting the Stone and that I'd come prepared with weeks of supplies. A memory of the two creeps who'd followed me rose in my mind.

I nibbled my lip and eyed the north again. Jagged peaks that were as black as tar rose from the Wood not far in the distance. Rocky terrain, steep roads, and who knew what kind of creatures waited for me up there.

Another gust of wind hit me, and my flames entirely flickered out.

"Oh Stars, screw it." I whispered a command, and my carpet leaped forward as I ignored the road heading north toward the mountains and instead flew to Inisville.

Tomorrow I would venture into the Wildland Mountains,

but tonight I would have decent sleep, cooked food, and an endless cup of hot tea.

Shivering, I flew slowly down the main street, then stopped at the only inn from the looks of it. A sign declaring *Wildlands Inn* hung above the door, and across the street, the lively music in its only salopas grew.

I hopped off, stacked my supplies by the door, then rolled up my carpet and tucked it into the outdoor storage space provided by the inn. Gritting my teeth, I carried all of my supplies into the inn's entryway in several trips, opting not to use my telekinetic magic, which would only draw attention.

Cold wind blew around me, and with only my pack left, I breathed a sigh of relief. I swung it onto my back and was about to enter the inn to finally check in, but a flash of steel caught my eye.

I swung around just in time to see a pair of sapphire eyes gleaming down at me. My jaw dropped, and I automatically took a step back.

"Kole," I said, my voice sounding as surprised as I felt. He'd approached me silently, from who knew where, and I hadn't even realized anyone was about.

Another fierce gust of wind kicked up, causing the dark hair on the top of the warrior's head to ruffle. He was dressed in warmer gear than what I'd seen him in previously. Thick black breeches, tall boots, and a long-sleeved tunic of royal blue with emerald stitching covered his broad frame. Stonewild colors. He'd had the foresight to change into something the locals were likely to wear, probably to blend in better than I currently was.

But as before, the same sword was strapped to his back, definitely *not* local.

Kole took a step toward me, closing the distance between us, and if he felt any surprise at seeing me again, he hid it entirely.

Instead, he reached around me, grabbed the handle to the inn's door, and opened it. "After you."

CHAPTER EIGHT

"What . . . what are you doing here?" I stammered. Loud music from across the lane still filled the streets, and a sprinkle of snow flurries began to dance in the wind.

"Getting a room. You?" His tone remained calm, but surprisingly, he arched an eyebrow.

I pointed above his eye. "You moved your eyebrow."

His cocked eyebrow immediately lowered. "Pardon?"

"Your face moved. Normally, it doesn't do that." His forehead furrowed ever so slightly, and I grinned. "You did it again."

As if realizing he was sharing facial expressions, his demeanor smoothed entirely. "How very observant of you, Miss Hollaran."

I just grinned more.

For the briefest moment, his gaze fell to my lips, but then he cleared his throat and nodded toward the door that he still held open. "Are you going in?"

Cold air swirled around us, the snow thickening, and the wildling sitting at the desk inside the inn shot us an irritated look. It probably didn't help that I'd already opened the door half a dozen times to bring my supplies in.

I ducked inside, and Kole followed, closing the door after himself, but I stopped at the threshold, almost making the warrior bump into me.

I twirled around and scrunched my nose up at him. "It is odd, though, to see you again, especially here of all places." I didn't tell him that I'd sensed his presence the other day after I'd heard that strange growl in the Wood.

"Is it?" he asked, his bland voice giving away nothing, as if it was completely normal that we were running into each other *again*, in the wilds of the shifter kingdom nonetheless, and in some tiny village to beat.

"Yes, it is definitely odd."

He shrugged. "Coincidences happen."

"Are you both checking in?" the wildling behind the desk asked, forcing my attention to her.

I pushed off the strangeness of our paths colliding for a third time and sidled up to the check-in desk. Crackling from the inn's fireplace overtook the howling wind outside, and the scent of mint filled the air. Candles burned near the desk, their subtle aroma permeating the entryway.

A *ramifin* waited expectantly, already standing with her

ledger open before her. Hooved feet clapped the wooden floor quietly every time she shifted position.

It was a small inn, with only the check-in desk, several hallways stretching from it, and a lone stairwell in the corner. A cozy fireplace with a glowing fire crackled across from the wildling employee, and the music from the salopas across the street could still be heard, but it was faint through the walls.

I smiled pleasantly at her, but her attention shifted momentarily to the large siltenite warrior at my back, and I was fairly certain the huge sword strapped to his back was the reason for her gulp. Or perhaps it was Kole's open demeanor and friendly smiles. I snickered internally at my sarcastic humor.

"He's harmless," I said, my lips tugging up. "An enforcer of the law, in a way. You're safer with him here, even with that sword of his."

A throat cleared behind me, and I was curious if my comment had rattled Kole's composure. It had thrilled me to see his eyebrow move and then his forehead furrow. The thought of an actual scowl brewing on his face elicited a pleasant shock in me that definitely bordered on the realm of disturbing. Perhaps several days on the road by myself, with only mental check-ins with Gwen and Ree to keep me company, was making me a bit desperate for excitement. Or maybe the Stone was affecting me again now that Kole was back. Who knew.

Smacking myself internally, I said happily to the wildling

staff, "But yes, checking in please, as you probably noticed from all of the supplies I dragged in." I waved toward the mess I'd made.

The ramifin dipped her long head. "I figured as much. Do you have a reservation?"

"No, but it's just for one night."

"Place your hand here." She gestured to the crystal ball that sat beside the ledger, and I placed my palm upon it.

Magical bands encircled my wrist, keeping my hand in place as the crystal's power siphoned my identifying information onto the wildling's ledger. My name and home address appeared, scrawling upon the page as though written from an invisible hand.

"Whiteolf, eh?" She cocked her head, her snout looking even more elongated with the movement. "You're a long way from home. We don't see many Mistvale fae up here. Hunting the Stone, are you?"

I offered an unconfirming shrug. "Have many ventured this way after the Wishing Stone?"

She shook her head. "Only a few beside you, thankfully. From what I hear, most have gone to the eastern coast, in the direction it was seen headed. Is the Stone why you're here too?" she asked Kole, her focus shifting to the warrior.

He didn't reply, and the ramifin hastily returned her attention to the ledger.

She finished her work, and with my information carefully catalogued, the inn employee held out her hooved hand for the necessary rulibs. I counted the coins from the small purse tucked in my cloak and handed it over.

Finally, she gave me a key. "Upstairs on the second floor, third door down."

I glanced at the staircase she waved to in the entryway's corner and sniffed, trying to detect a hint of food in the air, but the only smell that greeted me was the burning mint candles. "Is food offered here?"

She shook her head. "You'll have to venture across the street for that. Unlike most inns, we don't have a salopas as well." She shrugged an apology, but I smiled and waved away the trivial matter.

"It's fine. I'm happy to go across the street. What was your name by the way?"

Her head snapped back. "My name?"

"Yes, I'm Primelle, as you can see on the ledger, but nobody calls me that. Feel free to call me Prim."

"Ah, right, um, nice to meet you. I'm Nivinity."

I grinned, taking great pride in the fact that a Stonewild wildling had actually told me her name. I'd half expected her to ignore me given their reputation. "A pleasure to make your acquaintance, Nivinity. I'm sure I'll see you again before the night's over."

She blinked, as if unsure how to respond, but then she dipped her head.

"Bye for now." I waved cheerfully, strapped my pack to my

back, and began to collect my things, lifting each item awkwardly.

Nivinity glanced at Kole, who'd been unsurprisingly silent. "You'll have to have your information processed by the ledger as well, even if you're staying in the same room."

My eyes rounded to saucers, my mouth dropping. I swung toward Kole, but he was merely staring at Nivinity.

"No, we're not. I mean, he and I aren't—" I tried to slow my words, but my heart was suddenly racing. "He and I aren't staying *together*. We barely know each other."

Nivinity's eyebrows shot up. "Oh, sorry, I thought you two were a couple."

"No, we're not," I blurted, just as Kole said, "No need for an apology."

His more tactful response made my cheeks burn. I quickly gathered more of my goods and began shuffling toward the stairs. Of course, that was difficult. Between my pack, boxes of supplies, and the long cloak I was wearing, I nearly dropped everything.

It was only as I reached the stairs and *did* drop the box containing my cured meat and cheese that the warrior's aura brushed against my back. I wanted to smack myself at my clumsiness, but I didn't have a free hand to do so, so all I could do was watch as a wheel of cheese rolled across the wooden floor while the package of meat *thunked* near Kole's feet.

Perhaps I should be using my telekinetic magic even if it draws attention . . .

"Sorry about that." My cheeks warmed, and I tried to bend down.

Before I could grab what I'd dropped, Kole reached for the box and easily placed the meat and cheese back inside it. From there, he took the remaining boxes I held along with my pack. He did it so quickly, as if automatically.

Empty-handed, I shuffled from foot to foot. "Oh, um, thank you."

He abruptly stilled and glanced at what was in his arms. For the briefest moment, a look of surprise coasted over his features, as though he didn't understand how all of my goods were now being carried by him, but then he said gruffly, "I'll uh, take this up for you."

He climbed the stairs quickly, not faltering once under the weight of my supplies, and despite my heart pounding when a rush of his scent curled around me, I hurried back to the entryway to grab everything else, then flashed Nivinity another smile in hopes of distracting myself from my latest visceral response to the warrior. "I love that necklace you're wearing."

She brought a hooved hand to the small gem encased in silver at her throat and smiled shyly. "Thank you."

I *hmmed* a happy response, then climbed the stairs after Kole.

When I reached the second floor, my breaths came faster than they should have for a single flight of steps, but the warrior was already at my chambers, my supplies neatly stacked beside the door, and his height, impressive sword, and broad shoulders once again stole my attention and threatened to star in my next round of vivid female fantasies.

"Where are you staying?" I asked and beamed, hoping to cover up how easily he affected me. I inserted the key into my door's lock awkwardly since I still held two boxes.

He nodded at the fourth door. "That one."

"So we're neighbors," I replied, still struggling with the key. Seriously, it should not have been this hard, but Kole was standing so close to me, and apparently, coordination was no longer something I possessed.

The warrior reached out and took the key from me, our fingers brushing in the process. For the briefest moment, he once again grew still, but then he broke our contact and easily inserted the key and opened my door.

Warmth bloomed on my cheeks since my fingers still tingled from the brief touch we'd shared. "Again, thank you." I shook my head sheepishly. "I swear I'm not normally this clumsy."

His gaze lingered on my mouth again, much as he'd done downstairs. Abruptly, his nostrils flared, and he lifted his head. "It's not a problem."

His straight posture gave me a clear view of his lips and the strong columns in his throat. A memory of the kiss we'd shared in Whiteolf *again* blasted to the front of my mind, and thinking of the feel of his arms caging me in and the tangle of his tongue caressing mine once again threatened to derail my composure. Not that I currently *had* any composure . . .

Consequently, the uncontrollable urge to ramble to try and cover up my responses immediately took over. "It's so strange to see you again, all the way out here, nonetheless." I shoved my supplies through the door, then planted a hand on my hip. "Say, whatever happened to those two males that you apprehended? Did they walk free or go to the court system? They were such awful fae. I hope they got what they deserved. And did that wildling mother ever find you that night? She came to me when I was sleeping and gave me a handful of the most delicious berries. I was wondering if she did the same to you?"

I was nearly breathless by the time I smacked some sense into myself and stopped talking.

But Kole just eyed me, his expression blank, although he was staring at my mouth again.

Abruptly, he shifted away and withdrew his key. "I took those males to Fillow and left them for the kingsfae to take care of. I'm unsure where the authorities took them from there, and no, the wildling mother never found me and gave me berries."

"Oh, right, I kind of figured as much about the males, and I'm not surprised that you didn't get any berries if you left with them to travel back to Fillow. She probably couldn't find you." I ran a hand through my hair, unsure what else to do.

The key he held still sat idly in his door's lock, and it was then I realized that he didn't have any bags. I cocked my head. "Don't you have a pack or belongings you're traveling with?"

In a way, I felt entirely foolish given the sheer amount of goods I'd brought along.

But if he'd heard me, he didn't indicate it. His attention had dipped once again to fixate on my mouth, and I could have sworn that something flashed in his eyes. Heat, maybe, or *want?* But that couldn't be right. The warrior wasn't actually attracted to me. He barely wanted to speak with me, let alone be around me. Never mind how he'd kissed me in Whiteolf and practically devoured me in that moment.

That was a forced kiss, lest you forget that, Primelle Hollaran. Kole didn't choose to do that, I silently chided myself.

Yet just when I was certain that the warrior was looking at me with a hint of lust, despite trying to talk myself out of it, a crack of magic flared around his wrist, and he snapped himself upright.

My attention dropped to where his magic had just flared. *How odd.*

Forehead furrowing, he said in a rush, "No, I don't have any other bags. Good evening to you, Miss Hollaran."

With that, he turned his key and disappeared in a flash of speed inside his chambers.

CHAPTER NINE

My heart was still pounding even though all I'd done was unpack what I needed for the night, then stacked the rest of my things near the closet. But I couldn't get over the fact that Kole Swordwielder was on the other side of our shared wall, and that we'd run into each other yet *again*. Nor could I get over the belief that he'd been staring at my mouth in the hallway while I'd been having lust-filled thoughts.

Please, please, don't start acting crazy again just because he's near.

I sighed. That was all I needed. Although, given my reaction to him downstairs and in the hall, it was quite possible that ship had sailed.

I nibbled on my lip, frowning, and mulled everything over. Music from the salopas across the street continued to carry into my room, but it did little to drown out my thoughts.

I'd had days to think about my initial response to Kole, to

when we'd first met in that alleyway in Whiteolf, and then later that same day in the Wood. I'd been convinced my reactions were all due to the Stone, given that everything had happened so closely together. And that I, like Abel's unhinged behavior, was acting derailed due to the Stone's arrival.

Yet . . . since then, my insanity *hadn't* increased. The opposite in fact. The past four days I'd felt normal, just like I always did.

So what does that mean?

I rolled my eyes and finally accepted the obvious. "Seriously, Primelle. It doesn't take a genius to figure this one out. The Stone isn't making you crazy. You're simply attracted to Kole, and that's why you act like an idiot around him. That's all entirely due to your lovely self. Nothing more." I plopped down onto my bed and cradled my head. "Oh stars. How wonderful."

Even though I'd been attracted to other males in my life, if I was honest with myself, none had ever affected me like Kole did. For some stupid reason, my body, magic, mind . . . all of it, stood to attention when he was close by.

I muttered a sound of disgust. "Try to remember why you're actually here."

Bouncing, I tested my bed's mattress, then did a quick check of the room's security. Like most inns, simple wards were encased within the walls, deterring anyone from manipulating their magic through them. They were basic, though, not something that would keep a powerful magic wielder at bay, but it was enough to make me feel safe.

From there, I went to the door in the far corner, near the windows and beside the bathing chambers. It wasn't a closet, since I'd already found that, but oddly, the door was locked.

"How strange. Perhaps this is a secured closet?" But when I disengaged the lock and opened the door, a closet didn't greet me. Another solid door did.

Without thinking, I knocked on it.

A few thumps came from the other side, then the sound of another lock disengaging. Just as I realized where this door led and what it was, Kole was opening his door from the other side of our adjoining rooms.

So much for not acting like a crazy idiot.

I smacked a hand to my mouth to hide my embarrassment. "I'm so sorry. I only realized after I knocked that this was likely an adjoining chamber with yours. I didn't mean to bother you."

What I was coming to think of as his *very-Kole* expression didn't change.

Grinning like a buffoon, I called, "Enjoy your evening!"

I promptly slammed the door closed and re-locked it on my side, then placed my back against it.

Once again, my heart was beating so hard, but I tried to tell myself that it wasn't because of Kole's blazing blue irises or broad shoulders.

"Must reclaim sanity," I muttered. "If that's even possible."

Music continued to carry through the windows, and I eyed

the salopas across the street again. My stomach let out a loud rumble, and in a flurry of movements, I was securing my cloak around my shoulders and sailing out of my chambers because putting distance between myself and Kole Swordwielder seemed to be the only way to keep my head clear.

THE MUSIC in the salopas was in full swing. A lively wildling band played in the corner, swaying and shifting to their beat. Several patrons filled the tables in the small establishment, but there was plenty of free seating still available.

A barkeeper stood behind a long wooden bar, taking his time filling drinks and then placing them on enchanted trays that floated through the air to patrons.

As was common in most eating establishments, he was the lone employee in the room, although, I suspected fae or wildlings worked in the back, making the food.

When he glanced my way, I dipped my head in greeting, but all he did was narrow his eyes and give me a once-over.

Despite his snub, I kept my head high and approached him. Even if I wasn't local, and he had no intentions of acknowledging my presence, I figured he would still feed me. Rulibs didn't come from thin air after all, and everybody had to make a living.

At the bar top, I folded my forearms together and placed my elbows on the notched wood. He didn't even look at me, so

I stopped waiting for him to and asked, "May I please have a pot of mint tea and whatever hot food you have on special tonight?"

He finished topping off a large glass of *leminai*, then filled another. I was about to ask my question again in a sterner tone, but he finally replied, "Ten rulibs, then have a seat. It'll be over shortly."

I placed a ten-piece coin on the counter and turned stiffly.

Several other fae were watching me, their expressions cool, but at least the music was pleasant, the air warm, and the seats looked comfy enough.

Despite the unwelcoming atmosphere, I reclaimed my good mood and smiled pleasantly to those I passed, then sidled to a table near the crackling fire and waited for my food to arrive.

I didn't have to wait long, since thankfully, the barkeeper wasn't petty enough to take my rulibs and *not* feed me. Only two songs passed, and then a tray glided toward me with a large pot of tea and a steaming plate of sustenance.

My stomach growled, but while it wasn't an ustorill roast and herbed potatoes as I'd been dreaming of, it was baked hen drizzled in gravy and plenty of root vegetables and greens on the side. Simple, hearty fare and exactly what I'd been craving.

"Thank you, galaxy," I muttered to no one in particular.

I dug in, enjoying each bite and sip of tea as the music continued, and as I slowly devoured my supper, I figured it was a good time to do my daily check-in with my aunt and Ree.

Turning my attention inward, I released a stream of magic and resisted the urge to close my eyes. It was always easier to connect mentally over a long distance with all of my attention focused on my magic, but I also knew that would look weird, so I gazed toward the musical stage and gripped my hot mug between my palms as I connected with my aunt.

Prim? Are you all right? As Gwen had been every night that we'd spoken, she sounded worried the second our connection solidified.

Yes, I'm just fine. I actually booked an inn for the night. I'm currently in a small village in Stonewild called Inisville. It's much colder up here, and it's started to snow. The thought of camping tonight had my insides dying, so I opted to splurge on a room.

She sighed in relief. *That's probably wise, and I'm glad to hear that also means you're not alone if you're in a village. So you're still in Stonewild, then? Are you sure that's where the Stone landed?*

I shrugged, even though she couldn't see it. *The seekerill led me here, and it keeps telling me to go north, so at this point, I can say fairly certainly that the Stone is definitely somewhere in Stonewild.*

I felt, rather than saw, her nod. *Which direction are you heading?*

I'll be going into the Wildland Mountains tomorrow.

Her breath sucked in. *Be careful up there, Prim. That part of the Wood isn't for the fainthearted.*

I know. I will be. I took another sip of tea, then asked hesitantly, *How's Timith?*

A little worse, actually, but not by much.

I gripped my mug tighter, my fingers digging into it. *What does that mean?*

She sighed, and her tone dipped. *He's hardly drinking now. We really had to work to get enough fluids into him today. Thank goodness Verin is here.*

My heart began to thump. *Has anything else changed?*

Not enough that I think you should come home. You know if that were the case, I would tell you. And if you think you stand a true chance at finding the Stone, then keep going.

I nodded internally. *Has anything else been going on?*

Not really, other than Abel returning. Vissy told me he spent the week detained by the kingsfae. I can only imagine what he did, but thankfully, the kingsfae forbade him from hunting the Stone again, and unless he wants to be arrested a second time, he won't be leaving Whiteolf. Oh, and Opalin and Roosep have been asking after you daily, but I've kept them up to date. They're as worried about you as I've been.

Thank you for keeping them informed, and I'm not surprised Abel got arrested. I didn't say more. I hadn't told her how Abel had harassed me on that first day since I'd seen no point in needlessly worrying her, but I was glad he'd been forbidden from hunting the Stone again. One less thing to worry about. Although, I doubted he would be able to find me all the way up here. Still, I was thankful I wouldn't have to stress over that. *How are Opalin and Roosep doing anyway? I* added.

They're both well, but worried about you too. I don't think I could keep your updates from them if I tried. You know how relentless Opalin can be when she wants to know something.

I laughed softly. She was right. Opalin had a one-track mind if something intrigued her.

My aunt and I spoke for a few more minutes, then said our goodbyes.

Once I'd closed down our connection completely, I peered around at the other fae. Most of the patrons had stopped looking at me, the novelty of a newcomer obviously having worn off, and nobody was openly scowling at me anymore either.

Perhaps the fact that I'd kept to myself and had sat near the wall helped. As much as I enjoyed being friendly with others, I also knew that not everyone shared in my enthusiasm of meeting new fae.

I took a few more bites of food, my plate nearly empty, then I turned inward again to check in with Ree.

Ree answered immediately, her energy just as relieved and happy to hear from me as my aunt's had been. We spoke for a few minutes, each of us catching the other up on our day. But when I told her that Kole had shown up in this town just after I did, her shock barreled toward me.

Seriously? After your other strange meetings, he's now arrived in some tiny Stonewild village at the exact same time as you? She huffed. *Prim, this is getting to be too big of a coincidence. Is he following you?*

Lively music continued around me, and I took another sip of tea. *Honestly, now that you've mentioned it, it does seem like he's following me, but I doubt that's true. That makes no sense. I'm not a criminal nor causing any political issues. It's more likely that he's after the Stone than following me.*

An Imperial Warrior is Stone hunting?

I could just picture her flaming red eyebrows shooting clearly to her hairline. I shrugged. *Maybe the Council told him to.*

I could tell she was mulling that over. A moment later, she replied, *I suppose it makes more sense that he's after the Stone than following you. Maybe he has a seekerill too, or some version of it, and that's why you're both on the same path.*

I canted my head. I hadn't thought of that possibility. *I suppose that could be the case. Timith isn't the only inventor in the realm after all.*

And if he has the Imperial Council behind him, it's definitely possible he's got that kind of resource.

I nibbled on my lip. *So if he is after the Stone, do you think a king or queen, or even* our *king and queen, instructed the Council to get the Stone for them? Maybe one of the royals wants to claim its wish, but they don't want to be seen hunting the Stone directly?*

I felt her nod. *It's definitely possible, but that's not what the Council is supposed to do.*

No, you're right.

But if he's not Stone hunting, then he's following you, she teased.

I snorted and took another sip of tea and hoped she wouldn't detect how that comment made my stomach dip. *But why would he be following me? I'm nobody special.*

Not true at all. You're totally special, but you're correct that you're not someone the Imperial Council would be interested in.

I considered everything more. *You could be on to something, though. His time here could be related to the Stone, but maybe not in the way we're thinking. Perhaps he's doing kingsfae duties at the moment, which would be highly unusual given his skillset, but he did take care of Abel and those two males who attacked the wildling mother. And I've seen enough altercations that I know fae are acting badly. Remember those two creeps who were following me?* I shivered. *Bottom line, the Stone is making fae act horribly. Maybe the warriors have all been dispatched to keep the peace.*

She *hmmed* in agreement. *That's definitely a possibility, now that you mention it.* She laughed lightly. *You know, you could just ask him what he's doing in Stonewild.*

I snorted in amusement. *I could, but he hasn't struck me as someone who willingly shares his information freely.*

She laughed, and we chatted for a few more minutes about mindless, brainless things. It was so good to hear her voice and pretend that for a moment, my life was fully normal again.

She huffed out of the blue. *Ugh, sorry, Prim, but Siam is crying. I should go.*

No problem.

Talk tomorrow? she added.

I'll try, but no promises from here on out. I'm going into the Wildland Mountains in the morning, and likely even farther north into Stonewild after that. I'm not entirely sure what to expect. I may have to keep my wits about me and might not be able to afford any distractions.

Stars, Prim, be careful, okay?

I will. Love you, Ree.

Love you too. Connect with me next whenever you can.

Definitely. Bye!

She murmured a farewell, and I closed our link just as the door to the salopas opened, and a new group strode in. For a moment, all I could do was blink. In the time I'd been speaking with my aunt and best friend, the small establishment had entirely filled with fae, both siltenite and wildling.

The new crew who arrived consisted of a female and two male siltenites, and considering most in the salopas gave them barely hidden sneers, I figured they weren't local either.

I returned my attention to my tea, the pot almost empty, and leaned back in my chair, figuring I'd enjoy the music and the rest of my drink, then retire to my chambers for the night.

"Sorry to bother you, but are these seats taken?"

I glanced up to see one of the newly arrived males smiling at me in a pleasant manner and gesturing to the three empty chairs at my table. "Sorry to ask," he added, "but this place is rather full, and seats seem hard to come by."

I sat up straighter just as an enchanted tray floated over and collected my dirty dishes, only leaving my mug and the teapot behind.

I nodded and gestured to my mostly empty table. "Plenty of room now. I'll be leaving soon anyway, so feel free to sit here if you'd like."

The male smiled, his eyes conveying warmth that none of the locals did, and my blood thrummed in relief to see a friendly face.

"I'm Felix, by the way." He held out his arm for a handshake.

Smiling, I gripped his forearm. "Prim, nice to meet you."

He pumped my arm a few times, then grinned cheekily. "I take it you're not from Inisville either?"

I laughed. "What gave it away?"

He released my hand and ran his through his hair, his eyes twinkling. "The fact that you actually talked to me did not give it away at all."

I laughed again, and his aura washed over me, bringing with it the feel of a fairy who was often playful and quick to laugh. He seemed harmless, fun even. But looks could be deceiving.

Keeping my smile firmly in place, I considered mentally assessing him to read his thoughts and intentions. I could use my forbidden magic, just this once. I could let my magic stream out of me to filter through his mind, completely unbeknownst to him. It was an intrusion of his privacy, a complete violation, but I was also a female traveling alone, and I'd promised my aunt I would come back in one piece.

But the second that paranoid thought came to me, it left. We were in public, and he was only looking for a place to sit. Nothing more. Besides, my gut told me that Felix was harmless.

Scolding myself internally, I quickly brushed my crazy impulse off.

Completely unaware of what I'd almost done to him, Felix turned toward his friends, who were still putting in an order at the bar. Waving, he called over the music, "Jessip, Nym, head on over here when you're done. Prim's offered to let us sit with her."

He winked at me, and his friends soon crowded around my table, introducing themselves and thanking me for allowing them to sit with me.

I'd just filled my cup with the last of my tea, my mood lifting since the newcomers seemed as relieved as me to meet another friendly fairy along their journey, when the salopas door opened, and a new energy strode in.

I knew, without looking up, who it was. The brush of the familiar aura and the wary glances from the locals told me that Kole Swordwielder had also decided to grace the crowded salopas with his presence.

CHAPTER TEN

A cold gust of wind accompanied the warrior, and outside, the snow fell thick and heavy. The second Kole stepped inside the salopas, his gaze surveyed the room as though cataloguing who was present, what they wore, if they carried weapons, and what auras surrounded them. As usual, his expression remained stoic, and his Shield was locked down.

Several of the locals watched Kole, but unlike when I'd entered the bar, their demeanors stayed the same, as though knowing a predator had just entered their midst, and it was wisest not to draw attention to themselves.

When the warrior's attention reached my table, my heart thrummed, but determined to act normal in his presence, I lifted my hand and waved.

His eyes hooded slightly, but then his attention shifted to the other fae at my table. He slowly tracked the three newcomers, and given that his expression didn't change, it was impossible to gauge what he was thinking.

My heart ticked steadily upward regardless, and magic stirred inside me. As had happened more times than I wanted to admit, my inner abilities vibrated, as though standing to attention in the warrior's presence.

I huffed. I could hardly blame the Stone any further. This was one hundred percent *my* reaction to him.

Muttering quietly to myself, I tried to tamp it down, but my resolve wavered when Kole made his way to the bar. It was then I realized that he wore different clothes than he had previously.

The thick black breeches and tunic in Stonewild colors were gone. In their place, a loose long-sleeved navy top and a thinner pair of black breeches adorned his large frame. Heavy boots still covered his feet, but they didn't reach his knees as the others had.

Despite his more casual attire, his muscles still bulged beneath the clothing, hinting at strong lines and lean angles. The male was entirely cut, and I wondered what kind of training program he partook in to keep his body in that kind of shape. But one thing about him *hadn't* changed. As I'd also come to expect, his sword remained strapped to his back.

I was beginning to wonder if he ever took it off.

When Kole reached the bar, he stood casually at the end. Even at the bar top, the seats had been entirely filled.

Jessip, the lone female in the group I'd just met, leaned toward me. "Do you know that male?"

Her question snapped me out of the trance Kole had woven over me. "I do," I replied, then took another sip of tea. "We met a few days ago."

"He's very . . . big." She looked Kole up and down as he stood at the bar.

Nym nudged her. "Don't be getting any ideas."

Jessip laughed and stopped appreciating the warrior. "Oh, don't worry. I only have eyes for you, my sweetness."

Nym smirked, and Felix took another swig of his ale.

Unlike me, Jessip was tall with a lean build. However, similar to me, she wore pants and a long-sleeved top. We hadn't divulged many details to each other yet, but I was fairly certain they were also hunting the Stone, and I was guessing her group was from Faewood.

Jessip's aura felt shrouded in humid mist. I would have bet she had water elemental magic. And both Felix and Nym felt of soil and nature, likely terrain elementals.

"That's quite the sword," Felix remarked, pulling my attention back to the warrior.

Kole glanced our way, his jaw ticking once. It was the only indication of anything passing behind his steely mask, and I wondered if he'd heard us above the commotion. But it was such a fleeting movement that it could have been a trick of the light or a shadow hitting his face at just the right angle. Regardless, Kole still stood at the bar, making no move to leave, so I quickly looked around and searched for a free seat for my inn neighbor.

I spotted a stool near the stage, probably used to prop equipment against it if needed, but the wildling band tonight hadn't utilized it once.

"I'll be right back," I said to my new friends. Standing, I sashayed through the crowd, passing the full tables as the music continued thumping around us. Several fae had taken their thick tunics off until only their thin shirts underneath covered their frames, probably because the temperature in the room had climbed.

When I reached the stage, the wildling who was playing the horn gave me a wink. I swayed my hips to the beat and nodded toward the stool. "Do you mind?" I asked, trying not to distract him from his riff.

He dipped his head once, and I took that as permission to grab it, so I lifted the wooden stool, grunting slightly since it was heavier than it looked, but I somehow managed to heave it over my head so I wouldn't knock it into anyone on my way back to the table.

The entire time, I felt Kole watching me. He still leaned against the bar top in the far corner, but considering he'd helped me carry all of my supplies into my inn chambers, *and* had saved that wildling mother and her babies from the would-be murderers, *and* had gotten Abel off my back, I felt it was only hospitable to at least invite him to join us. Never mind that I was ridiculously attracted to him.

Once situated, I hopped onto the stool since I'd finished my tea, then waved over the crowd to Kole. "Come join us!" I called and pointed to the now-empty chair that I'd just vacated.

Kole stared at me for a beat. I half expected him to ignore my invitation. He didn't strike me as the sociable type, and I had a feeling Nym, Jessip, and Felix might be off-putting to him, but surprisingly, he pushed away from the bar and slowly made his way through the crowd.

I couldn't help but watch as he neared. Most of the fae scooted their chairs in the second he drew closer to them, and the fae standing between the tables stepped completely out of his way to give him room to maneuver.

"Must be nice," I sighed dramatically, "to have the entire realm be slightly afraid of you."

Jessip snorted. "If you carried a sword that big, I bet fae would move for you too."

I laughed lightly, and Felix leaned back in his seat and casually rested his arm on the back of my stool. His hand brushed my lower spine. "There are other ways to cause fear in fellow fae, Prim. You could rave like a lunatic. Act unhinged. Talk to fae who aren't there." He shrugged. "You could try that. I bet it would work even if you didn't have a huge sword."

Jessip snorted again, but I chuckled and gave him an impish look. "Are you speaking from experience?"

"He is, although not in the way you're thinking," Nym replied for him. "He was committed to several healing infirmaries during his lifetime. Our dear friend here suffers from occasional psychotic episodes."

My smile was immediately wiped clean. "Oh stars, I'm so sorry. I didn't mean to joke."

But Nym, Felix, and Jessip all burst into laughter just as Kole reached our table.

"They're toying with you, Prim," Jessip replied. "Felix has never been committed, although I've wondered on occasion if he should be."

Felix brushed his hand against me again, then lightly pinched my side, which got a squeak out of me. "Don't scare her off too much, Jess. I'm hoping to convince her to dance with me later."

I glanced upward, grinning, only to be met with Kole's attention locked on Felix.

"Hi," I said to the warrior, determined to act normal. "Would you like to join us?"

Kole hesitated for a heartbeat, his attention still on Felix, but then he turned my vacated chair backward and straddled it, having to angle his sword to do so. But the movement was so quick and so practiced that it was obvious he was used to sitting that way with his weapon.

Jessip's eyebrows rose. "Introductions, anyone?"

I waved at the Faewood fae. "Kole, this is Nym, Felix, and Jessip. They're not local either. And, everyone, this is Kole."

Felix elbowed me teasingly. "Has anyone ever told you how cute you are?"

My eyebrows shot up. "Cute? Hmm, I don't know. Maybe." Blushing, I leaned forward since Felix sat between me and Kole, then said to the warrior, "Did you order something to eat?"

Kole eyed Felix again, but since his mask had fallen into place, it was impossible to decipher his expression. "I did. The barkeeper said it'd be over shortly."

"Felix?" Nym said. "I almost forgot. I was going to ask you something about Teelive from back home. She told me . . ."

Since the Faewood friends began to discuss something about their friend, who neither Kole nor I knew, I settled back on my stool again.

Kole angled himself away from the table and said quietly to me from behind Felix, "I see you've already made some new friends, and quite quickly too."

"I have." I smiled cheekily and eyed his clothing. "And I see you've changed." I cocked my head. "But you didn't travel with any bags, so where'd you get the new clothes?"

Kole shrugged. "I have my ways."

A tray floated toward us and deposited drinks and food before all four of them. The barkeeper had easily doubled Kole's portions, compared to what he'd given me, and I had a feeling the warrior could eat all of it.

I eyed Kole, wondering what he meant by his evasive response, but Jessip stole my attention when she said loudly, "Anyway, enough about all that stuff from back home. So where are you two from?" She picked up her fork and began to eat.

"Mistvale," I replied readily. "Whiteolf, specifically. I live in the capital."

Kole remained silent.

"And . . . you?" Jessip said to Kole, her eyebrows rising.

Kole took another drink. "I tend to travel a bit. I don't really claim a residence."

I wasn't surprised by his answer. Imperial Council Warriors did live on the go, often moving from one location to another, yet I knew that somewhere in the realm, there *was* likely a residence in Kole's name. But if he didn't want to share his personal information, it wasn't for me to push.

I leaned back again and crossed my ankles. "What about all of you?" Even though I was fairly certain they hailed from Faewood, I had no idea what city they came from. "Where's home for you three?"

"Marrotum," Jessip replied. "We all grew up there. It's in Faewood, on the coast, just south of the Ustilly Mountains."

I took another sip of my tea. "I've never been there before. Is it a large city? Or a village?"

Nym took another swig of his ale, draining it, then signaled the barkeeper for more. "No, it's not large at all, and if you've never been there before, don't bother visiting. You'd be bored out of your mind. We have a total of three shops, twenty houses, and about eight hundred fishing nets. That's pretty much the entirety of our village."

I laughed. "Eight hundred nets? So it's a fishing village?"

"It is." Felix's hand brushed against me again. "All of us work on the boats. We grew up together at sea."

"Do you plan to live out your days there?" I asked just as another tray floated over carrying more drinks. The enchanted tray deposited five drinks on the table, one for each of us.

When I looked at them questionably, Nym said, "This round's on me."

"Oh, thanks." I tentatively picked up the mug of ale. Usually, I didn't drink. Alcoholic beverages tended to go straight to my head, but I figured it was only one glass.

"Solls," I said, raising my drink.

The others lifted their mugs too, and Kole did as well since we were all waiting for him to clink our glasses together.

"As for whether or not we'll all indefinitely stay in Marrotum . . ." Felix shrugged. "I guess that depends upon if we find the Wishing Stone or not." He shifted in his seat, his hand brushing me anew. "I, for one, wouldn't be staying there if I had endless riches."

The warrior eyed Felix, and his aura flickered, but Kole continued to eat methodically, clearing his plate in large bites, and he didn't join in the conversation.

I smiled and canted my head. "I was wondering if you all were hunting the Stone."

"Aye, we are." Jessip shrugged. "Although, our siblings all think us foolish for doing so, and don't even get me started on our parents."

"Same. My aunt wasn't a fan of me leaving to hunt it either. I'm sure many families in the realm have similar opinions since almost everyone fails at finding it." I cocked my head. "But what made you come all the way up here to look for it? I think most fae are on the eastern coast searching for it, perhaps even near your home village."

Nym side-eyed Jessip. "Are you going to tell her, or should I?"

A blush stained Jessip's cheeks, and she elbowed him. "You're never going to let me live this down, are you?"

"Well, if you're right and we find the Stone, even *I'll* stop teasing you," Felix remarked.

I leaned forward, eager to know what they were talking about. Inadvertently, I brushed against Felix when I shifted my position on the hard stool, and the fairy placed his hand on my thigh. But instead of removing it after I'd settled, he left it there.

He did it casually, as though touching me was something he'd been doing for centuries, and the familiarity of it rendered me speechless.

Felix smiled in my direction, then squeezed my thigh before removing his hand. "Sorry. You're just so damned cute. It's hard not to touch you."

I laughed shrilly, not sure how to respond. I hadn't been flirted with like this in so long that I failed at a witty comeback.

Kole's fingers wrapped tightly around his glass, and he leaned forward, knocking his shoulder with Felix in the process. Felix jerked from where he sat, hands flying to the table to steady himself.

"Sorry," Kole said dryly, then brought his drink to his lips again.

Since Felix was no longer touching me, and my shock at his blatant flirting had cleared, I raised my eyebrows at Jessip. "Well? Don't keep me in suspense. What brought you up here?"

Jessip ducked her head. "Stars and galaxy, it's rather embarrassing, but I had a dream. It told me to venture to the northern part of Stonewild, and that was where the Stone had landed."

My eyebrows shot up, and even Kole slightly inclined his head.

"A dream?" My eyes widened. "Do you have Mistvale seer abilities that allow you to see the future? Do you possess magic from two kingdoms?"

While it wasn't common to possess magic from more than one kingdom, having dual magic wasn't unheard of either. And even though some considered it rude to ask of another's magic, my shock at hearing Jessip's dream had apparently thrown my good manners out the window.

Jessip's cheeks darkened even more. "I wish I could say my psychic ability led us here, but that's not the case. I only possess elemental magic. It was just a dream, truly, but I swear it felt so real."

"Real enough that she was able to convince the two of us to

travel all the bloody way up here with her." Nym grinned, his eyes slightly glassy-eyed, and I realized that sometime in the interim, another tray of drinks had been brought to us.

"You never know. You could be right." I shrugged encouragingly, even though I hoped I found the Stone before they could. While I had nothing against any of them, my uncle's life depended upon *me* finding the Stone, and since only one fairy could claim its magic, that didn't allow me to share in its bounty.

"What about you, Kole?" Jessip asked him. "It sounds like Prim's Stone hunting too, but are you?"

I glanced at the warrior, curious to hear what he would say, but all he did was shrug and reply, "I'm not hunting the Stone. I'm here on work."

"On work?" I repeated, unable to help myself, and wondered if my guess that he was here to keep the peace had been right.

He inclined his head. "Indeed. Someone has to keep the crazy fae hunting the Stone in line."

The other three eyed the sword at his back and nodded, either curiosity appeased or too intimidated by the fact that he was obviously a law enforcer to ask more.

But a grin split my lips, and I sat up straighter. The question I'd been curious to learn the answer to since meeting him was finally revealed, and his response confirmed that my guess had been right. I couldn't wait to tell Ree.

Still, it was quite coincidental that Kole just happened to

have followed the same path as me, although, if I truly thought about it, it wasn't *that* improbable. There were only so many roads traveling through the Wood, and as luck should have it, Kole had chosen the same ones as me.

I drained the last of my ale and was about to settle back to enjoy the music, but Felix nudged me.

"Do you want to dance?" He nodded toward the cleared area by the stage where several other fae were dancing to the beat.

Kole stilled, but Felix jumped to his feet, then held his hand out to me.

I shrugged and placed my hand in his. "Why not? I love to dance."

CHAPTER ELEVEN

Felix entwined his hand around mine and pulled me toward the dance floor. Now that we were both standing, I realized how much taller he was than me. Even though my height was considered average, Felix was larger than I'd given him credit for, especially given how easily Kole had knocked him around.

He wove us through the tables and chairs, and once we reached the dance floor, he grinned down at me and began moving to the beat.

I readily joined in, smiling back at him and quickly getting lost in the rhythm.

Felix moved well, obviously having a natural inclination toward music, and when he spun me a few times and even dipped me on occasion, I couldn't help but laugh in delight.

"You're a good dancer," I commented just as we began moving to the third song.

"That's what my da always told me."

"Your da? Does he dance too?"

"He does."

"You must take after him."

He waggled his eyebrows. "I don't know. Maybe I do. It was how he convinced my mother to marry him, so I suppose that'll depend upon your answer to my proposal at the end of the night."

His words were said cheekily, so much so that I couldn't help but burst into laughter. I was quickly learning that Felix was a voracious flirt.

We spun, dipped, and twirled, and sweat began to slide down my back. More fae had joined us as well, even Nym and Jessip, but the space was only so large, so when I began bumping into those around me and my head began to spin from all of the twirling, I finally called it quits.

"I need a drink." My skin sparkled in the lights, sheening from our exercise. "I'm going to go back to the table."

Felix pouted. "Are you coming back?"

I laughed and poked him. "Maybe. Guess you'll have to wait and see."

"Oooh, a tease. I like that." He grinned and began dancing again, moving backward across the floor while making motions with his hands for me to follow.

Chuckling, I waved him off, then wove my way through the throng of fae. I wondered what time it was and glanced around, looking for a clock, but I couldn't find one.

While the night had taken a pleasant turn for the better,

the alcohol that had been swimming through my system was beginning to wear off, and I was reminded of the true reason for my journey. Being hungover tomorrow or sleeping in from a late night out partying wasn't in line with my plan. My uncle certainly deserved better than that.

A sword's pommel met my eyes when I returned to the table. Kole still sat there, drinking his ale, but he'd slightly angled his chair so he could see the dance floor.

When I approached him, he was looking away. Tiptoeing, I crept closer.

When I was only a hand's width away, I leaned down and poked his side. "Aren't you worried someone will sneak up on you with your back turned to the crowd?"

Kole didn't make a sound. He didn't even jump. "I knew you were behind me. You didn't sneak up on me."

I slid onto the chair beside him. "Did you? Or are you just saying that to save face?" I batted my eyelashes playfully and realized I'd had a lot more to drink than I'd meant to. I was unabashedly flirting with the Imperial Warrior and I didn't feel the tiniest bit nervous about it.

He gave me a side-eye. "Are you doubting my skills again? A lesser warrior would be wounded by your lack of faith in him."

"Ah! So you are a warrior. Now you admit it."

"I never denied it."

"But you're not a lesser warrior, are you?" I giggled slightly.

Ignoring my question, he sipped his drink again. "Did your dance partner leave you for someone else?"

"Oh no, he's waiting for me to return. He said he's going to propose to me at the end of the night."

The drink Kole was holding stopped halfway to his lips. "*What?*" he growled.

I laughed again. "He said it's how his da proposed to his mother, that he was able to woo her with his dancing."

He set his drink down. "You're joking."

I held up my hands in surrender. "I'm being entirely serious. That's truly how their happy marriage came about." I cocked my head. "Well, at least I think it's a happy marriage. Come to think of it, he never actually clarified if they are or not."

Kole finally brought his drink back to his lips and drained the last of it in one large gulp. The column of his throat worked, and his sword gleamed in the lights that somebody had dimmed as the night had worn on. When finished, he set his drink down, his movements precise. "And will I be invited to your wedding?"

"Of course!" I replied, delighted that he was joining in my game. "You could even partake in it if you want."

"Is that right?" He began to trace his finger through the wet ring his drink had left on the table. "In what capacity?"

"The officiant? Or perhaps you could place our sealing cloths upon us? Oh no, wait! I've got it. You could be part of the decorating party. I bet you have a way with colors and flowers. You would likely make the entire atmosphere stunning." I swatted at him playfully.

He stopped tracing his finger through the ring and lifted his head. Piercing blue eyes met mine. A light flared within them, turbulent and violent, but then he blinked, and it was gone. "I cannot say I'm much for decorating or being an officiant or placing sealing cloths on fae, but if you are unfortunate enough to marry someone such as Felix, I still wish you nothing but the best."

I snorted lightly. "Oh, come now. You couldn't have already formed such an extreme and poor opinion of him? You just met him."

"Why would that mean I can't have an extreme opinion of him?"

"Because you don't know him."

"I've seen enough."

I nearly choked on a laugh but then realized the warrior was no longer playacting. He looked entirely serious. "Do you always have this strong of a reaction to new fae?"

"Not usually."

"And what about me? Do you also have a low opinion of yours truly?"

His gaze traveled over my face, down my braid, and all the way to my toes. My skin heated, my flesh pebbling. Even though he wasn't touching me, his look held weight, as though he'd seared me.

"I do not have a low opinion of you, Miss Hollaran."

I released a breath. I suddenly felt lightheaded. "Well, I'm glad to hear that, because I find you quite charming despite your grumpy demeanor."

His eyebrow arched, and I almost pointed out again that his face had moved.

"Grumpy demeanor? I've heard that before, but charming? That's a first."

"You are charming. At least, I think so. Perhaps it's the stoic warrior persona you've adapted. I quite like it."

"Is that right?"

"Indeed. I haven't met many warriors."

I could have sworn that he was working to suppress a smile. "Have you ever met any?"

I cocked my head and tapped my chin. "Come to think of it, no. You're the first." I beamed at him, and for the very first time since meeting him, his lips curved, ever so slightly, as though his smile was on the precipice of being revealed.

I held my breath, waiting for his lips to arch into a true smile, but then Felix called, "Prim! Come on, love! I've been missing you!"

In a blink, Kole's expression vanished. I turned my attention back to the dance floor. Kole did too. His nostrils flared slightly as he watched the Faewood fairy.

"It looks like your future husband is beckoning you."

Sure enough, Felix was moving to the beat toward the edge of the crowd. He was smiling and swaying, his eyes on me, and his finger crooked, encouraging me to return to him.

But I didn't want to join him again. I wasn't here to dance and flirt, despite the fact that I strangely loved flirting with Kole. It was late. My uncle was dying, and I needed to get up early and head into the Wildland Mountains at dawn. Being groggy and having cobwebs congealing my thoughts from too much drinking and dancing was a sure way to end up dead before the day was over, especially since I was traveling alone.

"Another time!" I called to Felix.

His jaw dropped, and he brought a hand to his heart. Then he staggered back as though I'd shot him with an arrow.

I laughed again, unable to help it, and playfully blew him a kiss.

Felix caught my imaginary air kiss and brought it to his lips.

I chuckled and rolled my eyes.

At my side, Kole was watching Felix again, his attention zeroed in on the fairy who was once more dancing the night away.

"I think I'll be off then." I stood to leave, and surprisingly, Kole did too. As before, once he rose to his full height, the warrior towered over me. "Are you heading out as well?" I asked him.

"I am."

"Do you want to join me on my walk back to the inn, since we're inn buddies and all?" I elbowed him playfully, then grabbed my cloak and slung it over my forearm.

The warrior nodded toward the door. "After you."

I turned away, and something warm pressed into my lower back. The second I realized what it was, I nearly stumbled. Kole had placed his hand on my lower back to guide me toward the door.

Heat seared through my top, and my flesh tightened at the feel of his large palm. All at once, the memory of our kiss came blazing back to me, like a meteor shooting right through my body. Our shared kiss had been so hot, and this male had been able to make my entire body sing.

Kole's hand instantly fell away. "Sorry," he said gruffly. "I didn't mean to—"

"No, it's fine." I gave him a shaky smile over my shoulder and wondered why my lower belly was suddenly tightening or why my breaths felt shallow. He'd simply placed his hand on my lower back. That was it. Felix had put his hands all over me tonight, and it hadn't caused even the slightest reaction in me. But one touch from the warrior, and my body turned on fire. "You just took me by surprise. That's all."

His throat bobbed, and he nodded toward the door again. "After you," he repeated, but his voice was lower. Rougher.

My limbs were stiff as I made my way to the door. Kole followed again, and even though he didn't touch me a second time, I still *felt* the warrior. His aura pulsed around him. It was thick and weighted, like a storm cloud surging through the skies.

Stars Above.

We finally reached the door, but when I opened it, a gust of cold wind from outside nearly knocked me off my feet.

I stumbled back, right into Kole's chest, and his hands closed over my hips to steady me.

"You may want to put your cloak on." Kole's soft comment caressed the tip of my ear, and I realized he'd leaned down to speak to me, his lips nearly brushing against me in the howling wind.

"Oh, right, good idea." I closed the door since a few fae near us were grumbling that I was letting all the cold air in.

Movements clumsy and unsure, as if I'd never put a bloody cloak on before, made me look like an absolute idiot as I struggled with the garment.

"Allow me." Kole took the cloak from me and snapped it open, as if such a practice were easy, which I realized it was, but once again, my mind and hands did not seem to be communicating in the warrior's presence.

He draped my cloak over my shoulders, and my breaths stopped, actually *stopped*, when his large hands reached around to clasp the cloak at my throat.

"Thank you," I managed.

His face was still entirely devoid of any emotion, but beneath his Shield, his energy roiled. With a nod, he reached around me to open the door, reminding me of how he'd acted when we'd met several hours ago at the inn's entrance. It seemed the warrior had chivalrous manners.

Brain finally kicking into action, I said in a slightly teasing tone, "You know, Kole, if you keep opening doors for me, I'm going to start believing that you're a gentlefae."

Cold wind greeted us once more, but I readily walked outside and didn't stumble this time.

"Is that right?" he replied and followed. Outside, the dark night stretched around us. Snow had accumulated on the street and was still flying through the air. "Has a male never opened a door for you before?"

I shrugged. "A few have, but that's twice tonight from you, and you helped me with my cloak too."

His lips twitched, and it was obvious he was actively fighting a smile. "Well, you looked like you were struggling."

My cheeks warmed, and I was thankful for the low light, because the warrior was right. I *was* struggling, but I hoped to the galaxy that he hadn't realized it was because of him.

"Yes, well, cloaks can be quite complicated," I replied as we began to walk across the snowy street to the inn. "It's a lot of fabric. And only one clasp. And the hoods can be large and awkward. Truly, there should be a tutorial on how best to arrange them."

He made a sound low in his chest, but it was gone as quickly as it started. I stopped halfway across the lane and peered up at him.

"Kole Swordwielder, did you just . . . *laugh?*"

His face was hidden in shadows, the swirling clouds above blocking most of the moonlight. "No." His response came readily but sounded a tad defensive.

I burst into a fit of giggles and elbowed him playfully. "You did. You laughed. It's all right. You can admit it. There's no shame in laughing."

I grinned up at him, and he chuffed, but then slowly, his lips began to curve, and *finally* he awarded me with a smile. A true and genuine smile.

"Fine, you caught me. You actually made me laugh," he admitted.

For a moment, all I could do was stare at how the smile transformed his face. He was striking. No, that didn't do it justice. Stars, galaxy, and all the moons, he was *breathtaking*.

"Oh, but this is wonderful," I said theatrically to cover up how much his smile affected me. "I was beginning to believe you had no emotions at all."

He arched an eyebrow. "I have plenty of emotions, Miss Hollaran. I just don't wear them on my sleeve as you do."

Warmth radiated through me, and I poked him playfully in his chest. There was something about Kole, something that just begged me to play with him.

His gaze dropped to where I was touching him, and his aura kicked up another notch, so subtly that if it wasn't for my unique magic, I never would have noticed it.

"You should smile more, Kole. It suits you, and I'm relieved to learn that your heart under here"—finger still in place from poking him, I tapped his chest—"isn't made of stone."

His gaze met mine, and I could have sworn something

flashed in his irises. "No, Miss Hollaran, my heart isn't made of stone. Not even close."

He took a step toward me, closing the distance between us even more, and his aura pulsed. That strange glow filled his eyes again, so briefly, and I was certain I wasn't imagining it.

The warrior placed his hand over mine, flattening my palm to his chest, and my breath stopped. Completely *stopped*.

For a moment, we stared at one another. The air grew heavy around us, and Kole's focus subtly drifted to my lips, a look of *hunger* growing on his face again, just as it had in the hallway outside our rooms at the inn.

Abruptly, a flash of magic coiled around his wrist, electrifying the space between us, and in my next breath, the warrior was several feet away from me.

My breath rushed out of me, and I stilled because the warm air that had been swirling around me from Kole's body heat was gone.

Not entirely sure what'd just happened, I opened my mouth to ask him if he was okay, but a noise came from down the street. A snarl or a growl. Something that didn't sound fae but also didn't sound animal, and it sounded strangely . . . familiar.

Kole's head whipped in that direction, and before I could blink, he was standing in front of me, his broad back shielding me from the wind as he gazed toward where that growl had come from.

"Prim, go inside the inn. *Now*." His words were said with

such authority, such *intensity*, that my body began to move before my brain caught up with me.

Before I knew what I was doing, I'd crossed the remaining distance to the inn and was opening the door. Kole was watching me, as though wanting to ensure I did as he said, and when I stepped over the threshold, that same sound came again.

Part snarl. Part growl. Part *something*.

A chill raced down my spine as cold as the Cliffs of Sarum. Every instinct inside me told me to run. To hide. To escape.

Eyes wide, I peered out at Kole. Snow flew around him, the night dark and the wind cold.

"What are you going to do?" The thought of him tearing off down the street, in search of the creature that had made that noise, made my heart pound and my limbs shake.

"What I'm here to do," was all he replied, and with that, he disappeared in a blur of speed.

CHAPTER TWELVE

I knew I was supposed to close the inn door. I knew I was supposed to saunter over to the check-in desk and chat for a few minutes with Nivinity. I knew that I was then supposed to climb the stairs and retreat to the safety of my chambers and lock the door behind me.

I knew I was supposed to do *all* of those things, but Kole had just disappeared into the night, in search of whatever had made that shiver-inducing sound, and he was alone with only the sword at his back to protect him.

And even though he was an Imperial Warrior who had effortlessly taken down Abel and likely would have taken down the two bastard males as well, all I truly wanted to do was race after him to ensure he stayed safe.

My hands twisted, my fingers knotting together as I tried to shake sense into myself. Kole was a warrior. This was literally what he was trained to do. And while my magic was strong and I was tougher than I looked, I wasn't trained to deal with situations as he was.

It would be foolish to try to find him. *So why is every instinct inside me begging me to do just that? Why is my heart demanding that I protect him?*

The thought of harm coming to him made me want to vomit.

"Stars Above," I whispered aloud. Maybe I'd been wrong. Maybe the Stone truly *was* affecting me, because Gods and Goddesses, the impulse to follow him was so strong that I knew something was very wrong with me. Nothing reasonable and *not* magical could explain this type of reaction in me.

"Do you have strange nocturnal animals around here?" I called in a strained voice to Nivinity while peering out the window into the street again, but Kole was nowhere to be seen.

Nivinity stood at the check-in desk, her ledger closed and pushed off to the side. She craned her neck to look into the street over my shoulder, her hairy eyebrows drawn together. "We don't normally, but some other villages have reported strange occurrences at night."

I faced the wildling, and my eyebrows slammed together. "What kind of occurrences?"

Her large nostrils flared in her snout, her eyebrows tugging together even more. "Just weird sightings mostly, and some fae have reported hearing sounds."

"Sounds?"

She took a breath, and I could have sworn she shuddered.

"Weird sounds, not the normal that you would expect at night. Some are whispering that a creature from Silventine Wood has wandered into the southern Wood of Stonewild, a creature that isn't supposed to be able to leave the magic of that forest."

I shivered, a full-body shiver that blasted through me all the way to my toes.

There were several Woods in our realm that were filled with magic and animals that other Woods didn't possess. Silventine Wood in Stonewild Kingdom was one of them. The Shroud Forest on the Nolus continent was another. There were other forests too, and most fae knew to stay away from them. Ancient magic fed the soil in those Woods. Creatures roamed there that would happily eat fae for breakfast. Plants flourished in them that could easily choke the life from a fairy. *Deadly and nefarious.* It was the words that were often whispered when those forests were spoken of.

I shuddered anew. "Does anyone know for certain if a Silventine Wood creature has come down this way?"

Nivinity shook her head. "No, but it's probably best if you stay in for the night. Just a few nights ago—" She cut her words off.

I took a step closer to her. "Just a few nights ago, *what?*"

She shook her head. "Nothing, but be smart and go to bed. No reason to press your luck out there." She nodded toward the front entrance door.

"But what about the others that are still out?" I thought of

Nym, Jessip, and Felix, probably still drinking and dancing, none the wiser that a potentially lethal creature was prowling around this small village. And there were still other fae in the salopas, fae who had to find their way home for the night.

Nivinity lifted her hooved hands. "It's only a short walk across the street for the other travelers, and the locals have heard the rumors. They know to be careful. Besides, that male you know, the one with the sword . . . With any luck, he'll catch it and do us all a favor."

It struck me that she'd probably seen Kole race off into the night through the window. "Did you tell him about the creature? Is that why he went after it just now?"

She inclined her head. "In a way, yes. He was asking a lot of questions before he ventured to the salopas. He wanted to know if there had been any strange occurrences around here lately, and he pressed me for every detail about the rumors."

My lips parted, and I realized that Kole hadn't been lying. He truly *was* working, and that was why he was here, and perhaps, just perhaps, he hadn't revealed the full reason for his presence because whatever he was trying to catch wasn't meant to be known.

I'd guessed he'd been traveling through the Wood due to crimes that the Wishing Stone bred, but maybe that wasn't it at all. Maybe that was just a cover. Maybe ominous things were going on in the Wood, and maybe *that* was why he ended up in the same village as me.

But that didn't explain why I first met him in Whiteolf.

But just as fast, I reasoned that could be because he had to venture from Whiteolf to get here. For all I knew, that was where the Imperial Council headquarters were. After all, they were so secretive that nobody knew their exact location. But if he was ultimately hunting a creature from Silventine Wood, it certainly would explain why we'd kept bumping into one another. We'd been headed to the same location.

And now Kole was out there, potentially confronting that creature *alone*.

Fingers once again twisting into knots, I peered out the window, praying that I'd see him, while trying to talk myself out of doing anything rash, but only snow greeted me.

"Has anyone been hurt by whatever's out there?" Even to me, my voice sounded weird.

Nivinity released a breath. "Not here, thankfully, but we've heard that some of the fae whose villages are just south of here haven't been as lucky. Several have disappeared, and whatever took them has been on the move. It's going steadily north from what the rumors are saying, probably back to Silventine Wood." She shivered. "I suppose it would make sense if it's now around here. Truly, Prim, you should stay inside. It's safest."

I spun away from the window. "Fae have disappeared? As in, *gone*? Or taken? Or"—I gulped, barely able to get the word out—"eaten?"

She shrugged. "I don't know. Truly. It's just the rumors I've heard."

Her statement slammed into me, and it suddenly occurred to me why that growl I'd just heard had sounded vaguely familiar. It was because I *had* heard it before, that other night in the Wood. That was the night I'd also sensed Kole's presence nearby. Even then, he'd been hunting it, but he obviously hadn't caught it.

But just now, it sounded *so* close.

My heart thumped a steady tune in my chest, throbbing faster with every breath I took, as I imagined Kole out there alone with the *thing* that had taken fae, possibly eaten them.

I was opening the door before I knew what I was doing, acting on an instinct that I could neither understand nor ignore.

The last thing I heard was Nivinity calling a warning to me just as I bolted outside and raced down the street.

CHAPTER THIRTEEN

Snow flew around me, and every rational thought inside me told me that Kole would be furious if he knew what I was doing, but I couldn't *not* follow in the direction the warrior had gone. If something happened to him . . . If something hurt him . . .

I had no explanation for the panic that squeezed my lungs, so I shoved those feelings aside. Besides, I was of sound mind enough to know that while I wasn't as large and as skilled as Kole, I also wasn't a liability. If needed, my magic could over-power anything in the realm, including a deadly creature from Silventine Wood that had wandered too far south and was slowly making its way back to its home.

Cold air rushed past me, my breath labored in my mad dash, but my magic shot out of me hot and bright. I unleashed it since nobody was about. It flowed out of me like a charged, invisible river.

A sense of release traveled through me, as though my magic were breathing a sigh of ecstasy for the first time in many seasons. Finally, I'd opened the door to its cage and allowed it to do what the gods had blessed me with.

Heady power strummed around me, and as I sprinted, my magic assessed every living thing in my vicinity just waiting to take control of them, command them, and force them to do whatever I wanted at my slightest bidding.

Lifeform after lifeform registered in my mind.

A home with four souls I'd never met before was off to my right.

Three sleeping smaller souls, likely children, were asleep near a home's hearth to my left.

One soul was awake, and he was doing something in the home around the bend.

My feet pounded into the thickening snow as I searched for the essence that my magic had registered as *Kole*. Each life, each flicker of a heartbeat, had its own magical flavor. I'd encountered thousands of fae in my lifetime, most of whom I couldn't recall or identify.

But Kole's soul was new and fresh, and his magical flavor had been strong, making him easier to seek.

Wind whipped through my hair, tossing my braid behind me as my cloak's hood flapped against my back. The end of the town's street neared, and the dark Wood lay ahead.

Another snarl rose in the distance, carrying through the

night sky. It was faint but eerily similar to what I'd heard earlier.

Wherever it'd come from, it was no longer near the village. Perhaps Kole had chased it into the Wood. Or maybe it'd already attacked him, and Kole lay dying on the Wood's floor as the creature devoured him.

My stomach heaved, and my pace picked up. Arms pumping, I shot forward, thankful once again that pants adorned my legs.

The Wood grew closer, and my magic searched and sought. Concentrating, I pushed it farther ahead of me, stretching my mental fingers all around me and in every direction. Dozens and dozens of magical lifeforces answered my call. Animals. Wildlings. Siltenites. Within seconds, I had a location on every single fairy within the village.

I extended my reach even farther.

I filtered through everything, shifting through each magical essence as I sought Kole's.

A hum of familiarity abruptly hit me, nearly making me stagger. *There.* He was just northwest of me in the Wood, about a quarter mile away. He was alive—my magic was able to tell me that much—but around him, I detected *something*...

Prodding, my mental fingers assessed the creature more just as the Wood loomed. I'd never felt anything like it. Darkness. Evil intent. *Unbelievable* power. And . . . no heartbeat?

I struggled to understand that, especially since my magic

told me it was alive, yet I couldn't get a firm grasp on *what* it was and how it could be alive without a beating heart.

Still, I assessed it more and immediately wanted to mentally recoil given the icy film that encased the creature's mind.

Eww . . .

One thing I was certain of was that whatever Kole was stalking through the Wood was not something I'd ever encountered before, and the warrior was progressively moving closer to it, not even hesitating, and he was entirely on his own.

I reached the Wood and leaped into the foliage in the same beat, activating my sensory magic simultaneously to sharpen my eyesight and allow me to see more easily in the swamp of trees so I could increase my pace.

Leaves tore against my calves. Vines tried to obscure my path, but I ducked and moved, not slowing.

My lungs burned from my continued sprint, but I kept it up. I was growing closer to Kole and the creature, likely making a racket in the process, but maybe whatever that thing was, it would think twice before pouncing on Kole if it knew that two powerful fae were in its midst. Because, while I didn't know *what* it was, my magic told me that it wasn't stupid. The opposite, in fact. I would have bet rulibs that the creature was quite intelligent.

I closed in on their location. Kole stopped. My magic locked onto him, monitoring his every breath.

The warrior's aura soared, and I knew he'd either heard me

coming or somehow detected me. It didn't matter. I wasn't going to retreat, but I did slow down. Barreling toward the strange creature wasn't wise. For all I knew, before I got a firm grasp on its mind, it would leap right over me and attack me from behind.

I slowed to a jog, then stopped completely. Harsh breaths lifted my chest, my gasps audible, and it nearly killed me, but I quieted those too until I breathed silently. Still, my heartbeat pounded painfully.

Keeping my sensory magic activated, I scanned the area.

I stilled.

There it was.

Whatever the *thing* was, it'd stopped in the Wood, standing frozen, and it was only fifty paces ahead of me. Brush obscured some of it, so while I knew it was *there*, I couldn't see it clearly.

Kole was near it too, hidden behind a tree, but the edge of his shoulder was visible. Amazingly, the large warrior was nearly undetectable in the Wood despite his size.

I felt, rather than saw, the creature's interest shift to me. Something burned in its mind. An awareness. A knowing.

It'd known Kole was there too—my magic told me that much—but now that it sensed me, a new excitement grew in it.

What in the realm?

It was the only thought I had before a snarl emitted from the creature, that same stomach-lurching foreign-sounding growl that it'd made back in the village.

My blood ran cold. Everything inside me told me to retreat, but I sank lower into the brush, and it was only then I realized the Wood had gone silent. *Completely* silent. Just like the other night.

"Shite." The curse left me a second before the *thing's* ear-piercing scream wrenched through the air.

Before my mind could process what was happening, the creature shot toward me. It moved at blinding speed, blurring through the Wood so quickly that even with my eyesight activated and my mental magic on high alert, I could barely track it.

I staggered backward and gasped just as Kole lunged from behind the tree, sword raised, teeth bared.

He met the creature mid-stride, halting its run for me with the swing of his blade.

I stumbled back even more and nearly fell. They were only ten paces away, and Kole had slowed the thing enough for me to fully see it, and a *thing* was the only way to describe it.

It stood on two legs and looked like a fairy . . . but it wasn't. Sunken eyes. Hollowed cheeks. Pale and taut skin. Long fangs. And when it swung its arm toward Kole, black claws tipped each finger. Yet it wore ragged, dirty clothes.

Stars Above!

The warrior leaped back just before those claws tore his belly open. Kole's magic surged, cycling around him in growing intensity.

The creature snarled again and ripped its clawed hand

toward Kole once more, but the warrior became a whirling mass of limb, power, and steel. He slashed and slayed, keeping the creature from moving any closer to me, and his utter might filled the air around him.

For a moment, all I could do was stare. The male was pure wrath. Pure power. Kole moved in a song of indescribable beauty. Every twist of his limbs, dance of his feet, swing of his hand, was all precisely coordinated in an effortless, liquid rhythm.

Kole was death.

Powerful might.

Savage vengeance.

Primal skill.

I'd never seen *anyone* fight like him.

And the only reason I could *see* anything at all was due to my sensory magic. Otherwise, it would have all been a blur.

A tornado of magic swirled around the warrior as he kept the creature at bay, and every time I thought for certain the creature's speed would allow him to escape, Kole was there, matching him stride for stride.

Kole's sword abruptly arced through the air, and a surprised snarl tore from the creature's lips just as the warrior's blade met its neck.

A *thump* came.

I gasped.

The creature's head rolled on the forest floor, then a tangle of branches crackled as its body fell limply into the foliage beside it.

Dazed, I stood mutely, breaths coming so quickly that I began to feel lightheaded. But I made myself gulp in a lungful of air, just as the warrior swung toward me, his eyes blazing and pure rage emitting from his aura.

"Primelle Hollaran," he said in a deadly quiet voice. "What the *fuck* are you doing out here?"

I held up my hands in surrender because Kole was mad. Really, *really* mad.

The warrior stalked toward me, and I backed up, nearly stumbling again in the brush. "Kole, I'm sorry. I didn't mean to interfere, but when you ran off, I panicked, and—"

I stopped. *And what exactly? How exactly did I explain to him that an unreasonable instinct had come over me, and I'd been helpless to resist it?*

"The Stone is making me act crazy." I blurted. "I'm sorry. I shouldn't have followed you."

"The Stone," he growled.

"Yes, the Stone. I'm sorry." Eyesight still enhanced by my magic made every thunderous line visible upon the warrior's face. He was glaring at me, for once not even trying to hide his expression.

In my next breath, he closed the distance between us completely, his aura pulsing and rising, and then he was right in front of me, crowding my space.

I gulped, but I held my ground.

When he raised his hand, I flinched and automatically took another step back.

He seethed. "Do you really think I would hit you?" He grasped my chin with his raised hand and angled my head both ways as he looked me over. "It didn't hurt you?"

"No, it never came near me."

"There wasn't another one anywhere that you encountered on your way here?"

"No, not that I saw." *Or felt.* I was certain the headless creature behind him was the only one. "Wait." I shook my head. "There are *more* of those things?" It briefly struck me that perhaps the one I'd heard the other night had already been killed by Kole. Maybe this was a different one of the same species.

He finally released my chin, and his nostrils flared, but he stepped back and used a burst of self-cleansing magic to clean his sword. The black blood coating it disappeared.

Dear Goddess, black blood. *What in the realm had* black *blood?*

"Kole, what is that thing?" I wrapped my arms around myself, and I suddenly realized it was still snowing, and the temperature was even colder in the Wood. A shiver struck me. "Is it from Silventine Wood? Did it escape that forest?" I tried not to panic at the thought of the Wishing Stone potentially landing *there*, resulting in me encountering these creatures on a daily basis.

"It's something you should never hope to encounter again."

He gave me his back and stalked toward the creature, not pausing until he stood over its body.

A gust of Kole's air element flowed out of him, and the creature's decapitated head lifted in the wind and fell on top of its headless body.

A flash of moonlight penetrated the Wood's canopy, and I recoiled when razor-sharp fangs appeared in its dead gaping mouth, but the creature had ears like fae. Pointed and sculpted in a way that were similar to mine, but so many other aspects of it were different, not fae at all.

"Kole, *what* is that thing?" I asked again and stepped closer to him.

"Stay back." The warrior swung toward me, his eyes glittering in a way that even someone without my magic would have been able to detect in the dark. "Don't come any closer. It could infect you."

"*Infect* me?" I stopped, and another shiver struck me.

He swung back around, then pulled something from his pocket. He flicked it a few times, and a spark appeared at its end, but it went out as quickly as it'd appeared. He did it again, and another spark flamed, but as before, it extinguished.

A frustrated hiss tore from him, and his heightened aura formed a thick cloud around him.

"What . . ." I licked my lips, which had suddenly gone dry. "What are you doing?"

"I need to burn the body. Otherwise—" He shook his head. "I need to burn it."

I took a step forward. "I can help with that."

He cocked his head in my direction, but in a swirl of magic, I called upon my elemental power, and a stream of fire appeared in front of me. I molded it into a ball. "Stand back."

Surprisingly, he did as I said without questioning me. Once he was clear of the *thing*, I flung my fireball at it.

The creature ignited, and the sickening stench of burning flesh filled the Wood. I gagged, covering my mouth as the putrid aroma of decay swirled in the air.

Walking backward, Kole slowly moved toward me, never once taking his eyes off the hideous *thing*.

It was only after my fire had burned it completely and all that remained was a pile of ash that began to scatter on the wind, that I allowed my fire to extinguish. Once done, only a charred patch of soil remained on the Wood's floor. It was as if the creature had never existed at all.

Kole nodded his head in approval. "Time to go."

I'd thought that maybe his rage had calmed since he'd grown so quiet, but one look at his mouth that remained tightened in a thin line and one peek at his blazing blue irises, and I realized his rage hadn't cooled at all. No, it'd been *simmering*, and I wondered if I was about to be on the receiving end of it.

CHAPTER FOURTEEN

The warrior stalked ahead of me through the Wood, his strides strong and purposeful. I waited for him to berate me, yell at me, accuse me. Waited for all the things that I thought might be coming, but he remained silent.

But I knew better than to think his anger was cooling. Tension radiated along every line of Kole's body, and even though he walked ahead of me, he kept close tabs on my location. Anytime I fell even slightly behind him, he waited until I caught up.

He hadn't spoken with me, though. Not once. And that made his simmering anger all the more anxiety-provoking.

It was only when we emerged back into the village, and my toes were numb from the cold, and my teeth were near chattering, that he slowed enough for me to walk at his side.

Surprisingly, he didn't seem affected by the frigid temperature, even though he still wore the same casual clothes as he had at the salopas. And even though the wind had to bite through his top, he never shivered.

The street was thankfully empty. Music from the salopas still carried on the wind, and I hoped that Nym, Jessip, and Felix were still enjoying themselves, because if they'd run into what Kole had just killed in the Wood, I knew I would never see my new Faewood friends again.

As the inn neared, Kole placed his hand on my lower back, much as he'd done at the salopas, and guided me toward the main door.

"Not a word to anyone about what you saw. Understood?"

"Okay, but Kole," I said under my breath. "What *was* that?"

His jaw tightened, his usual steely mask absent. "Something we're trying to stop. That's all you need to know."

So he *was* here for Imperial Council business that had nothing to do with the Stone.

When we reached the inn, he opened the door for me, and if I'd been in a lighter mood, I probably would have teased him about his chivalrous behavior, but as it was, I could barely breathe, let alone make a cheeky comment.

When we both crossed the threshold, Nivinity straightened, and a relieved sigh escaped her. "Prim, you're back! Thank the stars. A dillemsill arrived while you were gone, telling me that everyone should stay indoors for the night. It was by order of the kingsfae."

I gave her a small smile and nodded, but Kole kept his hand on my lower back and guided me right by her.

The next thing I knew, I was climbing the stairs, then Kole was marching me down the hall on the second floor. When we reached my door, he held out his hand. "Key."

His demand snapped my head back, and my brain began firing again. Magic swirled in me, firing and igniting. "You're quite bossy."

"*Key*," he growled, and something in his tone had me complying.

I handed it over, and he opened my door, then ushered me inside.

I expected him to either leave now that he'd safely seen me to my chambers, or explode on me, but instead, he closed the door behind him and locked it. "I need to wash myself and thoroughly clean my sword."

Without further explanation, he strode across my room toward the bathing chambers and disappeared inside it. The sound of running water came next, along with the scent of his magic activating—self-cleansing magic from the fragrance of it—and I realized the warrior was taking his washing quite seriously if he was using both traditional bathing and magical cleansing.

Minutes passed before he finally reappeared.

My eyes widened. Like his sword, which now gleamed and sparkled, the warrior was spotless. Blood splatter that had been on his clothes was gone, and the lingering scent of that *thing* had vanished too.

"You need to wash as well, just in case." He nodded toward the bathing chambers.

I cocked my head. "But . . . it didn't come near me. I never touched it, and none of its blood got on me."

"You need to wash," he repeated.

Once again, that steely tone entered his voice, and while it was on the tip of my tongue to tell him to take a trip to the underworld, the rational side of me knew that he had a better understanding of that creature than I did. Maybe I *did* need to wash just to stay on the safe side.

I hurried past him into the bathing chambers. Inside, I did as he asked even though I was certain that none of that creature had touched me, but I still called upon my magic and doused all traces of the Wood and the day's grime from my clothes and skin. Following that, I also used soap and water.

Once my hair shone, my skin looked as fresh as it did after a bath, and my clothes billowed in a way that only freshly laundered items could, I rejoined him in my chambers.

He was still there, his sword once again at his back, except now he was pacing the room, and the simmering fury, which had been building in him since the forest, looked about to be unleashed.

Stars Above.

His eyes blazed as he looked me over, and he circled me

carefully, like a predator assessing his prey. The entire time, I stood stock still, not even daring to breathe.

"You cleaned every inch of yourself?" he finally asked after circling me twice.

"I did."

"You're certain?"

"Yes."

"I'm going to clean you too, just to be safe." A burst of his cleansing magic shot out of him. It smelled of him—of pine, cedar, and the sea. His essence clouded around me, bathing my skin and caressing me in a way that I was certain he didn't mean to make intimate, but Goddess, my knees began to weaken.

A sound emitted from his throat.

I glanced at him, but he wouldn't meet my eye. Instead, his jaw locked, and he didn't stop until his magic had fully cleansed me a second time, traveling over every dip and hollow of my clothes and skin. Exploring me inadvertently in the way that was needed to fully and completely bathe another.

The entire time I held my breath, even though this wasn't the first time another had bathed me. On occasion, a servant was tasked with doing a quick cleanse of their employer, but not in the way Kole had just done. Kole's cleanse had been intimate, and the thoroughness of it was usually only reserved for lovers.

But I knew the purpose of Kole's double check. He wanted to ensure that *thing* was gone, that no trace of it remained.

This was simply another one of his duties, even though my lower belly tightened in response.

Mortified, I lowered my chin.

Once done, his magic retreated, sucking back inside him so quickly that it slid over my body in a hurried brush, and that strange sound came from his throat again.

Cheeks blazing, I faced Kole and hoped he didn't notice the effect his magic had on me, but the warrior had his eyes closed. Just as fast, a whip of magic flared around his wrist, and he jerked his chin up.

Rapid breaths lifted his chest, and his hands fisted, large rope veins standing on the backs of them.

It was the most emotion, the most reaction, the most *anything* I'd ever seen from him. It was as if he'd entirely forgotten I was there, as though he'd retreated so completely inward that he wasn't aware that his every emotion had been laid bare upon his face for me to see.

My gaze dipped. Through his shirt, his hard body and chiseled chest were visible. Shoulders balled with tension held him rigid. Slabbed muscles and cut ridges were evident through his clothing, and, *Goddess*, everything about him made my mouth water.

My focus shifted to his waist, then lower, and my eyes widened at the very noticeable bulge in his pants.

I shakily ran a hand through my hair, loosening it from my braid. It'd been a rough night. A crazy night. It was obviously taking a toll on both of us, especially if the warrior had an erection that rivaled a temple's stone column.

But I knew it likely didn't mean anything. Most males would be affected physically if they tended to a female's body as thoroughly as he'd just done to me.

When Kole finally opened his eyes, I made myself not react, but his irises glowed like sparkling gems, and heightened energy surrounded the warrior like a rising tidal wave.

Despite the warrior's arousal and the intense urge I had to climb him like a tree, his rage was still palpable. Still *there*, but now it was coiling with something else, something dangerous.

He took a step closer to me, and his scent swam as thick as smoke around me.

"Now what?" I rasped. "I know that you're angry with me for following you."

"Aye, I am, but yelling at you will accomplish nothing."

"I'm sorry. I didn't mean to defy you."

"But you did, and you could have been killed."

"But I wasn't."

He growled. "But you could have been. You should have stayed at the inn as I told you to."

"I know." I ran a hand harshly over my hair, and he followed the movement, the glow in his eyes intensifying. "What was that thing anyway?"

His nostrils flared, blazing emotions once again shattering his steely composure. "How much did you see?"

"I don't know exactly, but enough to know that if creatures like that are what inhabit Silventine Wood, then there's no way I'll ever be able to retrieve the Wishing Stone if that's where it landed."

And that was true. I would never be able to close my eyes to sleep or let my guard down to eat. One could only go without proper rest or nourishment for so long, and if I had to spend days in Silventine Wood, then I was royally fucked.

"Silventine Wood?" His head cocked slightly.

"Isn't that where it came from?"

"Who told you that?"

"Nivinity. She said that other Stonewild villages have spoken of strange occurrences. They said a creature from Silventine Wood has escaped that forest's magic and is roaming the land. That some fae have disappeared." I waited for him to confirm that, but when he didn't, I took a step closer to him. "Is that where it came from?"

Instead of replying, the warrior went to the door that adjoined my chambers to his. He unlocked it, then swung it open.

"What are you doing?"

"I'm leaving the doors between our chambers open for the night, and for once, do as I tell you. *Don't* close them."

Shocked, I watched as he stalked back toward the main door, only to open it and disappear into the hall.

I followed him right out of my room, down the short distance to his chambers, and then into his own suite that he entered from the hallway. He strode across his chambers, unlocked his adjoining door, and swung it open too.

Now, even with our main doors barred to the hallway, each of us would still have easy access to one another's private spaces.

"Kole, what are you doing?"

"I told you. I'm leaving these doors open tonight."

I tapped my foot. "I see that, but why? Why do our doors need to be open?"

"Because."

I rolled my eyes. "Don't you think I deserve an explanation? This is incredibly intrusive on my privacy, and I haven't done anything wrong, nor have I broken the law."

He swung toward me, his eyes glittering, and the rage that he'd been carefully controlling exploded in his aura, yet despite that, his voice remained controlled. He held true to his promise not to yell, but his fury filled each word. "You defied my order when I told you to stay at the inn. You could have been *killed* because of that."

My mouth snapped closed. "Well, yes, I know I defied you, but—"

"But what? What's your excuse for that?"

That something overtook me. Something I can't explain and certainly couldn't ignore. Maybe it was the Stone. Maybe it was something else. Maybe I've simply gone entirely crazy in the blink of an eye.

Of course, I didn't say that. Doing so risked me being

committed to a healing infirmary, so I lifted my chin and said defiantly, "Why do I need an excuse?"

"Because you *did* defy me."

"I didn't realize it was said to me with authority," I replied, my voice also rising.

"No? What part of '*Prim, go inside the inn. Now.*' did you not understand?"

Fuming, I said through gritted teeth, "We're getting off track. What in the realm does any of that have to do with our doors remaining open?"

"Because there could be another one of those *things* out there. That's why."

His icy reply had me momentarily speechless. When I was finally able to speak, I whispered, "There could be?"

"It's hard to know for certain, but yes, it's possible."

"And you want our doors open to . . . protect me, should one come into the village again?"

He glanced away, his jaw ticking. "Yes."

Warmth bloomed through me, but just as fast, my hands began to twist. "But then others could be at risk too. We need to warn them. We need to let the village know that—"

"They already know."

"What?"

"They already know that it's unsafe to be roaming the streets tonight. They've been ordered to stay inside by their local kingsfae."

I thought back to what Nivinity had said below. "*Everyone was notified?*"

"Yes, Primelle." He sighed, and for the first time, I could tell the events of the night were catching up with him too. "The second I left you in that street, I contacted my superiors. Dillemsills were promptly sent out. While you were racing through the Wood, everyone else was being alerted to stay inside and shelter in place."

"You contacted them that fast?" I furrowed my brow. He'd done that on the move. But before I could contemplate *how* he'd done such a thing, my eyes widened. "Does the *entire* village know? Including Nym, Jessip, and Felix? They don't live here. What if—"

"They should know. Dillemsills were dispatched to all travelers, salopas, households, and farms in the surrounding area. Everyone was ordered to stay put until they were told otherwise."

"Oh," I said dumbly.

My thundering heartbeat began to slow, and for the first time, I felt like I genuinely understood why Kole was here. It wasn't because of the Stone. It wasn't to keep the peace. Not truly. That was just a cover. That *creature* was why Kole was here. The Imperial Warriors had been tasked to track down and kill whatever those creatures were, and apparently, there were more of them.

"Now, if you would appease me, you need to stay in your chambers." Kole placed his hand on my lower back, his heat searing me, and he guided me back to my room through our adjoining doors. From there, he locked my door to the hallway again, then retreated back to his room, only stopping at the threshold of our adjoining chambers to address me one last time. "I need to go back out. I have to check the Wood again to ensure there aren't more of those *things*, before restrictions on movements are lifted."

Before I could comment, he was gone.

The fairy lights were doused in his room, and the sound of his door closing and locking rang through my ears.

A second later, a pulse of magic washed through his chambers and into mine. It took me a second to realize he'd just placed protection wards around the perimeter of both of our rooms, stronger ones than the inn offered.

And realizing he truly was worried enough about my safety to do such a thing, I listened to his request and didn't follow him.

Instead, I changed into nightclothes and slipped under the sheets.

But despite the dark night, warm covers, my aching body, and tired magic, it still took forever to drift off to sleep. I kept thinking about Kole, that creature, and what was to come. And it struck me that he'd never told me what it was. Not really.

Regardless, tomorrow I was traveling north into the Wildland Mountains. Toward wherever the Wishing Stone had landed. Toward where that *thing* had come from.

And who was to say if another creature like that would be waiting for me along my path.

CHAPTER FIFTEEN

The fresh scent of coffee roused me in the morning.

Sleepily, I opened my eyes and immediately squinted. Sunlight blazed through my chambers' curtains, and I wondered what time it was. Groggily, I pushed to sitting. Long hair cascaded around me, falling across my eyes and disrupting my view.

I shoved it out of the way and searched for the clock. I finally found one near the window. Grumbling, I wasn't surprised that it was already after eight. It was much later than I'd planned on leaving, but after a night like last night, I decided to cut myself some slack.

Yawning, I stretched again, then realized the coffee I'd detected was due to a steaming mug of the delicious brew waiting on my bedside table.

Steam rose from it, so I knew it was either an enchanted cup that didn't allow the coffee to cool, or someone had just delivered it. I glanced around, wondering if the inn staff magically transported coffee to every traveler's bedroom chambers each morning, or if someone had—

My eyes widened, and I immediately rushed from my bed to the open adjoining doors Kole and I shared. I hadn't heard him come in last night. I had no idea if he returned, if he was safe too, if—

I barreled into his chambers.

And promptly stopped.

Kole sat in a chair near his bed, drinking coffee, and he was shirtless.

If he was at all surprised that I burst into his chambers, uninvited, with only my pajamas still adorning me, he hid it completely. And if he was at all embarrassed to be caught in a semi-state of undress, he hid that too.

But I couldn't.

Mouth dropping, I soaked up the muscles piled upon muscles that graced his chest. He looked smooth, hard, and surprisingly, no scars were in sight. The warrior was built like a slabbed wall, cut of angular granite, molded into the beautiful hard-rock specimen that depicted a perfect fae male.

And he was staring at me, his eyes slightly hooded, his only outward reaction, as he calmly sipped his coffee.

I, however, was not nearly as skilled in the art of *complete-and-total-devoid-of-emotion-upon-one's-face*, so I could only imagine the expression I wore.

"Good morning," he finally offered, his voice so deep a shiver rolled through me.

"Um, morning."

"Did you get your coffee?"

I gaped. "*You* brought that to me?"

He shrugged. "I went down the street to get a cup. I thought you might want one too."

"And you delivered it, just now?"

"I did. Sorry if I woke you."

"No, you didn't. That's not what I . . . I mean—" I snapped my mouth closed. The concern I'd felt at him being out during the night vanished now that I knew he was well, and quite frankly, I was at a loss to explain my dashing into his private chambers. "Thank you."

"You're welcome, and don't worry. I kept my eyes closed the entire time I delivered it, just in case you were—" He cut himself off, and even though his expression remained blank, his throat bobbed.

"Shirtless too?" I quipped, and despite the fact that I'd just woken up, a teasing smile twisted my lips.

He grunted, but I could have sworn that amusement lit his eyes as he took another sip of his drink.

I fiddled with the hem of my nightshirt, and he tracked the movements over the rim of his cup. Another roll of his throat came.

"Did, uh, or rather, were there any more of those creatures roaming the Wood last night?"

He shook his head. "Thankfully, no. The Wood remains clear."

"And the traveling restrictions have been lifted?"

"They have. A dillemsill wasn't sent to you because I knew I could tell you this morning."

I nodded and released a sigh of relief. "That's good. Have there been many sightings in the areas around here? I'm heading into the Wildland Mountains today, and well—" My hands twisted into my pajama top anew.

Kole glanced at my chest, and I realized the swell of my breasts was visible due to my fidgeting.

Kole stood in a flash and turned away, giving me his back. Muscles tightened and rippled along his shoulders. "It would be wise to reconsider your travels. It would be safest if you returned home," he said over his shoulder.

Words once again failed me, because, *Stars Above*, the male was built. I marveled as I took in his broad shoulders, tapered waist, and muscled thighs. In his breeches, even his toned backside was as taut as a bowstring.

Everything in me tightened. "Your sword."

He slowly turned, but his gaze stayed trained above my head. "What?"

"Your sword isn't on your back. I wondered if you ever took it off."

"I just told you it would be wise if you went home, and your reply was to comment on my sword?"

It was on the tip of my tongue to tell him that his

comment could be misconstrued in so many ways, especially after his impressive erection last night, but somehow, I managed to restrain myself. "Sorry, I did hear you, but I have to go where the Stone is, which means I'm going north."

"How do you know the Stone is north?"

An ancient book and my seekerill told me. I shrugged. "I don't know for certain, but that's where I believe it is."

A heavy frown descended over his face, and unable to help myself, I lifted a finger. "You're doing it again."

His frown turned into a scowl. "Doing what?"

"Showing emotion."

He sighed, and his glower disappeared. "You seem to have that effect on me."

A flush worked up my neck, and his gaze dipped, just for the merest second, to my attire again. While my pajamas weren't excessively revealing, they also didn't leave much to the imagination.

A sudden flare of magic came from his wrist, the same flare I'd detected before, and I couldn't help but wonder what aspect of his magic it was.

Jaw tightening, he looked away. "You should go."

"Oh. Right. Sorry. Thank you again for the coffee." Embarrassment flamed through me at his sharp dismissal, and I fled back to my chambers.

Once on my side, I turned to close my door, thinking the warrior would be where I left him, but Kole had moved.

And he was in a position that awarded him a clear view of me retreating.

Our eyes locked for the briefest moment, and I could have sworn that a glow filled his.

I quickly closed my door, and alone again, I sagged against the hard frame and shook my head. The strange pull he had on me and my illicit responses to him needed to stop.

Uncle Timith.

Uncle Timith.

That's why you're here.

I checked the adjoining door again, just to ensure it was truly locked, then I began to hastily pack my things.

The Wishing Stone was waiting to be found, and with any luck, I would find it today.

CHAPTER SIXTEEN

I wasn't finding the Wishing Stone today. Not even close.

I rummaged through the outdoor compartment outside of the inn where I'd stored my enchanted carpet last night. Snow drifted around my feet in the morning breeze. Several inches coated the main street, but the blast of northern air was the least of my concerns.

Because my carpet was nowhere to be found. It wasn't *here.*

"No, no, no. Where are you?" I searched through the outdoor storage shed again, and then again, hunting for my only means of transportation. I'd placed it in the shed's left corner last night. I was certain of that.

But other than a large trunk someone had set near that corner, an old, raggedy enchanted carpet that looked as if it would barely carry one fairy, multiple boxes that were too small to hold a carpet, and a few empty flower pots that I guessed the inn used during warmer months, there was nothing. Absolutely nothing. Someone had either stolen my carpet or it'd flown off on its own, the second not being possible.

Heart hammering, I left the shed and raced around the inn, searching the entire perimeter for my carpet. When that didn't yield anything, I went back inside and asked the front desk staff if they'd perhaps moved it. But they denied doing so.

And after doing another sweep throughout the entire inn and then back to the shed, I accepted the inevitable.

My carpet was gone.

"Shite!" I slapped my hand against the wall, gaining myself a new splinter in the process. Moaning, I sucked my finger, then pulled the splinter out and sagged against the wall. "What am I going to do?"

I'd been so careful on this trip. *So* careful. I'd avoided all conflicts following that first day. I'd even lost travel time when I'd sensed other fae wished me harm. Gods and Goddesses, I'd even carried all of my supplies *up to my chambers* last night just to avoid any thefts, only to have the one thing I desperately needed to travel taken from me.

My spirits plummeted. "Now what?" I whispered to myself.

Enchanted carpets weren't easy to come by, especially not in a village as remote as Inisville. If I'd been in Whiteolf or even Jaggedston, it might have been feasible to procure a new enchanted carpet today, but *here?* I would be lucky if one arrived a month after ordering it.

I slapped my hand against the wall again. "Stupid. Stupid. Stupid. You should have taken your carpet upstairs with you too, even if the blasted thing weighs a hundred stones!"

Granted, my carpet hadn't actually weighed that much, but it was heavy and awkward to carry, especially since I'd bought one on the larger size so I could carry all of my supplies. And since I was trying to conceal the extent of my abilities, I hadn't wanted to use my telekinetic magic. Although Kole probably could have easily maneuvered it up the staircase if I'd asked him to.

I balled my hands, anything to stop the rising anxiety clawing up my throat.

Feeling sick at what my future held, I took a deep breath and tried to see the bright side of things. Straightening, I forced a smile because I could order a new carpet. It wasn't like one wouldn't show up eventually, and perhaps spending more time in Inisville would allow me to better study my book from the Isle of Song . . . even though I'd read it cover to cover several times over.

My chin wobbled, but I strengthened my resolve to see the positive.

Perhaps I could learn more from the locals about that creature so I would know how best to avoid another encounter with one. Or maybe, just maybe, the cold weather that had filled the land with snow would pass, and by the time I headed out, it would be warmer.

I grasped onto those optimistic thoughts, desperately trying to pretend that this wasn't a total and complete disaster.

But my lower lip trembled despite my efforts, and I pushed away from the wall to begin pacing along the shed's exterior. Snow kicked up around my ankles, and a cold breeze brushed my cheeks.

"Think positively. Think positively," I chanted to myself again and again, then grabbed the lock of Goddess Nuleef's hair from my sack. I fingered the golden strands, the shiny material like silk. "It's not over. You'll get a new carpet. The snow might be melted by then anyway. Traveling could be warmer. And whatever the creature was, if there are any more in the area, hopefully, the rest will be long gone by then. This isn't the end. It'll be okay."

My pacing increased, but no matter how hard I tried to view this as a blessing, and no matter how many times I rubbed and prayed to the goddess, several cold hard facts remained.

I was now delayed, for who knew how long, and the Stone could very well be found by another fairy while I waited for a new carpet to arrive. It had already been a week since the Stone had shot across the sky.

I walked faster, my feet sliding along the slick snow. Tears were on the brink of forming in my eyes. My uncle might die now because of my carelessness. I rubbed the goddess's hair more. If only I'd been more careful. If only I'd—

A whoop of laughter came from down the lane.

I stopped short just as my three Faewood friends sailed down the street toward me on their enchanted carpet.

Nym, Jessip, and Felix sat securely upon it. Fresh supplies were strapped to it just behind them. In all likelihood, they'd just restocked on food and probably warmer clothing for their journey north. They obviously had the foresight *not* to store their carpet out in the open, where anyone could take it.

Felix waved jovially as soon as he spotted me. "Prim, my love, what a pleasant surprise!" The male grinned, his eyebrows waggling suggestively.

Nym and Jessip also waved, and they flew closer to me.

Jessip stopped at the inn's door, their carpet hovering in the breeze. "Morning, Prim."

"Good morning." I forced a bright smile, but moisture still coated my eyes.

"Glad to see you're safe and sound," Nym added. "Crazy stuff last night, eh? Did you get a dillemsill as well about needing to stay indoors?"

My smile wavered, and thoughts of the strange creature returned. "I heard," I replied vaguely, not wanting to dwell on that problem too.

Jessip cocked her head and peered closer at me. "Is everything okay? You look upset."

I blinked rapidly and forced my expression to smooth. "I'm afraid I've had a turn of bad luck, but it's nothing I can't fix."

"Bad luck?" Felix's brow furrowed. "Did something happen?"

I quickly explained that my carpet had been stolen, so my journey was delayed, but that I had plans to procure a new one. "I'll put an order in straight away. It's just something I didn't foresee happening, is all." I wrung my hands but kept my shoulders back, determined to make the most of this. I was about to tell them just that, but the inn's door opened, snagging everyone's attention.

Kole stepped outside, his dark hair glinting in the dim sunlight filtering through the thick cloud cover. His broad shoulders brushed against the doorframe, and his sword was once again strapped to his back. The warrior halted in place, being forced to stop since Nym, Jessip, and Felix's carpet blocked his path.

"Hi, Kole." Jessip waved in a friendly manner.

The warrior didn't reply.

Felix turned back to me, barely giving the warrior a passing glance. "Why don't you join us? We have plenty of room, and four heads are better than three. We can turn your stroke of bad luck into a lucky break."

"Really?" I perked up even though I knew that if I joined them, problems would arise eventually. If not on which direction to go, then on who would claim the Stone. After all, if we were lucky enough to find it, only one fairy could use its magic, and I doubted they'd let me.

"What's going on?" Kole's expression didn't change, but he surveyed the four of us.

Jessip waved toward me. "Prim's carpet was stolen during the night, so she's currently stuck here without transportation, but we've offered her a spot on our carpet if she wants to keep hunting the Stone. We have room after all." She patted the free patch of carpet beside her.

Kole took a step toward me, his tone lowering. "You're still journeying north? You're not going home?"

I tried not to be affected by the blatant concern in his voice or how his deep tone rolled right through me, as if on a path straight to my nether region. "Of course, I'm still going north. Or rather, I'd planned to be until someone stole my carpet, but now—"

"You're certain it's gone?" His aura flickered, and he peered inside the shed.

"Yes, definitely. I've searched everywhere for it, and it's not in there. I checked behind the inn too and asked the staff, but no one's seen it. Someone must have stolen it."

"Strange stuff must have been going on last night," Nym chimed in. "We all got a dillemsill about needing to stay indoors. Maybe that's when the thief took it since they knew nobody would see them." Nym scratched his head. "Do you know what that was about last night? About why we had to stay inside?"

Kole ignored him and swung toward me again, then nudged the boxes sitting at my feet that I'd laboriously dragged down the stairs on my own. "You shouldn't go north, Prim. You should go home."

His tone was heavy. Adamant. As if he truly cared for my well-being. And I didn't even want to think about what that was doing to my insides.

However, all three sets of eyebrows on my new friends shot up.

"She shouldn't?" Felix scowled at the warrior.

"But I have to go north." I peered up at Kole. "Retreating isn't an option."

"Why shouldn't she go north?" Felix pushed, a wave of suspicion descending over him.

"It's not safe. That's why," Kole replied in a clipped tone.

Nym, Jessip, and Felix all looked in confusion at one another, but Kole's attention stayed focused on me. "How are you going to transport your supplies without a carpet?" he asked quietly.

"We'll fit it," Felix said. "Prim can come with us. And four of us traveling together is safer than three if it truly is dangerous for her." Felix leaped off the carpet and reached for one of my boxes, but Kole stepped into his path, stopping him.

The warrior's aura swelled, and Felix bristled.

Kole gave Felix his back, then leveled me with a heavy stare. "Have you thought this through, Prim?"

I knew he was not only referring to his warning about continuing north, but also about the fact that I didn't actually know these three. And while the Faewood fairies seemed harmless, and I certainly didn't think they would murder me in my sleep, I also didn't know for certain that they wouldn't.

I also didn't know what kind of traveling companions they would be, or if Felix's harmless flirtations would morph into him wanting something more physical, which I didn't particularly want to pursue. And then the issue would eventually arise of who would claim the Stone if we were lucky enough to find it.

Challenges would lie ahead if I chose to travel with them. I nibbled on my lip. Kole was right. Impulsively joining them might not be the best option, but it wasn't like I had a plethora of traveling choices to choose from.

Felix glared at Kole and sidestepped him so he could clearly see me. "What's there to think through, Kole? We're offering her a ride because she no longer has one, and there is safety in numbers. She'll be safe with us. She'll be safe with *me*. I'll watch out for her."

I nearly snorted, because I was a hundred percent certain that if something truly dangerous occurred, I would be the one saving *him*.

"Is a ride all you're offering her?" the warrior said so coolly that he put the icy breeze to shame.

Felix smirked. "Well, that will be up to her to decide."

A pulse of energy shot from Kole's aura. Facing me squarely once more, he said gruffly, "I have room on my carpet. Come with me instead."

My eyebrows shot up. "You do?" I glanced behind him. "Where's your carpet?"

"Still in my chambers."

"Oh, of course." He'd obviously had the foresight not to leave it out here either, even though I didn't recall seeing a large rolled carpet anywhere in his private suite.

"You can still come with us." Felix waggled his eyebrows. "I promise to make it enjoyable."

Kole cut him a hard look, but I thought of the fun I'd had last night with the three—the dancing, laughing, and drinking. Felix was right. I could join them, probably even enjoy myself on this lonely journey.

But then I frowned. Fun and adventure weren't why I'd left Whiteolf and my family behind. Finding the Stone and claiming it were all that mattered, and I knew Kole's time up here *wasn't* because of Stone hunting. I didn't have to worry about him fighting me for it if my uncle's device led me to it. And then there was the matter of who Kole was. I would be safe with him should another creature come prowling. He'd proven that last night. We could even sleep in shifts if need be.

I eyed the warrior again. "Are you sure?"

For the merest second, a satisfied gleam filled his eyes, but then he blinked, and it was gone. "I'm sure."

I gave Felix, Nym, and Jessip an apologetic smile. "As much as I've enjoyed meeting you and spending time with you all, I think I'll take Kole up on his offer."

Felix pouted. "You're breaking my heart, Prim."

I rolled my eyes, but a playful smile tugged on my lips. "I'm sure you'll survive."

He shook his head dramatically. "I fear I won't."

"You'll make it," the warrior said dryly, then stepped closer to me. "I'll be back shortly. We'll leave soon. Just wait for me. Okay?"

I dipped my head, and Kole ducked back inside the inn.

"Now's your chance." Felix hopped back onto their carpet and held his hand out. "You can ditch him, and we'll be out of here before he knows it."

But too much relief was flowing through me for Felix's offer to be even remotely tempting. I blew him a kiss. "Farewell, my friends. Safe journeys."

Nym tugged on Felix to sit down. "You lost, my friend, and the warrior won. Take it like a gentlefae."

Felix sighed but continued professing words of love for me as they sailed down the street, and even though I knew he was just being silly and overly dramatic, another breath of relief filled me that I wasn't going with them.

Knowing that I could travel with the warrior, at least for a short while, had most of my nerves calming. However, there was still the matter of what to do once Kole and I parted ways. I would still have to travel back to Whiteolf eventually, and I couldn't do that by walking, especially if I needed to hurry back if my uncle took a turn for the worse.

I contemplated how long it would take for Kole to grab his

carpet and figured I would have enough time to place an order at the shop down the lane for my own.

Because while I hoped the warrior meant it that he didn't mind me traveling with him for the foreseeable future, I also knew that I couldn't rely on him entirely. If the Imperial Council demanded that he venture in a direction opposite of where I believed the Stone to be, the warrior and I would have to part ways. Even if that meant being on my own again in dangerous territory.

CHAPTER SEVENTEEN

An hour later, I was still waiting for Kole. I'd ventured to the general store and placed an order for a new carpet. I had it being delivered to a city in the northern area of Stonewild, which hopefully Kole would take me to if needed. Otherwise, I would have to hitch a ride with other fae in order to claim it.

But even though I'd kept an eye out the shop's window while I'd been placing my order, I still hadn't seen Kole emerge from the inn, not once.

So I waited and waited for him to return.

The sun rose steadily behind a thick cloud cover, and the frigid air didn't warm. Swirling masses of indigo, navy, and purple puffs roiled over the land, threatening another gale. Rain or snow would likely come again. I shivered. *No, not rain.* Snow would definitely be coming if those clouds decided to let loose.

I hopped from foot to foot, my toes slightly numb from

standing idly for so long, and I debated if I should go back inside the inn just to warm up.

But then another thought occurred to me, and my stomach dropped. Perhaps I should also check in with the front desk to see if Kole was still *here*. It was possible the warrior had changed his mind about helping me, and he'd ditched me through the inn's back door rather than breaking the news to my face. That could explain why he hadn't shown yet.

Oh Gods. I lurched toward the inn's door, but the second I brushed the door handle, Kole opened it with a carpet in tow.

I jumped back, and he halted, as if my presence took him by surprise as much as his did me.

His hair was ruffled, and his breathing was rapid, as though he'd been running, which made no sense whatsoever. The inn's quarters were much too tight to run through.

"You're still here." My shoulders sagged in relief.

He eyed me, and I could only imagine what I looked like. Frantic energy likely filled my aura.

"Of course, I am." He moved out into the street until his huge carpet was free of the door.

His enchanted carpet was large, colorful, and looked brand new. He maneuvered it easily, even having slipped it fully through the door without knocking anything over in our vicinity.

"Did you get lost?" I joked.

"No. I, uh, had to do a few things first. Sorry to make you wait." He began to unfurl the carpet. It rolled awkwardly, as though it'd been tightly coiled for months and was only just being allowed to breathe.

I shrugged. "That's okay. I'm glad you showed."

He peered up at me, and once again, his rugged masculinity threatened to steal my breath. "Did you doubt that I would?"

I wrung my hands and forced a smile. "No?"

His penetrating stare didn't waver. "I wouldn't abandon you, Prim. I promised you could join me. I was always going to show."

His tone left no room for argument, and something in me calmed. Even though I didn't know Kole well—if at all—his statement told me that if the warrior gave his word to someone, he kept it. "Sorry that I doubted you."

"It's all right." He returned his attention to the carpet, and once it was fully flat, it levitated automatically on its own. Thick magic puffed around it, and the strong scent of woven fibers filled my nose. It not only looked new, but it smelled new too.

Kole grabbed my supplies and began to stack them in the back. I joined him and studied the bright carpet colors that were in direct contrast to the angry sky.

"Do you require travelers to remove their footwear?" I bumped his elbow playfully.

He stopped mid-movement. "What?"

I nodded toward his carpet. "It's so clean. It looks brand new. I figured you may be one of those fae who don't allow anyone to wear shoes on their carpet. How else could it be so spotless?"

He reached for another box and said gruffly, "No, you can keep your shoes on."

My brow furrowed, but I finished helping him with my supplies.

Within minutes, everything was magically strapped into place, and we were ready to go. I glanced toward the northern skyline. The Wildland Mountain peaks gleamed with fresh white snow, and I thought of the creature last night. Of what potentially waited for us in the Wood.

Suddenly, I was very thankful that I was traveling with an Imperial Warrior whose very job was to hunt such things. I could only hope that Nym, Jessip, and Felix would be lucky enough to avoid them if any more were lurking about.

Kole jumped onto the carpet and sat, but he had to shift his sword so his blade angled off the carpet's side. He then patted the area beside him. "Ready to go?"

His large hand snagged my attention. His fingers were thick, his palm wide. Wind swirled his midnight hair around the tips of his ears, and my attention shifted to his mouth. Last night now felt like a whirlwind, but at one point, I knew he'd been as aroused as me.

My heartbeat kicked up, and I hurriedly climbed onto the carpet, then settled myself beside him. My leg brushed against his, but when I made a move to shift away, his hand settled on my thigh, halting me.

Warmth immediately seared through my pants from his body heat, and my muscles bunched.

His fingers tensed, and he quickly removed his hand and ran it through his hair. "Um, sorry about that."

All I managed was an awkward smile since I was still reeling from how easily he touched me.

Glancing away, he mumbled a command to the carpet, but nothing happened. His jaw locked, and he said it louder.

As before . . . nothing happened.

My brows furrowed together. "Kole, have you ever ridden this carpet before?" Seconds ticked by, but he didn't respond. "Kole?" I said again.

He growled, so low that it was more like a vibration in his chest. "No."

My nose scrunched up. "Then how did you get here? Didn't you travel here on this carpet?"

He wouldn't meet my eye, and once again, he didn't reply.

Sighing, I was reminded of his secretive nature and decided to respect his privacy even though everything about his new carpet made me endlessly curious.

"I take it you don't often travel by enchanted carpet?" I teased instead.

He made a noise in his throat, and a hint of embarrassment wafted from his aura. "What gave it away?"

I laughed and sat up straighter, smiling brightly. "You need to imprint the carpet to your voice before it follows your commands."

I told him the simple instructions, which I assumed all fae knew regarding carpets, but considering Kole followed my directions, I thought that perhaps this truly was new to him. Odd indeed, but I bit my tongue and didn't push further.

Once the carpet's magic recognized Kole as its commander, I nodded at him. "Try again."

Under his breath, he said, "Lift. Sail north on the road."

The carpet rose higher and immediately began gliding down the main street back to the Wood's road. Kole smirked.

I bumped the warrior's elbow again. "That's better, don't you think?"

For the briefest moment, his lips tugged up, and I felt positively giddy to see another elusive smile.

"Do you think the weather will hold?" I gazed skyward. Threats of an impending gale continued. The wind was positively fierce, but unlike last night, a breath of warmth filled me since Kole's body heat radiated out of him. Blessedly, I soaked up every bit of it. "But I suppose even if it starts snowing again, at least it's not as cold as it was last night."

"Not yet, at least. Weather can be unpredictable this time of the season. There's no telling what's in store for us."

"Is that so?" I peered up at the warrior. "Do you know this area well?"

"Not as well as the locals, but I've been here before."

We sailed out of Inisville, and the carpet settled into flight along the Wood's road, going north as commanded.

"Do you have a certain destination in mind today?" I asked

him. "Other than going north?" I would ride with Kole for as long as I could, but if the seekerill told me to go in a different direction from him, we would have to part ways.

"Nowhere specifically. My orders are to stay on patrol."

"Ah, wonderful. In that case . . ." I pulled out the seekerill and checked the needle. A cold breeze rushed over my cheeks as the carpet glided along its predestined path, and Kole's heat continued to be a blessing. My spirits lifted, even when the needle showed that I should go more northeast, but the road we were on tracked steadily north instead, with no intersection in sight. I shrugged. "Close enough. Let's stay on this road for now."

Kole eyed my device as I tucked it back into my pocket.

"Is there any chance we could go faster?" I asked him.

He issued another command, and the carpet shot forward.

Grinning, I relished the speed as the land whizzed by us, and the fact that I was once again making headway caused my heart to soar.

We sailed over the Wood's road, and the Wildland Mountains loomed, yet even with potential creatures lurking in the forest, my smile didn't abate.

Kole glanced down at me, and asked in a curious tone, "What was that device you put in your pocket?"

My lips parted, surprise momentarily biting my tongue that the warrior had initiated a conversation.

"Oh. Well . . ." I withdrew it from my pocket and showed it to him. "This is actually my uncle's. He invented it."

I opened the small metallic box and showed him how the thick needle, which floated over a flat piece of babbo wood, moved in the direction its magic guided it. "It's similar to a compass, but it follows an object that you alert it to. It can follow anything. Its magic is incredibly precise and accurate."

"May I?" He held his hand out, and I placed it on his palm. He picked the box up and inspected it more, then handed it back to me. "How interesting. And your uncle invented that?"

"He did. He's a brilliant inventor."

"So brilliant that he knows how to create a device that can find anything?"

"Indeed. He's one of the most brilliant fae I know. Normally, we use this device to find our way home. If I activated the magic on our residence in Whiteolf, that's where the needle would be pointing right now."

"But Whiteolf is behind us, so what's it alerting us to?"

"The Wishing Stone."

His eyebrows shot clear to his hairline.

I giggled, unable to help it. "You look surprised."

"You said it's pointed toward the Wishing Stone. I think that warrants some surprise."

"True, but considering that until yesterday I never saw any emotions on your face, you can perhaps understand my delight at how you look right now."

His eyes narrowed, but his eyebrows dropped back to a normal level. "Okay, I'll bite . . . how do you know that device is leading you to the Stone? Nobody knows where the Stone is."

"Seekerill."

He cocked his head. "What?"

"Technically, it's called a *seekerill*. That's the name of this invention."

"All right, in that case, how do you know your *seekerill* will lead you to the Stone?"

"I don't, but I'm hoping it will." I grinned again and didn't bother telling him about my book or constellation scroll. It was too fun to observe his confused reactions.

He continued watching me, and a small smile played upon his lips. "You are a strange one, Miss Hollaran."

"Perhaps, but delightfully strange, no?"

His mouth cracked more, then lifted in a genuine smile. My heartbeat inadvertently raced.

"Aye, I can agree that you're delightfully strange."

My chest locked up, my lungs refusing to work. Heart thumping, I shifted my attention to the Wood and took a deep breath, using the cold air to ground me, and cold it was. It'd grown darker, which was odd considering the sun was still rising, but the swamp of trees around us could explain it, along with the thick cloud cover. The Wood here was denser than I'd ever seen it. Patches of foliage even drifted entirely across the road, as though the Wood refused to be tamed in these parts.

"And your uncle, you said he's an inventor?" Kole's deep voice pulled my attention back to him. I couldn't have ignored him if I tried. Something about his tone, his scent, his feel, his *everything*, had latched onto me, as though a rope had been cinched around my head and forced it to turn in whatever direction he lay. Perhaps Kole was my personal seekerill. "Are you and your uncle close?"

I cleared my throat. "Yes, very. Even though he's my uncle, he's more like a father to me. I've lived with him and my aunt nearly my entire life."

"Not with your parents?"

I shrugged, but the old pain that had once caught me in a death grip as a child anytime somebody mentioned my parents didn't appear. Enough seasons had passed that I'd grown used to their passing. "No, my parents died when I was an infant so my uncle, who's my father's brother, has been the only father I've ever known."

"May I ask how they died?" he asked quietly.

"It was a carriage accident." I swallowed, dryness creeping into my throat, but I also knew Kole didn't ask questions of other fae like this, and I hoped that if perhaps I opened up to him, he would do the same with me. "It happened in the Clawfur Mountains. That's where I was born. I was told their carriage slipped off a mountain road during a freak storm and plunged into a river below. If I'd been in that carriage with them, I would have died too. Following their accident, my aunt and uncle came to take care of me. They were so supportive, and even though I was only a baby, they still allowed me to grow up in my parents' home until I turned eight, then we moved back to the capital so my uncle could be closer to the palace for his work. He works for the king and queen of Mistvale Kingdom."

Kole was quiet again, his gaze intense. "Did your uncle continue working for the crown while he lived so far away?"

"He did. He's such a brilliant inventor that the royals didn't want to lose him, but eventually, they pressed him to return, so we had to. I've been living in Whiteolf ever since."

He nodded, then said gruffly, "I'm sorry you lost your parents."

"I've had thirty-two summers to get used to it. It's fine. Truly."

His brow furrowed. "You're thirty-two?"

"I am. And what about you?" I held my breath, wondering if he would answer.

"Eighty-seven."

A flurry of warmth drifted through me. Something told me he rarely disclosed that to fae. "Well, in that case, we're about the same age."

"Indeed."

Quiet descended between us once more, and when we passed underneath a rare opening in the Wood's canopy, a small ray of dim sunlight hit my face.

"So how long has your uncle been doing inventions for the Mistvale royals?"

I bit back a smile, trying to hide the fact that his interest in me made me feel positively gleeful. "For hundreds of full seasons." The lightness in my voice faded. "Well, at least he used to. He's not working at the moment. He's too sick to work."

Kole's face gave away nothing, but I could have sworn that something brewed behind his cerulean irises. "How sick?"

"Very. It's actually why I'm hunting the Stone. I'm hoping to find it so I can cure him. Nobody's been able to heal him, and he's likely to die within the next few weeks if we don't do something. At least, that's what the palace healers have said."

He nodded, not responding, but that flicker happened in his eyes again.

Another moment of silence passed, and then Kole asked in an even more serious tone, "Do they know what his sickness is? Palace healers are notorious experts in their field. I'm surprised they haven't cured him."

I shook my head. "That's the problem. Nobody knows what's wrong with him. He became ill gradually. Initially, it started with indigestion, then a fever, fatigue, and weakness. Each day he grew a little bit worse. And now—" I cut myself off and blinked rapidly. "Now, he can't get out of bed. He won't eat or drink, and my aunt has to force fluids into him. When I left, he was asleep in his chambers, in the dark, and he looked so thin. Skeletal almost following weeks of poor appetite." Images of his emaciated frame had carved themselves into my mind like unwanted engravings.

Kole's aura rippled behind his Shield. "That's a strange illness."

"Exactly. It's an unknown ailment, whatever it is." I sighed angrily. "It's also why nobody knows how to help him."

"Yet you and your aunt never contracted it?"

"No, that's the odd thing. It doesn't seem to be contagious."

Kole watched me again. "Is it just the three of you in your home?"

"Yes, well . . . no, I suppose. We have a live-in servant. She has a room on the main floor."

"A servant?" His eyebrows rose slightly.

"Yes, I know, I know. Having servants sounds so pompous, but it's because of my uncle's position. He's always been paid quite well, so my aunt and uncle have always employed household staff. Their current servant is named Verin. They hired her earlier this season after our previous servant left to be closer to family. The poor thing. Verin hadn't been with us long before my uncle fell ill, but she's been a huge help in his care." I thought of how Verin had always been shy and meek but still tried her hardest. She was brave too. She'd never batted an eye over my uncle's illness, always offering to help when others were too afraid to.

"And she hasn't fallen ill either?"

"No, she's stayed healthy as well. Thank the stars."

Kole watched me for a moment, his gaze penetrating.

I bit my lip, anything to stop it from trembling, but then I forced a smile as we sailed down the road. "But no matter. I'm going to find the Stone, and I'll save my uncle. He's going to be fine."

"You're quite a positive thinker."

"Always have been."

"Was that a learned trait?"

I laughed. "Oh no, my aunt is anything but optimistic, and while my uncle isn't as pessimistic as her, he's more of a realist, I suppose. My endless optimism is for me and me alone. I was definitely born this way."

Kole's lips curved, ever so slightly, and a streak of triumph bolted through me that I'd made him smile *again*. "So your ball of positive energy is innate?"

"It is. And what about you? Would you say you're an optimist?" He gave me a flat look, and I couldn't help but laugh again. "I take it, that's a no?"

"I'm positive if there's a reason to be," he said dryly.

"But that reason doesn't present itself often?"

"I imagine I would align more with your uncle. I would consider myself a realist versus an optimist. In my line of work . . ." He shrugged. "It's not always pretty. Optimism can be hard to hold onto."

My pulse thrummed, and I asked cautiously, "Have you been an Imperial Warrior for long?"

"Going on thirty summers, but I'm still considered one of the new ones."

A smile spread on my lips that he'd readily offered that much personal information, and I decided to try for another tidbit. "So which kingdom were you born in?"

I waited for him to say Faewood, since I knew he had an air

element, but he glanced ahead and said slowly, almost cautiously, "I wasn't born on the Silten continent. My parents moved around the realm a lot when I was a kid."

My head cocked in surprise. "Yet, you have Faewood magic?"

"I do."

"That's interesting." Normally, the land's magic was what imbued Silten fae with their abilities, but it wasn't impossible for a Silten fairy to acquire another kingdom's magic, as I had, even if they hadn't been born upon that land.

I figured that was what had happened to Kole, even if his parents were overseas. "In that case, where were you born? If not on our continent?"

He opened his mouth to reply, and my stomach dipped at learning such an intimate detail about the stoic warrior, but a sound ahead snagged his attention.

Kole growled, and his aura spiked.

I followed his gaze, and my eyes popped, because lining the road just ahead of us were six fae, standing shoulder to shoulder, blocking the Wood's road.

And they all held weapons.

CHAPTER EIGHTEEN

"Stars Above. This doesn't look good," I whispered as anxiety churned within me.

I frantically assessed the Wood more, looking for a way to avoid the group we were quickly approaching, but the canopy above was thick and woven so tightly together that we wouldn't be able to fly over them.

"What are we going to do?"

Kole's attention stayed on the males. "Let me handle this."

Our carpet was nearly upon them, and the six males widened their stances. All of them smiled menacingly. My stomach dropped even more. Their sinister grins were as sharp as the blades in their hands.

When only ten yards separated us, Kole commanded the enchanted carpet to career to a halt. The supplies behind us heaved in protest, but their magical bands held, and we hovered silently.

Kole scanned the trees around us, his nostrils flaring as he scented the wind. Even the Wood had grown eerily quiet.

I did the same, but instead of smelling for more fae, I released a stream of magic and sought additional lifeforms around us. But no siltenite consciousnesses pulsed back to me, only nervous wildlings and other woodland creatures that remained hidden and still.

"It's just the six of them," I said under my breath to the warrior, then sucked my magic back inside me. "No other fae are lurking about."

Kole glanced at me, but he didn't question how I could know that. "Stay here."

He leaped from the carpet and strode forward, not showing the least bit of hesitation at being confronted or outnumbered by males who obviously weren't here to offer us tea and refreshments along our journey.

Kole stopped halfway to them, his arms loose at his sides. "You're blocking the road."

One of the males in the middle, the tallest one with a wiry build, sneered. "You noticed that, did you? How very observant you are."

Kole's demeanor didn't change, not even a flicker. "I'll say this once. Move."

All six laughed, and the two near the end eyed me. One leered. The other made a rude gesture with his tongue.

A jolt of energy surged in Kole's aura, and his head tilted as he assessed the end two.

"There's a fee to go farther." The middle male rapped a baton against his palm, the motion slow, precise, and clearly meant to intimidate. "A hundred rulibs if you wish to carry on."

"Is that so?" Kole's tone remained impassive. "I don't recall fees being placed on this road previously. Under what jurisdiction are you claiming this for?"

The male beside the tallest one snorted. "The jurisdiction of *we're shifter fae who live here, and this is our territory.* That's who."

I sat up straighter and glanced around, but even though there were no signs of a discarded carpet or goods strewn through the Wood, I wondered if Nym, Jessip, and Felix had ventured this way. I could only hope they hadn't. We'd passed one intersection a few miles back, and I prayed that they'd taken one of the other paths.

The male at the end jerked his chin my way. "If you and your pretty lady wish to travel farther, you'll need to pay up. If not . . ." He ran his tongue suggestively over his upper lip. "I certainly wouldn't mind taking her as payment."

"As if." I scoffed at the male, not feeling threatened in the slightest considering it would only take me seconds to shred through him completely.

But Kole's aura swelled even more, and in a low, lethal voice, the warrior replied, "She's *mine.* You touch her, and you die."

My eyebrows shot up at the warrior's possessive admission.

Mine. I hadn't heard that claim since Whiteolf, when Kole had been playacting during Abel's delusional attack.

But I shook my head and quickly reasoned it was simply because of where we were, and it was a tactic Kole was consciously using in hopes of avoiding bloodshed. All fae males were possessive of their females, *mine* being a common word among those who were mated, but shifter males were notoriously violent about protecting their females. With any luck, these males would think twice before doing whatever they'd planned.

The end male snickered, but when Kole's challenging stare hit him directly, his gaze averted.

"She'll only remain yours if you pay the fee," the middle one countered. He stopped rapping his baton and held out a palm. "Pay up."

Kole's tone dipped. "I won't be paying."

All six males took a step forward simultaneously, and I knew from that coordinated movement that they were all the same type of shifter. They had to be a pack animal or one that stayed in a herd. Whatever they shifted into, they hunted as a unit.

Tensing, I stood from the carpet. "There's no need for a fight. Do as he says and move."

But the males didn't stop. Their group progressively closed the distance to Kole, weapons in hand, stances readying for attack.

The one on the end eyed me from head to toe, and since I

was now standing, his gaze paused on my breasts. He licked his lips again, then palmed his crotch suggestively. "I think I'd rather not move. You're a nice piece of arse. I'll gladly take you as—"

A blade abruptly sliced through the air.

In my next breath, the male's head rolled from his shoulders. Before I could comprehend what'd happened, his decapitated head fell with a *thunk* to the Wood's road.

Sword in hand, Kole raised his weapon dripping with fresh blood.

My jaw dropped. In less than a blink, Kole had drawn his weapon and *killed* the male.

Stars Above. So much for no bloodshed.

"As I said, she's *mine*." Kole lifted his sword higher. Glistening droplets of the male's blood pooled around his lifeless body, sparkling like rubies in the dim light. "Does anyone else care to disrespect her?"

Shocked expressions passed among the remaining five males. Eyes wide, shoulders stiff, they stared at their dead friend.

"You killed Peelin," the tallest one finally said, disbelief evident in his tone.

"I told you I was only saying it once." Ice filled Kole's voice. "You chose not to move. He continually made lewd comments about my female, and I *warned you* that she was mine."

"She's not yours anymore." The tall one met Kole's stare

directly. "You just sealed her fate. We'll each ride her a dozen times, and when we're done, we'll slice through her pretty neck and watch the life drain out of her."

Magic surged inside me at his violent threat just as a roar from the males filled the Wood. The remaining five shifters exploded into action.

Battle cries emitted from their mouths.

Vengeful expressions coated their faces.

In a blink, they'd circled Kole and lunged at him as one.

The criminals moved in blurred speed, in precise coordinated movements, and my heart shot into my throat.

I called upon my magic, about to take all of them down at once, but I paused.

Moving even faster than the criminals, Kole arced his sword, his grace and precision rendering me into stunned immobility.

Steel met steel as the five males brought their weapons down on Kole, yet Kole's sword met every move inflicted to kill him, countering their blows just as fast.

Heated magic surged around the warrior, his arms twirling faster, his legs blurring into impossible speeds. Air shot from him in gusts too, knocking back the males just as fast.

I was so completely shocked by how he moved and manipulated his air element that I kept my magic within me. It was just like the fight I'd witnessed last night. Kole's intrinsic magic swelled, clouding around him in a powerful aura as his body and sword became one.

He dipped. Lunged. Impaled. Danced.

Kole was death on wings, and every slice of his sword and gouge of his hand was like watching a symphony of music come to life.

He moved so fast it was difficult to track him, and it was only my activated sight sensory magic that allowed me to watch him at all. He was that fluid. That swift. And the last thing he needed was me helping him.

Something stirred in my chest. Something *yearned* as I watched him.

But one thing I was certain of. An ancient and primal power embodied the warrior, as if the gods and goddesses had placed him upon this realm to slay and fight. To do exactly as a warrior should.

I didn't interfere, even though my Mistvale magic was crackling inside me, just ready to be let loose. But I knew enough, and I'd seen enough to understand that Kole wasn't an Imperial Warrior for nothing.

And he was truly breathtaking to watch.

He cut down the males, one by one, and even though their shifter origins gave them unnatural strength and speed, they were no match for Kole.

Blood rushed in rivers along the road, and groans filled the air as each male lay dying or dead under Kole's hand.

When only their leader remained standing, he raised his baton, now scarred and punctured from Kole's vicious attacks. With one last cry, the shifter swung with everything he had.

But an arc of Kole's sword had his baton splitting in two.

The force of Kole's blow had the male pitching off balance. He went down on his knees, and on my next breath, the tip of Kole's sword sliced clear through his throat.

The male's eyes went as round as the moons, disbelief and shock filling his last expression, a second before his head and body fell in opposite directions.

Breathing hard, my knees sagged in relief that the fight was over, but then I surveyed the carnage, and my stomach churned.

Death spread out before us like a bloody banquet.

A severed arm.

A gutted belly.

Slitted throats.

Two decapitated males.

Six siltenites had died at Kole's hand in less time than it took me to dress in the morning.

Calmly, the warrior walked to a tree and wiped the majority of the blood from his sword onto a leaf, then he cleansed himself and his weapon with his magic.

Once all traces of gore were gone, he sheathed his sword, then jumped back onto the carpet to sit beside me.

"Are you all right?" A violent storm churned in his irises, the energy from the battle still apparent in his aura.

I nodded a *yes*, too stunned to speak.

He whispered a command, and the carpet took off, and he

did it so easily. So thoughtlessly. As if flying right over the males' body parts and torn flesh was nothing.

"You're going to leave them on the road?" I finally managed. "Like that?"

Kole didn't even glance behind us. "Let the evidence remain of what happens when one crosses an Imperial Warrior. The wildlings who witnessed it will spread the word."

Kole's eyes were as hard as diamonds as he stared straight ahead, his demeanor stoic.

He never looked back.

———————★

NEITHER OF US spoke again as we traveled onward. But the entire time, Kole steadily surveyed the Wood, as though waiting for another attack. Anticipating it.

Despite his silence, energy pounded through the warrior's aura, growing and swelling with every mile that passed beneath us. He had his Shield locked down tight, but I could still sense him. *Feel* him.

Rage filled the warrior, and it was so palpable that I could practically taste it.

Since I never used my forbidden magic, I didn't enter his mind to read his thoughts, as tempting as that was. But I guessed he was likely stewing over the skirmish, or perhaps feeling indignant that those males had dared to defy his orders, or perhaps now that the battle was over, he even felt regret that he'd murdered six fae.

Whatever the case, I didn't ask as I let him work through whatever inner war he was fighting.

I didn't shift away from him, though, because while Kole's violence might have scared some, I didn't feel fear. Deep down I knew the warrior would die to protect me. Whether that be because of an oath he'd sworn to the Imperial Council or because he felt the need to protect all innocent fae, I didn't know, but the fact remained that I *knew* Kole would protect me with his life.

I was sure of it.

Mine.

Once again, that word he uttered collided with my thoughts. I nibbled on my lip, frowning. Kole had said that to those males so easily, so *convincingly*. But I reminded myself it was only because we were in Stonewild, in the land of shifters whose song was threaded with possession and claim.

Several times, I glanced subtly at Kole, but the fury strumming through him didn't abate, so I kept my mouth shut and respected his need to work through whatever was raging within him as the miles passed beneath us.

MIDDAY CAME AND WENT. The sun had passed its peak, breaking through the thick cloud cover to show its slow descent into the western sky. Hours had passed since the attack on the road. Hours of silence. Hours of contemplation. And hours in which Kole and I hadn't mentioned the six dead males he'd left behind.

Kole finally broke the quiet in the afternoon, startling me since his voice sounded so guttural. "What would you have done if you'd been alone and that had happened?"

My focus snapped to him. "What?"

He continued staring straight ahead. The Wildland Mountains loomed around us. Rocky terrain had grown, and the thick swamp of trees had finally begun to thin. We were moving steadily upward, snaking through the trees toward the stony peaks above.

Yet even though this terrain was new to me and wildly beautiful, all of my attention focused on the warrior. On his tone. On his pounding energy.

A thunderous expression brewed upon Kole's face. Once again, the warrior's emotions were leaking through, his carefully constructed mask cracking on every surface. And I didn't need to read his mind to know that the past hours of silence hadn't abated his fury in the least.

"What would you have done if I hadn't been with you?" he repeated. "Those males would have raped you, even if I hadn't killed their friend."

I angled my head, confusion strumming through me. "I know."

"Yet you insisted on traveling here despite the dangers."

"No harm's come to me."

"But it could have." He turned toward me, and all of the emotions swirling inside him hit me full force, and the underlying essence of what he truly felt startled me completely.

I jolted back, and it struck me why he'd been so quiet. I'd been wrong about what he'd been feeling. He hadn't been enraged at the males for defying him or regretting the fact that he'd killed so many or contemplating if that battle could have been avoided.

No, it wasn't rage at all. Kole had been quietly *terrified* at the thought of what would have happened to me if he hadn't been there.

"That's why you've been so quiet?" I gentled my tone. "Because you think they would have raped me if you hadn't been at my side?" It hit me again what he'd said to the shifters. *Mine.* For the briefest moment, it felt as if the warrior believed just that. That I was his. His to protect. His to care for. His to cherish. That such a word hadn't been said simply because fae males understood it. But because he'd meant it.

But I wasn't his.

We barely knew each other.

I frowned, but I felt more curious than indignant that he thought me so weak. "Where is this coming from, Kole?"

He held my gaze, unflinching. Dark hair curled around his forehead in the wind. Eyes as blue as the Adriastic Sea regarded me steadily. "They would have done unspeakable things to you, Primelle. Disgusting things. Things that would make your insides shrivel. I could scent it on that male who stood near the end. He was just waiting for the opportunity to hurt you."

"And that's why you killed him?"

Kole blinked, but none of the emotion in his energy abated. Nostrils flaring, he shifted his attention forward. "He deserved it. No male like that should be allowed to roam the Wood."

It wasn't lost on me that he'd evaded my question. But Kole was right. That male would have gladly raped any female who happened upon them. I'd sensed that too.

I swallowed down the sickening thought of what that male had likely done to other lone females who had been traveling this Wood, without a warrior at her side or psychic magic that was strong enough to protect herself. And I was suddenly glad he was dead.

"Well, he didn't hurt me. None of them did, and now none of them will hurt anyone else either."

"But they *would have*." His tone dipped. I only then became aware that he was breathing faster, and his hands were balled so tightly that his knuckles were white. "That's my point."

My arms loosened. I'd never seen the warrior this transparent. I'd seen hints of it at times, even a few moments, but not like this. Kole's carefully controlled exterior had completely fallen away, as though it'd never been his emotional armor to begin with.

"Kole?" I laid my palm on his forearm. Heat billowed up

from him, and his muscles stiffened. "They never would have hurt me. I wouldn't have let them."

"Six against one, and you truly believe that?"

Normally, my reply would have been biting if any other male were acting as Kole was, but the warrior's expression stopped me, because when his gaze cut to mine, once again, I sensed what was truly lurking beneath the depths.

Not anger.

Not hatred for those males.

Not contempt for me.

But fear.

Bone-chilling *terror*.

I squeezed him. "You saw what I did to those two criminals in Mistvale. I'm not defenseless." When he didn't respond, I squeezed him again. "Nothing happened to me, and nothing would have happened. Believe it or not, I could have taken all six at once, just like you did." Trying to lighten the mood, I added, "Just because my muscles aren't as impressive as yours doesn't mean I don't have my own strengths."

But he didn't rise to my inviting humor, and his tone turned anguished. "You shouldn't be alone up here, Prim. Not in this area. It's wild in this portion of Stonewild. The kingsfae are few and far between. Shifters up here follow their own set of rules as you saw back there."

I shrugged. "Then I guess it's good that you're with me."

He abruptly raked a hand through his hair. "Dammit, Prim. This is serious."

I sighed loudly. "I realize that, Kole, but you're underestimating me."

He growled. "That's not what I'm trying to do."

I bumped him, once again attempting to lighten the mood, and said teasingly, "No, but you're kind of implying that by acting like I don't have the sense to understand where I am or the danger I'm potentially facing." I waved toward the trees and rugged terrain. "It's not only uncouth fae that roam these parts but predators too. I knew up here that it would be difficult to rest, let alone sleep. I knew that I'd have to keep my wits about me at all hours of the day and night. I *knew that*, which is why I always sleep with a ward around me at night and have blades under my clothing"—I lifted the hem of my pants and pulled the knife stored in my boot out—"and it's why I have so many supplies with me. I'm on my own out here. Trust me. I get it. You don't need to worry about me."

A heartbeat of silence passed, and then he said quietly, "I can't help it."

I bit back a smile and slipped my knife back into its sheath. "Make no mistake, my aunt shares in your sentiment, but I'll tell you the same thing that I told her—I *had* to do this. I couldn't not hunt the Stone with my uncle dying at home, when absolutely nothing was saving him. I had to at least try, even if it was a dangerous journey." I nudged him again, and some of the fear in his aura calmed. "I could give you a demonstration if you want, to show you just how capable I am. Would you like to be rendered defenseless so you can rest easy that I'd be fine?"

He side-eyed me, then chuffed lightly. "You could take me down?"

"In a blink." I batted my eyelashes flirtatiously.

His eyes narrowed, but his lips curved, and at last, a sense of lightness began to overtake his aura.

That strange sensation stirred in my chest again, stretching and yearning toward the warrior, and it felt strangely gratifying to know I could turn the tides of his emotions.

"No need," he finally said gruffly. "I believe you."

"Good." I smiled sweetly up at Kole, and his attention dipped to my mouth. My heart began to thrum. Energy stirred inside me anew, that *thing* wanting me to go to the warrior again. To lean into him, to tilt my lips up to meet his, and to kiss him again with complete abandon as I'd done in Whiteolf.

Kole's eyes grew hooded, and he fixated on my lips. His gaze grew *hungry*, but out of nowhere, magic cracked around his wrist, and a painful shock emitted from it, strong enough that I slightly felt it too.

The warrior hissed and snapped his energy forward, then said in a tight voice, "We should stop soon and eat something."

I nodded, not responding, and the thick sexual tension that had begun to form between us felt as if ice water had just doused it. "Right. I'll start pulling some food out."

I shifted to the back of the carpet, putting space between

us, and once again felt the need to remind myself of why I was on this journey.

Find the Stone, Prim. That's where your focus needs to be. It certainly shouldn't be on flirting with an Imperial Warrior and fantasizing about what it would be like to lie with him. You're only here to save Timith.

With that reminder firmly in place, I cracked open a box of supplies.

CHAPTER NINETEEN

With Kole's tense emotions finally subdued, we relaxed into comfortable silence for the rest of the afternoon. A part of me wished we could return to the easy conversation we had before encountering the six males—especially because Kole had been about to reveal where he'd been born—but while Kole's terror had abated, he'd also closed off, as though retreating somewhere inward to a place of retrospection and quiet.

Sighing, I decided to use the opportunity to mentally check in with my aunt and let her know I was okay. Our conversation was quick, since she was in the middle of trying to get Timith to drink, and once I disconnected from Gwen, I sought my best friend. Who knew when I'd next have such a fortuitous opportunity to speak with her.

My connection to Ree formed immediately, as if she'd been waiting to hear from me.

Prim, how are you? Is everything okay?

Internally, I laughed humorlessly. *Okay? Well, I suppose that's one way to put it. It's been an interesting day, that's for sure.* I quickly summarized what had happened that morning with my stolen carpet, the Faewood group who had offered me a ride, and then Kole's insistence that I travel with him instead. And when I got to the part about running into six shifter males who meant to rob us, maim us, rape me, or who knew what else, Ree's breath sucked in. And even more so when I told her that Kole proceeded to kill all of them.

Are you serious? He murdered them?

Well, I don't know if it counts as murder when he's an Imperial Warrior who was attacked first. You could argue that he was defending himself and me.

But killing them was a rather extreme reaction, don't you think? Wouldn't the kingsfae have arrested those males instead and brought them to the courts to meet their justice?

I nibbled on my lip, then nodded. *Yes, that's likely what the kingsfae would have done, but I'm quickly learning that Imperial Warriors are governed by their own set of rules. Even though Kole apprehended those two males back in Mistvale and had Abel arrested in Whiteolf, the shifter males we encountered up here were . . .* I paused, shuddering. *They were out to kill, Ree, not just take our rulibs. I'm sure of it.*

Stars Above. I could practically feel her shiver. *In that case, never mind. If you think Kole killing them was the best way to deal with them, I trust your judgment.*

I toyed with the hem of my shirt, Kole none the wiser that I was communicating with my best friend back in Mistvale. *There's more, Ree. He said something really odd to those males.* I stopped myself from shaking my head, in case Kole started to suspect that I was either talking to myself or carrying on with some other delusion. *He warned them not to touch me. He called me his, or rather, what he actually said was* mine *to the shifters, and that if they touched me, they'd die.*

A moment of silence came from her. *Mine? Like the* mine *males use when they've claimed a female?*

We sailed around a steep bend in the road, and a blast of cold wind shot into me. *Yeah, that kind of* mine.

She paused, then said, *That's definitely weird.* Another moment of silence came from her. *Do you think he said it because you're in Stonewild? You know, the land of shifters and whatnot? Even though all mated fae males speak like that, shifters are notorious for that kind of language.*

I sighed. *Yeah, you're right. I thought the same thing, too, initially. I don't know why I'm overthinking it.*

Maybe because you've had a really shite week, and this is just one more bizarre thing you're dealing with, she replied dryly.

I laughed. *That could definitely be it.*

Out of the corner of my eye, I saw Kole give me a perplexed look, and I realized I'd just laughed out loud.

Smothering my amusement, I wiped my expression clean and changed subjects with Ree. *How are Siam and Bennif?*

She shrugged. *They're good. Nothing exciting or as death-*

defying as what you've been experiencing, thankfully. She filled me in on her husband and child, and when I asked if she'd brought that meal to my aunt and uncle, I felt her nod.

And how are they? I held my breath as I waited for her answer. Even though I'd already spoken with my aunt, I wanted another perspective. Ree didn't see my uncle every day. She might have a completely different viewpoint on how he was doing.

Similar to how they've been before. Your uncle hasn't taken a turn for the worse, so please don't worry about that, because I know that's what you're worrying about. But it's heartbreaking to see him. Gwen was appreciative of the meal, but I don't know if they'll eat it. She seems too stressed to eat.

My heart cracked. *Eating has been hard for both of us, even though Verin is constantly trying to feed us.*

I know, Prim. I'm so sorry.

I toyed with the hem of my shirt again. *What else is new?*

She told me more of the daily going-ons in Whiteolf and what she'd read just that morning in the *Whiteolf Tribune* about the Stone. *Nobody's found it yet, obviously, since magic hasn't clapped the realm, and they're predicting that over half the fae who had originally left to hunt the Stone have already returned home. They also reported that arrests are up on the continent by thirty-eight percent.* She laughed lightly. *I think everyone knew that was coming. But how's your hunt going? Is the seekerill still working?*

I palmed the device, safely stowed in my pocket. *It seems to be.*

Do you truly think the Stone will be that easy to find, given the book you borrowed from the Isle of Song and your uncle's invention?

I thought of what lay ahead, of where the seekerill was currently leading me. Silventine Wood. *Something tells me it won't be.* I told her where I was likely going, where all evidence was pointing, and the second I mentioned Silventine Wood, her breath sucked in.

Oh Gods, Prim. You can't be serious. You're truly going to venture into Silventine Wood if that's where the seekerill leads you?

If I want to find it, I'm not sure if I have a choice.

But that Wood is deadly.

I winced. *I know.*

Is Kole going with you?

I subtly glanced at the warrior. The entire time I'd been speaking with Ree, Kole had sat silently.

I don't know. I suppose it depends on what his superiors order of him.

I'll pray to all of the gods and goddesses that he accompanies you if you have to go there.

A shiver ran through me, because she was right. Venturing into Silventine Wood alone could end in disaster. *Thank you.*

Ree and I spoke for a few more minutes, then said our goodbyes.

You'll contact me again soon, right? she asked. *And you promise to tell me if you do go into that Wood, so I can send help if needed?*

Not that help would get there in time, but I didn't remind her of that. *I'll try.*

Love you, Prim. Gods and Goddesses, please stay safe. Okay?

I'll do my best. You can count on that, and love you too. We whispered another goodbye, and once again, I was alone in my head.

⟶★

EVENING HAD ARRIVED, the day growing darker faster than it would have south of us. It reminded me of what I was facing, if I did have to venture to Silventine Wood. It probably saw nighttime even earlier than this.

I nibbled on my lip as the darkness around us grew. I would have to be smart and prepared if the seekerill led me *there*. My wards wouldn't fully protect me, even if I managed to keep them over me while also flying on a carpet, which meant I would have to come up with a different plan.

An intersection loomed in the darkness ahead, and Kole slowed the carpet. The moons had begun to rise, and twilight had set in.

When we reached the intersecting roads, Kole stopped the carpet entirely. "Which way?"

I started. It was the first time he'd spoken in hours, but at least he sounded calm. Normal. His fury and terror had vanished entirely.

My eyebrows rose. "You're going to let me decide?"

"I thought that was obvious." He gestured toward the seekerill in my pocket.

Frowning, I cocked my head. "What about your job? Aren't you here as a warrior on patrol? Don't you have to be in a specific location?"

"My orders are to stay on patrol. I've been on patrol all day."

I realized he was right. Kole was indeed traveling the Wood of Stonewild. We'd encountered more fae since leaving the body parts along the road hours ago, but other than one hunting party also searching for the Stone—who was traveling south and away from where I believed it waited—the rest had been locals. And even though I'd kept an eye out for Jessip, Nym, and Felix, we hadn't seen them since departing Inisville. And thankfully, none of those *things* that had escaped from Silventine Wood had made an appearance either.

I smiled tentatively and pulled the seekerill from my pocket, holding it on my palm. The needle spun.

The sign at the intersection's center showed four directions we could follow. East led to the port city of Wagsworth, southeast to Jaggedston, northwest to the Bay of Rocksmund, and directly north ventured to Silventine Wood.

The needle's spinning stopped and pointed in one direction. North. It clearly pointed toward the road leading to Silventine Wood.

"Shite," I whispered beneath my breath.

Kole also eyed the seekerill. "North it is."

He whispered a command to the carpet, and we sailed through the intersection. I knew I could have been imagining it, but it felt as though we were being watched in the Wood, as if the deadly animals that roamed Silventine Wood had all broken free and were just waiting to pounce on us when our backs turned.

I knew I was imagining it, but I still shuddered.

"Everything okay?" Kole asked, his tone guarded, and it struck me that he was initiating a conversation again.

I smiled encouragingly. "Yeah, I was just thinking about what lies ahead. My imagination is starting to run away with me."

His lips curved. "You're not a believer in wildesnare or treefang, are you?"

I laughed. "No, not since I was a wee child and actually believed my aunt's bedtime stories."

He laughed too, and my heart warmed to hear that easy sound. "Me neither, but we should stop soon. It's growing dark, and even though none of those mythical creatures have ever actually been proven real, this part of the Wood is best left alone at night."

"Why's that?"

"*Larpanoons* are said to roam here, and those are *very* real."

My eyes widened. Larpanoons were some of the deadliest animals in the land, and it wouldn't matter how strong of a ward I placed around myself on the Wood's floor. Their claws could shred through magic. "Stars Above, I nearly forgot about those."

"Exactly. It would be best if we found a cave or a rocky enclosure that we can brace with not only magic but stone too. Thankfully, even those beasts can't gouge their way through a mountain."

"Do you know this terrain well enough to find such a place?"

He shook his head, and he eyed the mountainous land-scape. "No, but keep your eyes peeled. I imagine we're not the first fae to be searching for a place to rest around here. There's bound to be somewhere."

"What about another village? We could stay at an inn." I pulled my map from my sack.

"I don't think there are any nearby."

"I'll take a look." Forehead furrowing, I spread my map out in front of me, scanning the parchment until I found the inter-section we'd just passed. When I saw that Kole was right—the nearest village was over fifty miles east and would have required taking the road to Wagsworth—my hope withered. North of us, there was only one more small village, and it was over a hundred miles away from where I'd asked for my carpet to be delivered. "You're right. Shite, shite, shite."

Kole glanced my way. "It's not that bad, is it? We'll find a place."

"No, you're right . . . but that's not why I'm upset. I just realized the enchanted carpet I ordered in Inisville is going to be delivered east of here. I'll have to backtrack to get it."

He frowned slightly. "Why did you order another carpet? I told you that you could ride with me."

"For the moment, yes, but what if your superiors order you to go elsewhere? I won't be able to join you because I need to find the Stone."

"My orders won't take me elsewhere."

"How can you be so sure?"

"Trust me. They won't be changing. I'm to patrol this area of Stonewild. I can keep giving you a ride."

"Truly? You're sure?"

His gaze met mine, and in the growing moonlight, his sapphire irises glittered like gemstones. "I'm sure. I'll stay with you until your hunt is done."

A blast of relief hit me that was so strong, I nearly slumped back. "Thank you." Yet, I nibbled my lip and wondered if he knew what he was promising. "But what if my hunt leads me into Silventine Wood?"

"I'll stay with you, Prim, and if you're going into Silventine Wood, I'm definitely staying at your side."

CHAPTER TWENTY

After twenty minutes of flying and searching for an area to rest, we spotted a rocky alcove in the distance.

It looked to be only a short flight through the Wood, and it appeared promising enough that we agreed to veer the carpet off the road.

Leaves brushed against us during the short journey through the Wood, and above, the clouds cleared enough for stars to appear.

When we reached the alcove, the trees parted to reveal a plethora of stone. Jagged boulders rose from the soil, and tangy scents of *crisilite* filled the air, the low-lying shrub growing in abundance around the rocks.

"This looks like it may work." I hopped off the carpet, Kole doing the same.

We treaded through the area, and as Kole had suspected, we weren't the first fae here. Footsteps littered the gravelly terrain. Thankfully, they were all siltenite tracks, not larpanoons.

"Prim, look at this." Kole's deep voice came to me from around a large rock, the sound of his timbre causing a shiver to dance down my spine.

I joined him, and he gestured to an outcropping of mismatched boulders that created a small opening between the rocks.

It wasn't a cave, since several large boulders sat atop one another to make the enclosure, but inside the piled rocks was an area big enough to sleep in and stand fully. Even better, the hole to enter it was small enough that it would be a tight squeeze, especially for Kole. However, that small opening was exactly what we needed. Even a larpanoon, with all of its deadly magic and flesh-shredding ability, wouldn't be able to enter it.

I grinned. "This is perfect!" I clapped in delight, and a twitch lifted Kole's lips.

He quickly began to gather my supplies. Most of my boxes wouldn't fit directly into the enclosure with us, but we found another area where we could wedge them in between the rocks. Following that, we each lifted several smaller boulders to safely cover everything inside. Even if scavengers prowled this area while we slept, my supplies and his carpet would remain unharmed.

"A ward would still be prudent," I said to no one in particular, then wove my hands through the air, whispering a spell my aunt had taught me seasons ago, until a shimmering veil of magic fell over everything. Now, even if thieves sought to steal our items during the night, they wouldn't be able to get past my ward. Well, not without a lot of cursing and counterspells, that was. I figured by that point, they would be making enough of a racket that either Kole or I would wake up, and we could fight them off.

"If only I'd thought to do that back at the inn," I added, realizing I was talking to myself, but not bothering to stop.

"What's that?" Kole stood near the enclosure's entrance. He was stuffing a few bedrolls and supplies through the opening.

I waved toward my warded boxes. "I was just wishing that I'd put a ward around my carpet last night, but I hadn't considered it because the shed belonged to the inn, and I didn't want to lock other fae out."

Kole shrugged. "It turned out all right, didn't it? Even if your carpet was stolen." He took his sword off and threw it through the opening, then he began to wedge himself between the boulders, grunting a few times as he did so.

I crossed my arms to watch and muffled a laugh.

He arched an eyebrow at me. He was mostly through, but his broad shoulders remained on the outside, which he was trying to force through the narrow opening. "Is something funny?"

I immediately flattened my expression and coughed. "No, not at all. I shall endeavor to watch you with a straight face."

He snorted lightly and resumed his struggles.

A few more grunts and two curses later, and Kole was finally inside.

"Let's hope you don't need to leave frequently to relieve yourself," I called sweetly.

His soft chuff came from inside.

In the distance, a howl rose, but it didn't send the hairs on the back of my neck rising. It was a wolverine from the sounds of it, a deadly predator in its own right, but not something a fully grown siltenite needed to fear.

I peered inside the opening. It was dark since the moonlight didn't fully penetrate the rocky shelter, but Kole was able to comfortably stand and the ground looked even.

I hastily shimmied my way through the rocks, not having nearly as hard of a time as Kole, but the boulders still rubbed against my clothing.

Once inside, I stood beside the warrior, and his scent billowed around me. Cedar, pine, and the sea. My insides tightened, and once again, my body responded to him, as if on its own accord.

To distract myself, I hastily activated my elemental fire until I had a ball of light burning in my palm. I flamed my fire higher until it shone brightly and illuminated everything in the enclosure. Gray rocks greeted us on all sides, but the interior was surprisingly cozy.

Kole eyed the fire hovering above my palm and said in a

dry tone, "I thought you said you only possessed magic from one kingdom?"

I blushed. I knew he'd caught me in my fib last night when I'd burned the creature. Shrugging sheepishly, I replied, "Sorry. I didn't mean to lie about my magic."

"I wouldn't have told anyone, if that's why you kept it from me," he said quietly.

I eyed him, and something about his comment rang true. "No, I imagine you wouldn't have."

He gestured to what he'd stuffed into the enclosure. "Should we unpack?" he asked.

Thankfully, Kole had already gathered kindling and firewood. I nodded. "Yeah, I'll get a firepit going."

While Kole pulled out food for an evening meal, I created a small pit near the rocky wall, then placed the kindling and larger bits of wood in its center. Once complete, I dipped my flame into it.

The kindling immediately caught fire, and it wasn't long until it burned naturally. Leaning back, I admired my work. I could have used my magic to keep the fire burning all night, but that would have been exceedingly tiresome, so once the wood burned my flame on its own, I released my magic.

"Nice trick." Kole's deep voice filled the space and vibrated right through me.

I beamed. "A fire element certainly comes in handy when one's camping."

A sound emitted from him that sounded suspiciously like a chuckle.

"Was that another laugh I detected?" I teased.

"No. You're hearing things."

I snorted.

Kole handed me a plate filled with cheese, a few fresh plums, and thick bread covered with honey and butter.

"Oh, honey bread. My favorite!" I sat on the pebbly ground, and Kole sat across the fire from me.

Firelight flickered over his face, dipping his features into shadows.

Once again, awareness of him hummed through me.

I took a bite of cheese, then bit into a juicy plum. The butter and honey on the thick bread were divine. I hadn't realized how hungry I was until I began eating.

Kole's jaw worked as he chewed. "Are you harboring any other magic you haven't shared?"

A feeling of warmth drifted through me that he'd initiated a conversation again. On top of that, he'd asked his question casually, so I easily could have answered him cheekily and not been serious if I'd chosen to.

We both knew why that was, the unspoken reason hovering between us, because while sharing one's magic was considered trivial by some, it was a sacred rite to many others.

I'd always felt I landed somewhere in the middle. While I didn't share what I could do with most, I'd also confided that I possessed magic from three kingdoms to Ree and a few others.

But nobody knew about my hidden magic, apart from my aunt and uncle.

And right now, I knew Kole's question was the same. He left it open for me to answer, but his meaning was clear. *You don't have to share if you don't want to.*

"I have sight sensory magic too." The words flowed out of me, and in that moment, I knew what it meant. I trusted Kole completely. For whatever reason, I did, and I wasn't going to analyze it. "I possess magic from Mistvale, Faewood, and Ironcrest."

His strong jaw worked more. "Magic from three kingdoms? That's impressive."

My heartbeat ticked up. "And you? What kingdoms do you hold magic from?"

His silence filled the enclosure, and I could feel it, his need to protect his secrets, to keep himself safely guarded. But then he shifted from where he sat, the pebbles skittering lightly beneath him.

"I have an air element, as you probably noticed in Whiteolf when I slowed your fall." His words were low. Hesitant. As if this *sharing thing* was new to him. "It's the only Silten Kingdom that I have magic from, but I have other talents, although not of this continent."

"Oh?" I cocked my head and took another big bite of the sweet and buttery bread. Beyond that one word, I didn't push. Something told me that Kole didn't reveal to many what he'd just shared, so as he'd done for me, I wasn't going to force or push him if he didn't want to offer more.

He bit into his plum, eating almost half of it. He stretched out more, his long, muscular legs filling the space around him, and I didn't think he was going to elaborate, but then he stated, "I'm part Solis fae. I have affinities that most on this continent don't possess."

My eyebrows shot up. While having a mixed origin wasn't unheard of, it wasn't common either. Most fae in our realm kept to their continents. Some moved, of course, as Gwenery's Nolus grandmother had all of those centuries ago. But in general, it was a frowned-upon practice. Pride kept our realm's fae among their own kind, each fae race believing they were superior to all others and not seeing the point of moving to a "lesser" area.

"Does that have anything to do with you growing up in various areas of the realm?" I asked.

"It does." He paused, and I wasn't sure if he was going to divulge more, but then he said, "My mother's Silten fae, but my father's Solis. I spent a good portion of my childhood on the Solis continent among my father's family."

"Is that where you were born?"

"It is."

A smile bloomed across my face, my spirits soaring to ridiculous levels. It was silly, but I felt honored. Privileged to have learned this information. "That's why your eyes are so blue. They're Solis eyes."

His focus dropped to my mouth, to where I was still grinning, but he immediately averted his gaze. "That's right."

I cocked my head, happy energy still strumming through me. "But your hair's dark."

He shrugged. "A trait I inherited from my Silten mother."

I arched an eyebrow, my tone turning teasing. "But no wings?" All Solis had wings. It was a trait that set them apart from other fae.

He smirked. "No. No wings." He took the last bite of his plum and discarded the pit in the fire.

I finished my bread, cheese, and the rest of my fruit. Once he and I had cleaned the dishes and stowed them away, I began to roll out the bedding and couldn't help but study Kole more as I did so.

Hair as black as night covered his head, yet eyes as blue as sapphire gems graced his face. His skin tone was a shade darker than mine, but I figured that could be due to the sun versus an inherent trait.

Overall, his coloring wasn't unusual on the Silten continent, but it would have been on the Solis continent, considering they all had pale skin, white or silvery hair, and crystalline blue eyes.

Yet Kole's eye color was so vivid. So breathtaking. No Silten fae had eyes like that. That trait of his was pure Solis.

I pulled my lone pillow from my sack, placed it on the bedding, and finished with the arrangement I'd made. It still struck me that Kole hadn't divulged what his exact magic was yet, but I knew since he was part Solis, it could literally be anything. Unlike Silten fae, the land didn't breed the Solis magic. It was usually inherited, and sometimes, completely new magic appeared in Solis families that had never occurred before.

But until Kole chose to share what his affinities were, I wasn't going to push.

Shrugging my thoughts off, I smiled pleasantly. "There, that should do it." I looked up to see Kole watching me.

He stood frozen, his energy rising beneath his Shield. "We'll be sleeping side by side?"

It was only after he pointed it out that I realized I'd placed bedding for both of us right next to each other. "Oh, um, no, I didn't mean to—"

"It's all right," he said gruffly. "It's safest to stay close. Just because we're in this enclosure doesn't mean nothing from outside can get in."

I pictured the *thing* from last night. It was similar in size to us, and unlike a larpanoon, it had arms and hands. It could definitely find a way to wedge itself through the enclosure's opening. A shudder racked me.

Kole dusted the sand off his clothes, and it suddenly hit me that his attire was the only apparel he had along.

"I can loan you something if you want to change," I offered.

His expression didn't budge, but his words were full of

amusement when he replied, "Do you really think that anything you own could fit me?"

I scrunched my nose up. "Well, you do make a good point, but I'm sure that I could find someth—"

"No need to. I'll grab a few things."

I barely had time to process what he'd said when he disappeared.

My jaw dropped. One second, the warrior was standing before me, and the next, only a rustle of wind was left in his place.

The warrior had vanished before my very eyes, which meant he was *definitely* Solis fae.

CHAPTER TWENTY-ONE

When Kole reappeared fifteen minutes later, shock was still barreling through me.

The warrior's hair was damp, as though freshly washed, and he was wearing clean trousers and a loose top. In his hands were a pillow, another large blanket, and his sword.

He set his sword against the rocky wall, close to where he could reach it, and the firelight flickered on the steel near its handle.

"I wish I could commission a portrait of your face right now." His expression was smooth, but a hint of delight rolled through his tone.

My mouth opened, then closed, then opened. "You can *mistphase?*"

"What gave it away?" He dropped his pillow next to mine, then lay down on the makeshift bed I'd made for us. A cloud of his fragrance wafted around him, and I had the asinine urge to deeply inhale.

I lay down too, but I propped myself up on one elbow so I could peer down at him. Thoughts shifted through my mind rapid fire. "Is that why you don't travel with any luggage? Because you just return . . . where? Home? Your barracks? You can change clothes or get what you need whenever you need to?"

"Yes."

It wasn't lost on me that he didn't clarify if he'd returned to the Imperial Warrior's barracks or his personal home, but his admission did explain how he'd appeared in different clothes at the salopas the previous night, especially since he'd arrived at the inn empty-handed.

And he'd obviously mistphased to wherever he'd gone just now to change, bathe, and gather a few things for the night.

My mind turned faster. "And the carpet, earlier today, when you were gone so long . . . did you mistphase somewhere to buy it?"

"Also, yes. I had to go to Jaggedston to find one. Took a bloody long time too since I had to go to three shops before I found the size we needed."

My pulse ticked steadily upward. "You went to *three* shops?"

"I did."

"All so you could offer me a ride?"

His throat rolled in a swallow. "Perhaps."

My insides curled, and I bit back a smile. I had no idea why the warrior would go to such lengths to help me, but I was thankful that he had. If not, at this moment, I would have been with Felix, Nym, and Jessip.

Trying to brush off how much his gesture meant to me, I asked, "But how do you mistphase that often? I thought mistphasing required a lot of magic?"

"It does, but I'm magical enough."

"Truly? So is that how you've been traveling throughout the realm, by *mistphasing*?"

"You seem to be on a roll here."

Even though it hit me that the stoic warrior had just made a joke, I couldn't stop my curious questions from continuing. "But how do you patrol the Wood by mistphasing? How does that allow you to do your job?"

"I walk when needed, mistphase other times. I travel light and prefer it that way. My superiors know that and have given me free rein."

"But if you can mistphase that easily, why are you here at all? Why not go back to your home to sleep in a comfortable bed tonight?"

"And leave you alone with larpanoons prowling the Wood?" His disapproving look told me exactly what he thought of that.

"I would be fine."

He made a noise in his throat. "I'm not leaving you, Prim.

Besides, my orders are to stay on patrol, which means I need to stay here, day and night."

I lowered myself, no longer propped up on my elbow, and began to play with a lock of my hair.

If Kole could truly mistphase as easily as he claimed, it also explained how dillemsills had been dispatched so quickly in Inisville. Kole had likely mistphased back to his headquarters to tell his superiors about the creature that was lurking around the small village and then had mistphased back to the Wood to find it. Meanwhile, the Imperial Council had likely sent out the dillemsills to warn the local fae.

Stars, moons, and all the galaxies.

I undid my braid and threaded my fingers through my hair, combing through the thick locks. My long hair splayed out around me, and I stared up at the rocky ceiling as shadows danced across it in the firelight.

I mulled through it all, and another fact hit me.

Angling my head, I eyed him again and was startled to find that he'd been watching me.

He quickly looked away, and I licked my lips, not wanting to say what I was about to, but it was selfish of me to monopolize his time. Perhaps, despite my reassurances to him that my magic would keep me safe, he felt obligated to stay and protect me. And as much as that fact made my heart soar, I needed to let him know it wasn't necessary. The truth was, despite how much I was coming to enjoy this quiet, serious warrior, he didn't owe me anything.

"You know," I said hesitantly. "I could have just *bought* your carpet from you this morning. I could even buy it from you right now. There's no need for you to travel with me and have me impede your work, especially if this isn't how you normally travel. You could sell it to me. You don't need to keep accompanying me."

His silence filled the enclosure, only the crackling fire making any sound.

A moment passed.

And then another.

"Is that what you would prefer?" he finally asked quietly.

No. The thought came to me unbidden but immediate. It was the truth. I didn't prefer to travel alone, and I was enjoying his company, even if he was still mostly an enigma to me.

For whatever reason, I liked Kole, or what I'd seen of him at least. I liked his subtle humor, his stoic and hard-to-read demeanor, and his behavior that could be interpreted as grumpy by some, but I had learned it was simply his guarded nature. And I'd seen enough to know that he felt a need to protect those around him. He was brave. Strong. Kind too, even if six males had died at his hand today.

So while I didn't know him well, I *did* know that I admired what I'd seen so far, and I welcomed his company and wanted to get to know him further.

"That's not what I meant," I said the words sheepishly, not wanting to dwell on the fact that my stomach was flipping again. "I just don't want to be a nuisance to you."

"You're not." His reply was immediate. Firm.

I bit back a smile, and another moment of silence filled the space. My heart thumped to the beat of every quiet second.

Since it didn't seem like Kole was going to speak again, I changed the subject and said in a teasing tone, "I'm still reeling that you mistphased home to take a bath. Is that why you always smell so good? Because you can bathe regularly?"

"You think I smell good?"

You did not *just say that out loud, Primelle.* But considering the subtle flare of male satisfaction that tingled in his aura, I apparently had.

Warmth bloomed over my cheeks, and I said in a rush, "I just meant, it must be nice to know how to mistphase so you can go home and do that kind of stuff, or whatever."

He angled his head to look me in the eye, and I could have sworn that his satisfaction grew, but his face remained impassive. "I could teach you to mistphase . . . if you wanted."

"Teach *me* to mistphase?" My eyes widened. "But I'm wholly siltenite. I'm not Solis or of mixed blood as you. I can't mistphase."

"You could. Any fairy with strong enough magic can mistphase. It's simply not done on other continents because other fae don't know they could learn, and those that do, are too prideful to take instruction from a Solis tutor."

My jaw dropped. "Are you serious?"

"Quite. Mistphasing is only related to the strength of one's magic. That's it."

I pushed to sitting, amazement barreling through me. "How? How is that possible? Why don't other fae know that? Tell me *everything*."

His lips twitched. "Most don't know because the Solis fae don't tell them. But there's also a lack of tutors who understand the complexities of mistphasing between each fae species. I doubt there are many, if any, Silten tutors that can teach mistphasing. But some Solis tutors have learned the differences, because mistphasing *is* different for each of our realm's fae, and since I'm of mixed heritage, I was given instruction from an early age in order to determine how I would mistphase. My tutor taught me both Silten and Solis mistphasing, since she didn't know how my magic would manifest, so I learned both. Turns out, I mistphase like a Silten fairy."

I leaned forward, and my hair cascaded around me. "You know *both* ways?"

His attention drifted to where my hair had fallen over my breasts. His eyes turned slightly hooded. "I do."

"And you're offering to teach me?"

"I am."

"Do you think I could actually learn?"

"If you have magic from three kingdoms, you're definitely strong enough, so yes, I think you can."

I jumped to my feet. "Can I learn now?"

He chuckled lightly, then stood in a blurred move, his speed once again taking me by surprise. "I don't see why not."

I sucked in a breath. "How do you move that fast?"

He shrugged. "It's my warrior affinity."

He shared that so casually, so *easily*, that my breath caught. It also explained how he could fight as he did. His Solis magic literally gave him that capability.

I tried to mask my joy at how readily he'd shared that detail. To cover it up, I said in a teasing tone, "Ah, so this was the other magic you were alluding to, and do you have more than one Solis affinity?"

I cocked my head curiously, because like Silten fae who typically only had the magic of the kingdom they were born into, most Solis only had one affinity. But as also occurred on our continent, I'd heard that some Solis possessed *more* than one affinity.

Instead of answering, Kole held out his hand. "Enough talking. If you want to learn to mistphase, we best start now. Take my hand, and I'll transport us outside."

I grasped his hand. It was hard, calloused, and completely swallowed mine. The feel of him threatened to command all of my attention, so I forced myself to keep my focus on what he'd said. "Wait . . . you can mistphase me *with you?*"

"Yes, I have enough magic to carry us both." He pulled me closer, and since he towered over me, I had to tilt my chin back to meet his eye.

His irises sparkled. My heart galloped, and not just at the thought of mistphasing. Once again, I was struck by the sheer beauty of this male.

"Ready?" he asked.

"Will it hurt?"

"No, but it can be rather jarring."

I chuffed, but the fact that I could learn how to mistphase had a moment of regret hitting me that my aunt and uncle weren't here to witness it.

They'd always been so proud of my immense magic and abilities. I had no doubt that Uncle Timith would have been cheering for me and encouraging me to give it everything I had.

My frown grew. Timith would likely never see me mistphase, not unless I found the Stone.

"I promise you'll be fine." When I didn't reply, Kole's eyebrows drew together. "Prim, what's wrong?"

Startled, I smoothed whatever expression I wore. "Nothing. Sorry. I was just thinking of my uncle. He would have loved to see me learn how to mistphase."

"There's no reason you can't show him one day."

"You're right. I shall learn how to mistphase, save him with the Stone, and then I'll show him how I can disappear in a blink."

"So optimistic." Kole's tone was gentle, almost tender. He cleared his throat. "You know, I could mistphase us to wherever that seekerill is leading you if you'd like?"

Hope surged through me, but then I paused. I didn't know for certain that the seekerill was leading me to Silventine Wood. It was just a hunch. And I also didn't know what mistphasing would do to my uncle's device. For all I knew, transporting the seekerill like that could disrupt its anchor on the Wishing Stone, and I couldn't take that chance.

"Actually, as tempting as that offer is, I better leave the seekerill here. I don't know what mistphasing will do to it." I took the device out of my pocket and carefully stowed it near my bag. "There, now I'm ready."

"I'm going to pull you close to me since this is your first mistphase. Okay?" A rough edge filled his tone.

I nodded, and Kole pulled me into his arms, his scent flooding me.

His large frame closed around mine, his chest hard and rigid with steel-like muscle. Strong arms encircled my waist, and *Stars Above*, my body instantly responded.

A wave of arousal crashed over me, and the warrior sharply inhaled. Just as fast, a flare of magic zapped his wrist.

He gritted his teeth, then rasped, "Close your eyes."

I did as he instructed, and in a rush of magic, the ground dropped out from beneath me.

CHAPTER TWENTY-TWO

Kole kept his grip on me, and I clung to him tightly even though my entire body had morphed into mist and shadows, air and wind. The realm was a blur, and then—

Snowy sand shifted beneath my feet. Nighttime sounds filled my ears. Fresh air brushed over my cheeks.

My eyes flashed open.

A dark and beautiful sky with the three moons blazing in its depths and colorful waves of magic from the galaxy greeted me.

I sucked in a breath, and Kole's unique fragrance pummeled me anew. My fingers dug into his top's soft material, but his clothing did little to hide his steel-like strength beneath it.

His muscles clenched, but he didn't release me. "Are you all right?" His mouth drifted down to my ear, and he was *everywhere* around me. His chest, his arms, his face, the long length of his body. He held me so close, and I didn't want him to let go. "It can be quite strange, especially for those who've never mistphased before."

Nodding, I moistened my lips. "I'm okay. I think." I had the craziest urge to sink into him until our bodies were molded as one. I wanted to bury my face in his neck so I could kiss him. Lick him.

His grip on me tightened. In the moonlight, his face was dipped into shadows, but there was a glimmer in his eyes. It was almost *primal*. And I could have sworn that *hunger* filled them too.

A huge flare of magic sparked on Kole's wrist.

In my next breath, he stood several feet away.

My eyebrows slammed together. *What in the realm?* Similar magical flares had come from his wrist enough that I was beginning to wonder if it was another type of magic he possessed. Perhaps a Solis affinity that I was completely ignorant of.

I opened my mouth to ask him, but he said, "Would you like to learn how to mistphase now?" An edge filled his voice, and he rubbed his wrist.

I hastily surveyed where we'd traveled to. It took me a moment to actually comprehend what I was looking at since the warrior's energy was pounding into my back.

Kole had mistphased us to just outside of the rocky enclosure, to an open area littered with pebbles and scattered shrubs. Soft light from my fire flickered through our cave's opening, the only light in the dark night apart from the moons. We hadn't gone far at all.

"We're just outside the cave," I managed, but my voice sounded funny. Too breathy and light.

"It's best to stay in the open so we can see any predators and return to our shelter immediately if needed."

"That makes sense, and yes, I'm ready for whatever you can teach me."

Starlight blazed in the night sky as Kole faced me, still staying an arm's length away.

He gave a curt nod. "To a Solis fairy, mistphasing is as easy as picturing the area in the realm that they wish to travel to, and if they've never been there before, they focus on a location's name or picture it on a map, and their magic automatically transports them there. But for a Silten fairy, it's not quite as simple. For Silten fae, we must turn entirely inward, to the very core of our magic, but *how* one mistphases depends upon the kingdom's magic they were blessed with."

I cocked my head. "But I have magic from three kingdoms."

"True, which is why I believe you're magical enough to mistphase, but it also makes this trickier. You'll need to figure out which of the three you'll use to mistphase. For me, I connect with my air element, and I have to let my Solis affinities fall to the wayside. In order to mistphase, I have to let my air embody me completely, then I use my air to fly away . . . so to speak."

I swallowed and wondered if he even realized he'd just said *affinities*, in the plural form. He had more than one Solis affinity. I was sure of it. "So if I have mental, elemental, and sensory magic, which one do I focus on?"

"Which one is your strongest?"

"My mental."

"Then that's likely the magic you should concentrate on, but not necessarily. My warrior affinity is stronger than my air element, but I still use my air to mistphase. My tutor told me that's unusual. So most likely, you'll use your mental magic. Now, to start, you'll need to disconnect your mental magic from your sensory and elemental abilities."

I frowned, wondering how in the realm to do that. My magic was all balled together inside me, like a glowing orb that I called upon at will. When I wanted to use my mental magic, I simply tapped into it, but I didn't separate it from the others. I didn't even know how to do that.

"How in the realm do I separate them? And if I somehow can, then how do I use just my mental magic to mistphase?"

"Separating one's magic is exactly why it's harder for siltenites than Solis fae, but it can be done. I'm living proof." He stepped closer to me, and his scent once again commanded my attention. "It's also why most siltenites can't mistphase.

Those who only possess magic from one kingdom are likely not magical enough to do so, and those who do possess enough magic struggle to get beyond the first step."

I sighed. "All right, so assuming I *am* magical enough, and assuming I *can* somehow separate my magic from one another, then what do I do with my mental magic to move myself?"

"If mental magic is truly the magic you'll end up using to mistphase, you'll need to figure out how to tap into it to transfer. That could be by using imagery or projection or telekinesis or something else. It depends upon what kind of mental magic you have."

My nose scrunched up. "But I have several types of mental magic, so which one do I use?" The words flowed from my lips so easily. So few fae knew about the extent of my abilities, but once again, I felt like I could trust Kole.

He frowned slightly. "In that case, that's a good question."

I took a deep breath. "Assuming it's my mental magic I need to use, and assuming I can separate it from the others, and assuming I can figure out which aspect of my mental magic I use to mistphase, then where should I travel to?"

"Distance takes practice. You likely won't be able to go far the first time. I would recommend just going to the other side of this clearing."

"Okay, I'll try."

A small smile lifted his lips, and it hit me how open he appeared. There was no mask. No curtain hiding his emotions. No veil suppressing his reactions. Just pure, unfiltered *Kole*.

And I liked it. I liked it more than I wanted to admit.

"Close your eyes. Concentrate on separating your magic," he instructed.

I did as he said until all I felt was the wind on my skin and Kole's pounding aura. Scrunching my eyes tighter, I focused on the throb of my power, the steady pulse of it. But my magic was everywhere. It was a part of me, just as my blood, my lungs, and my vital organs were. It lived within me, so to separate it . . .

"How do I untangle it?" It was embarrassing to admit that I had no idea how to do that. What Kole was asking me to do was so different from anything I'd ever been instructed to do as a child when Timith and Gwenery had taught me how to tap into my power.

"You said your strongest magic is mental. Maybe shift your attention to your mind. Focus on that area, and try to separate it there."

I did as he said, concentrating on the magic that encased my mind. *Mental magic. Focus on my mental magic only.*

Yet despite the swirling mass of it filling my head, my fire and sensory magic were still there too, still filtering through the psychic magic that encompassed my very essence.

I huffed but kept trying to do as he implied. "This is harder than I thought it would be."

"It's all right. Keep trying." His tone was calm, patient, and I could have sworn he'd stepped nearer to me.

But I forced myself to concentrate on my magic only, not on his proximity. *Filter through it. Sort it out.*

But it was like wading through a tub of water of three different colors that all swirled together and had become one, and somehow, I was supposed to separate the fluid into three separate buckets. Only thing, I had no buckets. Just the large tub.

Still, despite that crutch, I tried and tried and tried.

I had no idea how long Kole and I stayed out under the night sky as he coaxed and encouraged me. His patience seemed never-ending, but I finally admitted defeat after who knew how long.

"I can't, at least, not tonight. I'm sorry, but this is proving much more difficult than I hoped it would be." I opened my eyes, and my breath sucked in.

The warrior stood right in front of me, his chest so near that all I would have to do was lean forward, and we would be touching.

A glow filled his irises despite my total and complete failure at this.

My stomach flipped. "I am a horrible student, it seems."

"Not at all, and no need to apologize." His voice was deep, slightly husky, and it made my entire body vibrate to attention. "It would have been a miracle if you'd learned how to do it tonight, but I have no doubt that eventually you will."

"Really?" I laughed self-consciously. "Because, what you're asking seems impossible."

"It might feel that way, but keep working on it. Once you're able to fully separate your mental magic from the others, mistphasing should be possible."

I nodded, then offered him a grateful smile. "Thank you for trying to teach me."

"We can continue working on it in the coming days."

His willingness to keep helping me sent a bolt of pleasure down my spine, but I also knew our time together was finite. Once I found the Stone, I would be racing back to Whiteolf to save my uncle, and Kole would be continuing on with Imperial Warrior business.

A pang of remorse filled me, but he was right. We had a few more days until then, and I might as well make the most of it.

To AVOID HAVING to enter the enclosure through the small opening again, Kole mistphased us back inside our makeshift cave.

As before, he held me closely for the mistphase, and once we materialized, my fingers were gripping him anew.

Warmth from the dying fire brushed us, and Kole gazed down at me, his eyes hooded as our chests hovered only inches away from one another. He was so *hard.* And so *still* beneath my grip.

Out of nowhere, his hand ran up my back, caressing me,

but his touch was light enough that it could have been unintentional, yet something rose in his aura. Something delicious and inviting, and I could have sworn that the same faint glow pulsed in his eyes as it had outside.

Everything inside me wanted to sink into him, and that strange feeling in my chest returned. I shifted forward, my core beginning to burn with *want*, but just as fast, Kole blurred away from me to the other side of the cave and gripped his wrist.

The separation from him was so abrupt that a chill seeped through my body. One second, he'd been in front of me, and the next, he was gone.

Brow furrowing, I looked at where he held his arm, but I hadn't detected that strange magic again on his wrist, yet he was glowering and eyeing it again, almost as if anticipating his magic to rise.

It struck me that whatever that magic was, it was irksome to him, and it seemed likely that such magic came from another Solis affinity that he'd chosen not to share yet.

I ran a shaky hand through my hair. All in all, this struck me as a time when it was best to give Kole his space.

"I, uh, I think I might read before bed." I kneeled by my bag and shoved my arm down the length of it, and when my fingers landed on my romance novel, I pulled it out.

I'd packed it on a whim, not thinking I would actually have time to read it, but suddenly, I was so grateful that I had. I was too keyed up to sleep, and since Kole was currently scowling at the fire, and at his wrist, alternating between the two, it appeared he was no longer in the mood to talk. In other words, reading seemed like the perfect way to wind down.

Turning on my side, I lay down on the bed and thumbed through the pages. I'd been midway through the book, the romance building and the stakes heightening. Given all that had happened with my uncle, it'd been over three weeks since I'd picked it up, but I remembered each detail with startling clarity.

Heavy energy pulsed into my back. Kole didn't say a word, but he dropped down behind me on his side of our makeshift bed, and the covers dipped. He lay as still as a stone, his energy palpable, but at least, he wasn't glowering at the fire anymore.

Despite his throbbing energy, I began to read, and by using the dying firelight and my sight sensory magic, the words were crisp and bright.

I scanned each page and soon got lost in the story. Amazingly, my ability to completely get enraptured in books took over, and before I knew it, I was living through the eyes of the heroine. The dying fire in the cave melted away, and the rigid warrior at my back fell to the great beyond.

A smile curved my lips when the heroine and hero found themselves on the lawn outside of a banquet they were attending. The hero convinced her to accompany him to the distant gardens, and soon, it was only the two of them, since the rest of the partygoers had stayed in the ballroom.

The entire book, I'd been waiting for this moment. Each of

the characters had felt their attraction growing. Their need for one another blossoming.

The hero pinned the heroine against a tree's trunk and began to kiss her. His hands roamed over her skin, his mouth on her neck, as he—

"His hard rod pulsed against her belly, and the need to have him inside her sang through her soul."

Kole's deep timbre jolted me out of the story, and his voice was not only tinged with amusement but something else, something . . . heated.

I snapped the book closed. Mortification burned my cheeks. At my back, I became aware of the warmth from Kole's chest. Like me, he was on his side, but I had no idea when he'd turned to face me, or for how long he'd been reading over my shoulder.

"I didn't realize you had such *graphic* taste in novels." A slight tease filled his voice, but his undercurrent of *want* was there too.

"It's just a bit of light reading before bed," I breathed, since the shock of how he'd just read that filthy sentence aloud was still barreling through me.

"I thought you were an academic scholar?"

"I am, but that doesn't mean I don't also read books for pure enjoyment." I cocked my head, and I tried to remember if I'd ever told Kole my profession, but then he shifted closer, not touching me, but *stars*, I was suddenly aware of every particle of his being, and his entire length was only an inch away.

How I'd not realized he'd moved so closely to me while I'd been reading, I didn't know.

He leaned down and inhaled. I could have sworn that he was drinking in my scent. He inhaled sharply again and shifted even closer, nearly touching me.

"*Fuck*," he said so softly under his breath, I almost didn't hear it.

Panting, I didn't say more. I couldn't breathe. I could barely think. My entire body was on the precipice of igniting, both from my book and from Kole's rising energy, and I had a feeling Kole was on the verge of touching me. *Really* touching me.

I was about to turn, to let him know that I'd welcome his advances, that I wanted him too, but a crack of magic filled the air, then a hiss of pain from Kole.

Before I could face him, coldness washed over my back, and the blankets tugged and pulled. I didn't have to move to know that he'd just put distance between us again.

Energy rolled through his aura, but his head thumped against his pillow. "Goodnight, Prim," he said, his voice sharp. "Sweet dreams."

Confusion swamped me, and I tentatively rolled over, but the warrior had closed his eyes even though his aura was *pounding* out of him.

The firelight flickered in our makeshift cave, dimming more as the embers died.

What just happened?

The warrior had been on the verge of touching me, perhaps *more* than touching—I was certain of that—but Kole had stopped himself just as fast, right after his strange magic had flared.

What in the realm is that magic? I'd never heard of one's magic causing pain before, but I also didn't know much about Solis affinities. Maybe the reason he hadn't told me about his other affinity was because it was more of a curse than a blessing.

Regardless of whatever had just happened, the warrior had made it clear he didn't plan to act upon any attraction tonight, and the last thing I wanted to do was cause him more pain if his magic was stopping him from doing so.

"Night, Kole," I finally whispered.

I settled myself onto the covers too, then forced myself to close my eyes while trying to forget my bursting arousal. But my core throbbed. Between Kole's allure and my smutty book, I definitely would have taken him up on his offer for release. It'd been so long since I'd been with a male, and Kole was the epitome of a sexy male.

Sighing, I turned on my side and faced the wall again. Behind me, Kole shifted too, and even though he was once again trying to hide his aura, it pulsed into me in steady, strong waves.

I scrunched my eyes closed even tighter. *Uncle Timith. Uncle Timith. Uncle Timith.*

Concentrating on my sick family member helped dispel

some of my arousal. Besides, I needed to remember why I was here. Even though the warrior elicited responses in me that I'd never felt before, our paths had only temporarily crossed.

And if we did have an affair, if we did find a way to overcome whatever pain his affinity inflicted on him, it would likely be quick and fleeting . . . over before it truly began.

CHAPTER TWENTY-THREE

Morning sunlight and a cold breeze drifted around me. Warmth pressed into my back, and I snuggled deeper into it. Heat. So much *heat* surrounded me, and it felt positively blissful.

A throat cleared in the distance, but I burrowed deeper against the intoxicatingly firm warmth. I wiggled more, and a hard rod abruptly pressed against my backside. Someone hissed.

My brow furrowed in my dazed state. The hard thing against my rump reminded me of something.

Something . . .

My eyes fluttered open, and the sensation behind me disappeared. Cool air abruptly coated my backside.

"Good morning," a male said roughly.

His deep voice rumbled through me, and my toes curled, but just as fast, I realized *who* had spoken.

Kole.

I blinked more, taking in my surroundings. Solid rock appeared in front of me, only feet away, since I was facing the wall. Sunlight drifted into the enclosure too.

Alertness coasted through me rapid fire. It was morning, and I'd just spent the night beside the warrior in our makeshift bed, and I could have sworn that I'd felt him not even a second ago, and I'd been pressing myself against his—

My eyes flashed wide open. *Stars, moons, and all the galaxies.* I'd just ground my arse against his morning erection.

Kole pushed to a stand, his movements barely making a sound. Chilled air made my flesh pimple, and I peeked over my shoulder.

He was straightening his clothes, his back to me. It was obvious the warrior wasn't going to acknowledge the fact that we'd just been spooning, or that I'd been grinding myself onto him. His closed-off actions reminded me that he could very well possess a Solis affinity that prevented him from experiencing intimacy.

Kole grabbed his sword and said gruffly, "I'll be back in a minute."

He disappeared in a blink of mistphasing magic, and I was alone in the cave.

Fast breaths lifted my chest. In front of me, cloudy puffs emitted from my mouth since the air was so frigid. Without Kole's heat, the cold quickly set in.

Shivering, I wrapped the covers around me more and

called upon my fire element to rush through my blood, warming me. But I missed Kole's warmth. His body heat was much more appealing than my elemental magic.

Once I was warm enough not to feel like an icicle, I shoved the covers off and made quick work of dressing and cleaning my teeth, then I grabbed a few supplies for breakfast.

Not long later, I was in the midst of slathering jam on bread while a pot of water heated over my newly formed fire in the makeshift pit, when Kole reappeared.

As before, he reappeared as suddenly as he'd left, but instead of looking like he'd just rolled out of bed, his hair was damp, his face was cleanly shaven, and fresh breeches and a new tunic adorned him.

The sword I was coming to associate as being an extension of himself draped down his back, and an air of coldness clung to the warrior, as if he'd bathed in a frigid lake.

I stopped slathering the jam and eyed him hesitantly. "Good morning," I offered.

His gaze met mine, his mask entirely in place. Not one trace of emotion flitted across his features, but his aura was roiling.

"Morning."

I so desperately wanted to know what that magic was around his wrist and if such magic truly existed that prevented one from enjoying intimate relations. I could only imagine how awful that would be, and I wanted him to know that I didn't judge him. If anything, I sympathized with him. That had to be torture, especially for a male as virile as Kole.

But he looked away and said, "I'll get everything packed up." His movements turned quick and jerky, and my stomach tightened because it was obvious Kole wasn't willing to share that part of himself yet.

Disappointed, I returned my attention to the breakfast I was making and knew it had the potential to be a long day.

———————⋆

KOLE PACKED everything in blurred speed, then secured it to the carpet while I finished making breakfast. We both ate the jam and bread and drank a cup of tea in silence. Never in my life had I been more aware of a male's every move, but I didn't know how to breach this newfound awkwardness between us.

"Should we go then?" I forced a smile.

Kole's gaze landed on my mouth, settling there for a heartbeat. He started, jerking his chin away, and gave a swift nod. "Yeah. Let's go."

He mistphased both of us outside, but instead of holding me close as he had last night, he only took my hand, and the second the transfer was over, he released me.

Sighing, I made an effort not to touch him at all once we were on the carpet.

But just as the carpet lifted and we began to glide back to the road, a thought occurred to me that explained *why* Kole was fighting this *thing* between us so hard. And it had nothing to do with a strange Solis affinity.

Horror filled me as my thought took root. Perhaps a *relationship* was keeping Kole from being intimate with me. He might be married, and that magic flaring around his wrist could be due to a Solis marriage vow that I was ignorant of. It could be that it was Solis magic reminding him of his *wife*, not preventing him from being intimate.

My eyes widened to saucers. That seemed much more likely than it being his internal magic, because I'd never heard of natural magic before that prevented relations.

My cheeks burned hotter. If he were with someone else, that would definitely explain why he kept pulling back.

But then I thought of our one kiss in the capital. He'd reciprocated that kiss. Quite enthusiastically, if my memory could be trusted, but maybe it was because of how quickly I'd kissed him and how I'd taken him entirely by surprise. Perhaps his Solis magic hadn't had time to catch up.

Feeling entirely nauseated about it all, I did my best to keep several inches of distance between us. But that was easier said than done. The carpet was only so big after all, and a few times when we glided around turns, I brushed against him before I was able to right myself.

It didn't help that a new tension lined the warrior's shoulders, and he'd clammed up completely, not saying a word to me since we'd left the rocky enclosure.

It began bothering me so much that not even an hour into

our ride, I couldn't stop the question from tumbling out of my mouth. "Do you have a wife, Kole?"

The warrior's dark hair fluttered in the wind, and his head jerked my way. Looking down, his eyes glittered in the morning sunlight, and I could have sworn confusion filled them. "*What?*"

"Are you married?" I pressed. "You know, *with* someone in your everyday life? Is that why magic keeps flaring around your wrist? Is it from the marriage vow you promised?"

He shook his head, and his eyebrows folded together. "You think I have a female back home? A *wife?*"

I twisted my fingers together. "Um, yes? Or . . . no?"

For the briefest moment, his nostrils flared, but just as fast, his expression closed off, and he returned his attention to the road ahead. "No, I'm not married, and I'm not with anyone either. I'm as single as they get."

A heartbeat of silence passed between us, and I wondered if my initial suspicion had been the right one after all. He likely had a Solis affinity that prevented intimacy.

"Oh." My brow furrowed, and while his statement alleviated my guilt over disrespecting a potential spouse, it only made me feel entirely awful that such a trait had been cursed upon him.

But something told me Kole wouldn't appreciate me feeling sorry for him, so to cover it up, I gazed at the rising sun and said as cheerfully as I could muster, "'Tis a lovely sunrise." I plastered a smile on my face for good measure and fell back on my usual fake cheer and positivity. "I love this time of day. There's so much new magic, and the beauty always captivates me."

Kole glanced at me again. His sapphire eyes were particularly bright this morning, swirling and igniting. "Yes, it is pretty."

I beamed up at him, and his focus drifted to my lips, nose, then down my neck. His attention shifted rapid fire, and the aura around him thumped higher with every second that passed. He stared at me so intently, again . . . *hungrily* even.

Everything in me softened at his obvious arousal for me, but before I could comment, a huge flash of magic flared around his wrist, and he hissed and whipped his hand back, confirming my suspicions entirely. But just as fast, a burst of magic appeared in front of us, and a dillemsill popped into existence, right on the edge of the carpet.

Everything happened so fast that it took me a minute to understand that a messenger bird sat in front of us.

The second that comprehension dawned, my heart immediately plummeted.

"Oh stars, are you here with a message from my aunt?" My hand shot to my throat, dread instantly filling me.

But the bird ignored me and turned to the warrior. "Kole Swordwielder, you've been summoned back to headquarters. You're to return immediately."

Relief hit me at the same time Kole's jaw ground together,

but just as fast, he smoothed his expression and dipped his head. "Message received."

The bird ruffled its feathers, then began to spin, moving faster and faster until it resembled a whirlwind. With a final spark of magic, it disappeared, going back to wherever it'd come from.

I held my chest. My heart was still galloping. "I'm so glad that wasn't a message from my aunt telling me my uncle had taken a turn for the worse." I took another deep breath. "Is that how you get summoned by the Imperial Council?"

"It is." His lips thinned. "I need to answer that call."

"Of course, no problem. I can keep going on my own, if you're okay with me continuing to borrow your carpet?"

He raked a hand through his hair and worked his jaw again. "That's fine. You can use anything of mine you like."

"Do you think you'll be gone long?"

"Depends upon what they're summoning me for. I hadn't intended to leave you today. Not up here." He glanced around at the barren, unforgiving landscape.

Snow and ice filled the land. We'd traveled so far north that the only land farther north than our current location was the tip of our continent, then the Brashier Sea, and then the arctic region in the fae lands, where the Solis continent lay. Considering the northern tip of Stonewild Kingdom brushed against the Brashier Sea, the Solis weren't that much farther north, not in these parts.

I bumped Kole's arm, trying to lighten the mood and tamp

down on the remorse I still felt for him, especially since a storm cloud had begun roiling in his aura. "I'll be fine. Just relinquish the carpet to me so I can command it, and catch up with me when you can."

He frowned anew, then scanned the area once more.

"I don't see any larpanoons nearby or any of those hideous creatures that escaped Silventine Wood," I said lightly. "And if any come prowling, I'll force their limbs to sleep and will fly right by them."

He was still frowning, but he shook his head. "Right. Of course you could. I've seen how strong you are." Intense, shining blue eyes met mine. "I'll be back soon. Okay?" He pulled something from his pocket and gave it to me. It was round, the size of a marble, and was an opaque green.

I cocked my head. "What's this?"

"A tracking charm. It's how I'll find you. Just don't lose it, and I'll be able to mistphase to exactly where you are."

I nodded and didn't ask for more details. Kole suddenly seemed edgy, and I was reminded that he was working after all, and something had just come up that required him to return to his headquarters.

I offered him a dazzling smile. "Don't worry. I'll be fine. I'll see you when I see you."

His expression clouded, but then he shook himself and nodded. "Yeah, of course, I'll be back soon."

CHAPTER TWENTY-FOUR

I didn't know how long Kole was needed by the Imperial Council, so I settled in for the journey on my own. With Kole's tracking charm buried deep in my pocket, I checked my seekerill as the carpet sailed steadily north. The seekerill's needle continued to point exactly where I dreaded going.

Silventine Wood.

"Goddess help me." I snapped the lid closed and shoved it back into my pocket.

Anxiety swirled higher inside me. I released a harsh breath and turned my attention inward to call Ree. I needed to let her know that I was still safe and unharmed since I'd told her I would do my best to keep her updated. I also still hadn't told her about the creature outside of Inisville and Kole's true reason for being in the Wood. The six shifter males yesterday had taken precedence in our brief conversation.

I had so much to tell her, but first, I did a quick search of my surroundings, especially now that I was on my own.

The snowy Wood had thinned out, and I could easily see that no fae or predators lurked about. Above, the cloud cover had finally fully cleared, and the sun shone brightly. It would be safe to connect with her, but just as I was about to, a noise came from behind me.

"Yoo-hoo!" someone called. "Is that Prim up there?"

I looked over my shoulder, and my lips parted in surprise. Jessip, Nym, and Felix barreled around a dip in the road and raced toward me on their carpet.

Relief hit me that my Faewood friends looked unscathed. Obviously, they hadn't encountered those six shifter males before Kole and I had.

"We thought that was you!" Jessip called good-naturedly as they neared.

They sailed their carpet forward to glide alongside mine. When they reached me, Jessip frowned. "Where's Kole?"

"He had to leave for a bit."

"Did he get maimed?" Nym brought a hand to his chest, his expression aghast. "Is that why he left? Did he need to seek a healer?"

I shook my head. "No, he got summoned for a work thing and is fine." I smiled broader. "I wondered if I would see you all again. I'm happy to know you're all still safe."

Felix waggled his eyebrows. "Of course you're seeing us again, love. You're my future wife after all. And why wouldn't we be safe? Nothing is too dangerous to keep me from tracking you down."

I snorted in amusement even though he was laying it on thick. "You know that I haven't said yes to our nuptials yet."

Felix sighed, getting a laugh out of Nym and Jessip.

"I see that I need to get you on the dance floor again." Felix straightened and rapped his knuckles against his thighs. "Right, my mission after we find the Stone has been set. Once I have you in my arms again, you'll be changing your tune." He grinned so cockily that I laughed anew.

Nym guffawed. "That might be wishful thinking, Fee. Dancing with you doesn't make females want to marry you. Otherwise, you'd already be married a dozen times over."

Felix smacked his friend in the chest. "That's only because Prim hasn't been properly courted by me yet. But I plan to do that too after our next dance."

Nym smirked, and Jessip rolled her eyes.

Still smiling, I asked, "Did you all find a safe place to rest last night?"

Jessip sighed dramatically. "If you can count sleeping in a tree, well away from the Wood's floor, a safe place, then yes, I suppose we did."

I winced. "Oh no, what happened?"

Nym made a horrified sound. "A larpanoon came prowling around in the wee hours of the morning. Luckily, we got up the tree in time, but then none of us could leave the tree to retrieve our carpet and get out of there because the larpanoon kept circling the tree's base, but thankfully, it finally left at sunrise. We didn't get much rest, though."

"Or *any* rest," Felix corrected.

My chest tightened. "That sounds close."

"It was." Jessip ran a hand over her braided hair. "Count me out of ever traveling to this region of the continent again." She cocked her head. "What about you? Did anything exciting happen to you since we parted?"

"Do six shifter males accosting Kole and I on the road count?"

Jessip's eyes grew as round as the sun. "You're joking."

"I wish I was."

Felix sidled closer to me on their carpet. "Do tell."

I quickly summed up our encounter with the six fae but left out the gory details of the males' deaths and instead said that Kole took care of them, without elaborating.

Nym shuddered. "That sounds even worse than the larpanoon. So when will Kole be back?"

I shrugged. "I'm not sure, but I'm assuming sometime today."

"You should definitely travel with us until then." Jessip eyed the snowy Wood ahead of us. "This area of the continent gives me the creeps, especially if you're a lone female on the road."

"What she said," Felix added. "As my future wife, I consider it my duty to protect you."

I rolled my eyes but couldn't stop my smile. "Thank you. I would love to join you all."

"It's settled then." Jessip surveyed the road again, her nose scrunching up. "I can tell you that once we find the Stone, we're out of here."

Her comment reminded me that despite their friendliness, we were still in direct competition with one another, but I didn't want to think about that just yet. It was possible that the Stone had landed so deeply within Silventine Wood that it would take a few more days to find it. We could still enjoy each other's company for a while.

But regardless, hearing about their larpanoon experience and remembering the six males Kole and I had encountered were reminders of the challenges I would be facing if I *didn't* find the Stone soon.

It was just one more thing I needed to consider.

THE MORNING PASSED in a flurry of cold wind, desolate roads, and chipper communication with my three Faewood friends.

Since most other fae left hunting the Stone had been fooled by the direction of its tail, where we traveled was nearly deserted.

After passing the last village before Silventine Wood, I began to wonder if Kole would be back before I reached the ominous forest.

I hadn't heard from him, he hadn't mistphased back, and no dillemsill ever appeared.

A part of me wanted to try linking consciousnesses with him, but since we'd never connected mentally before, it could prove difficult to find him. Still, I could try.

But as soon as that impulse hit me, it left. Kole didn't know my magic could do that, and my attempts at reaching him could only end up alarming him since the feel of my magic brushing against his mind could be mistaken for an ailment or the feeling of going psychotic.

I sighed. Even though I knew his work took precedence, I still wanted to know if he was okay. But more than that, I wanted him with me. Having him at my side had made me feel much more secure in this region of the continent, but I tried not to worry about that and instead concentrated on making headway.

⸺⭑

Hours passed as the day flew by. Throughout the afternoon, I stealthily checked the seekerill several times. Its needle stayed true to its course. North. I was growing closer to the Stone.

And when I checked it again as evening neared, my breath sucked in. The needle began quivering, alerting me to the fact that I was almost to where its endpoint lay.

When that happened, I snapped the lid closed. Breaths

coming faster, I slipped the device into my pocket since my three friends were all glancing the other way. Apparently, I wouldn't need to spend days in Silventine Wood searching for it. If the needle was vibrating like that, it meant the Stone was even closer than I'd thought.

A hill loomed ahead, and only low-lying crisilite shrubs surrounded us. When we crested the swollen land, the entire northern region came into view, and just beyond that, the glimmering and icy Brashier Sea waited.

My lips parted in wonder. The last time I'd seen that sea, I'd been traveling on a ship to the Isle of Song to retrieve *Legends of Our Realm*. It was hard to believe that had only been a few short weeks ago.

But at sea, there hadn't been a deadly forest to contend with, only waves and potential storms.

"Dear Gods, there it is." Jessip shaded her eyes in the early evening, staring straight ahead.

Nym and Felix swore quietly, and I swallowed the knot of anxiety that had suddenly grown in my throat.

Silventine Wood glimmered on the landscape, filling the area before the sea, and the eerie metallic shimmer along its border let us know that we'd nearly arrived.

I shuddered. The Wood's name had come from that very perimeter. A silvery metallic haze enshrouded the forest, like a dome of gleaming metal. It was said that after one passed through the border, the color changed. Some days, the Wood's interior would be dark and sinister. Other days, it appeared vibrant and colorful.

But that was one of the reasons this Wood was so dangerous. It was alive in its own way. The soil was rumored to be incredibly magical and had a lifeforce all of its own. Plants writhed like fae's limbs. Animals prowled beneath the ground's surface. It was even said that the trees communicated, as though an all-seeing omnipresent consciousness controlled the Wood's creatures.

"I've heard a god died here eons ago, and his soul lives on in the ground." Jessip toyed with her fingernails, picking and scraping at them. "And that's why it's so magical and so labile. Some say the god's soul is unable to escape from here, and when he's slumbering, the Wood is dangerous but still survivable, but when he awakens, dark acts occur."

"That's just a rumor." Nym elbowed her. "There's no proof of that."

"Yet it would be wise to take heed," I replied. "I've heard the same." I didn't elaborate that I'd read details about this Wood many summers ago when I'd still been at the university. Even though such rumors had never been proven, there'd been enough dangerous acts and enough fae had experienced such oddities that it did make me wonder.

"Are we *really* going in there?" Felix's playful tone turned cautious, his usual flirtatious nature curbed.

I arched a questioning eyebrow at the three of them. I was

definitely going into the Wood, whether I liked it or not, but all day we'd been carefully avoiding the topic of how long we would stay together. It was as though the four of us knew that while we might be friends now, soon, we would be rivals.

Jessip offered a wavering smile as both of our carpets sailed down the hill.

"Well?" Felix pressed. "Are we?"

"My dream showed us here, so I guess, *yes?*" Jessip shrugged.

"Dreams can be wrong," Felix countered. "Come to think of it, I cannot believe we came all the way up here because of a damn dream."

Nym huffed. "Well, we didn't just bloody traverse the entire continent to turn back now. I say we go in."

"Even if we get *killed?*" Felix slugged him in the shoulder. "Think about what you're saying, Nym."

I eyed the three of them. "Felix is right. It would be wisest to go home now and not venture in there."

Jessip scoffed, then elbowed me lightly, her gesture easy since the distance between our carpets wasn't far. "Sounds like you're hoping to keep the Stone all for yourself, Prim."

She said the words jokingly, but a gleam had entered her eyes. It was the same with Nym. I knew that despite the two of them being concerned about venturing into the deadly Wood ahead, they would do it. They were going to see this through until the end. And while Felix seemed the most apprehensive,

I would have been shocked if he were able to talk them out of it, because Nym was right. They'd come a long way to turn back now.

I watched the energy change around my Faewood friends. Slowly, the joking and laughter subsided, and I knew the time had come.

My lips downturned, because my concern that we would become rivals was occurring right before my eyes, and the last thing I wanted was to end up in a race to the Stone or worse, have them follow me as I led them right to it, and then have us directly fighting for it.

I gave them all a sad smile. "As much as I've enjoyed your company, I think this is where I say goodbye."

"What?" Felix's mouth dropped. "You can't be serious, Prim."

"It's for the best."

"But you're planning to go into that Wood too, right? You can't go in there *alone*. You'll never make it out." His lips thinned, and for once, his tone was entirely serious.

I lifted my shoulders nonchalantly. I was so used to fae underestimating me that I didn't bother to correct him. "Regardless, it's best if we part ways. I would rather our memories of one another end on fond terms versus a bloody battle to the Stone."

"Bloody?" Nym laughed lightly. "Just what kind of fae do you take us for?"

I smiled, but it was forced. "I'd rather not take the chance. In everyday life, I know that would never occur, but in *there*"—I pointed to Silventine Wood—"it's said fae can change, that the magic can take hold of them. You three have a bond that I'll never share. I'd rather not test how solid that bond is if we're all competing for the same thing."

Felix's eyes dimmed. "I would never hurt you."

"Just as I would never intentionally hurt you, but still, it's best to part ways."

Nym nodded, and eventually Jessip agreed too.

Their response came readily enough that it solidified that while they might have been fun companions to booze with at the salopas and joke around with today as we all traveled north, they weren't actually my friends. Not truly.

We were more strangers than anything, and if it came down to me or them, I knew they would pick them—as all fae would.

"Best of luck to all of you." I waved in farewell and commanded my carpet to part from theirs.

Felix opened his mouth, and I could practically hear the protest forming on his tongue, but I zoomed eastward, veering off the road to travel over the shrubs before he could say anything else.

The road ended soon anyway, right at the perimeter of the Wood's entrance, so it didn't matter if I was no longer following it. Nobody had dared construct anything into Silventine Wood, and since most of the Wood extended all of the way to the sea, there was no need to extend the road farther anyway. Once one reached the water, there was nowhere else to go.

I took a deep breath and guessed at how long it would take me to reach the forest's perimeter. I had a feeling I would be there before nightfall, and I just hoped Kole had returned by then.

Otherwise, as Felix had feared, I could be entering the Wood alone.

———————✶

I CAREENED toward the Wood's perimeter, heading in a northeast direction as my anxiety grew. It felt as though serpents slithered around my insides, biting and coiling.

Thoughts kept pummeling me too. Horrible thoughts of what could happen.

Magical plants that tried to devour me.

Larpanoons the size of large domals attacking me.

Herds of that terrible creature that Kole had killed in Inisville chasing me through the trees.

Every thought I had brought more fearsome images to life. I was near sick by the time I pulled the seekerill out again.

"Stop, Prim. Just *stop*." I eyed the device. It still bore north, but also slightly east. I breathed a sigh of relief. I could continue traveling outside of the forest. I didn't need to go in yet. But eventually, I would have to.

"Use your magic when you're in there," I whispered to myself. "Keep a cool head. *Don't* let the forest trick you or sway you from why you're there. Uncle Timith is depending on you."

I safely stored the seekerill back in my pocket, and my pep talk helped slightly. Some of the anxious tumbling in my belly calmed, and I took a deep breath.

I debated contacting Ree. Even though I'd meant to earlier, I'd never done so. But now . . . I grimaced. Now, I had no idea what could come out of that Wood. For all I knew, one of those *things* would, because if others had escaped, more could too. It was best to stay focused. I would have to contact her later.

I followed the direction of my seekerill and knew that the longer I stayed out of the Wood and on its perimeter, the better, and thankfully, the northeast direction held. It was my only saving grace since there was a small patch of open land between Silventine Wood and the Adriastic Sea. The low-lying ground cover continued, making it easy to see if any large predators were near. So far, my good luck held.

I rubbed the lock of Goddess Nuleef's hair over and over. I'd stowed it right by Kole's tracking charm, deep within my pocket.

So far on my journey, I'd managed to avoid true harm, and I couldn't help but wonder if her hair was the reason for that. Even though my carpet had been stolen, I hadn't been injured by other fae, and despite the slight hiccup my stolen carpet had caused, it'd also brought me time with Kole, which had resulted in increased safety.

My heart pounded at the thought of him. He still hadn't returned, and surely, if he *couldn't* return, he would have sent a dillemsill.

I tried not to worry over it, but evening had arrived, and while I didn't relish the thought of venturing into the Wood at night, I also didn't want to spend the night sleeping alone out here either. So far, I hadn't found any suitable shelters. Just endless brush and ground cover between the forest and the Adriastic Sea.

I couldn't even use the carpet for safety. Commanding the carpet to rise high in the sky, so I could sleep upon it well away from the ground was dangerous. Carpets didn't stay activated indefinitely. It was possible while I was sleeping, it would deactivate, resulting in me falling off and plummeting to my death.

I groaned. None of my options seemed ideal.

I studied the landscape more, and my usual cheer waned. It was either sleep out in the open and hope that I avoided being killed at night or stay awake until sunrise and hope that Kole had returned by morning.

Nibbling my lip, I slowly realized that it was best to keep moving forward. Uncle Timith was dying, and I didn't have time to wait.

But all of my fears were coming to a head.

I was by myself.

The Stone was in Silventine Wood.

And from the looks of it, I would be venturing into that magical forest on my own. Tonight.

Two fae would have been better than one when venturing into the Wood, but Kole was also on duty. For all I knew, his commanders had sent him to an entirely new portion of the continent, and they hadn't allowed him the time to alert me to his delay.

My stomach bottomed out. I had no idea when I would see him again, or even *if* I would see him again.

"You have to assume you're on your own, Prim." My brow furrowed, and I eyed the Wood, then pulled out my seekerill.

The needle spun, moving and quivering at lightning speed, then it abruptly stopped and pointed directly to the Wood. It vibrated so aggressively, *eagerly*, and that only meant one thing.

"Stars. I'm almost there."

I weighed my options. If I followed it now and kept my wits about me, it was possible I'd find the Stone before sunrise. Given how the seekerill was acting, the Stone was *close*.

I glanced at the sky. It wasn't that late yet. The sun was nearing the western horizon, but at least an hour of daylight remained, and I wasn't tired. I was still mentally sharp.

I glanced behind me to the Wildland Mountains. Their dark peaks, while still tall, had grown distant. And nothing surrounded me but empty brush.

It was now or never.

With a whispered command to my carpet, I veered directly toward the Wood and didn't look back.

Fierce determination bloomed through me. The time had come.

I was finding the Stone *tonight*.

CHAPTER TWENTY-FIVE

The Wood's metallic border glimmered. My carpet rushed toward it, and the closer I got, the more I could *feel* the forest. Its border rose in a haze, like a pearly soup of gleaming silver. It was beautiful in its own way, but something about it screamed *other*.

Magic heated inside me, and I extended my mental fingers forward, intent on pushing through the border to seek any creatures that could be waiting for me on the other side.

But when my magic hit the Wood's barrier, it scattered, and an electrifying hum filled my mind.

I hissed, the sensation bothersome, but not painful. Putting more of my magic into it, I pushed and surged until my mental extension reformed and began to force its way through the Wood's encapsulating dome.

Breathing deeply, I concentrated more. As I neared the edge of the Wood, my magic finally penetrated the border.

On the other side, hundreds of lifeforces greeted me.

My breath sucked in, and I mentally spanned my magic out. There were *so many* creatures of varying degrees and sizes. Some were intelligent. Others weren't. And some were so foreign that I didn't even know how to categorize them.

"Dear Gods."

I sucked a breath in but didn't slow. I hit the Wood's barrier at full speed, and a glimmer of magic surrounded me. The realm turned into a cloudy shimmer. Sparkling dots appeared in the air, touching and caressing my skin.

Stars, galaxy, and all the moons, but the Silventine Wood was *assessing me.*

It released me to the other side, and my heart immediately jumped into my throat.

Darkness greeted me.

Thick, unrelenting *night.*

Even though the sun still hovered in the sky on the outside of the Wood's barrier, no sunlight penetrated the Wood's canopy. The only saving grace was that it was warmer in here. No snow either.

I immediately halted my carpet. A low chatter filled my ears, like thousands of buzzing insects filling the quiet, but nothing fluttered near me.

My eyesight shifted of its own accord, my sensory magic activating. Objects came into view. Thick plants, trees, and vines hung everywhere. Above, several pairs of eyes watched me. They glowed in the darkness, but my magic told me they were the less intelligent creatures that I'd initially detected.

I sent a pulse of magic toward them, more curious than anything to learn what they were, but before my magic could reach them, they blinked and then disappeared into the tree.

My heart pounded like a drum, and I hastily consulted the seekerill again. The needle still vibrated eagerly, aggressively, and pointed straight ahead.

I palmed the device tightly, knowing that if I dropped it or lost it, I was entirely fucked. I called upon a stream of the carpet's magic and tethered the seekerill tightly to the fibers, directly in front of me so I could watch if the needle turned.

Once certain that it wouldn't budge, I whispered a command to the carpet and cautiously began to move forward.

I kept my breathing silent, my movements still. The last thing I wanted to do was alert any creatures or nefarious plant life to my arrival, although if the Wood's perimeter had already done that, then it was too late.

Still holding the lock of Goddess Nuleef's hair tightly, I commanded my carpet to pick up speed, using my sensory magic to see clearly.

Something rustled in the bushes, only thirty paces away. A head lifted. Horns appeared on a creature I'd never seen before. It was large, easily the size of a small domal, and two large fangs extended from its gums.

It hissed at me, and its tail flickered and made a rattling sound like an ominous snake about to strike.

I watched it out of my peripheral vision, hoping it would let me pass peacefully, but just as it began to disappear from my view, it lunged.

It moved so fast, flying toward me in a gigantic leap. Its gaping maw opened, and several rows of razor-sharp teeth appeared.

"Stars!" I shrieked and instinctively shoved myself to the far side of the carpet. It was nearly upon me by the time I blasted it with mental magic. My magic coiled around its consciousness, commanding it to sleep and be still.

It fell with a thud, right into a patch of vines—another plant I wasn't familiar with. If my heart didn't feel like it was about to explode, my academic side would have found the discovery of a new plant species fascinating.

But as it was, fear raced through me anew, making my heart pound in a painful beat, and not even an unknown plant created any interest in me because that horned creature had moved *so* fast and with such certainty that I knew it thought I was its next meal.

The beast lay still on the ground, horns ensnared within the foliage. Vines roped around its body, and a horrible sucking sound filled the air. Blood welled up from the creature's hide as the plant began to devour it.

I shuddered and zoomed away as fast as I could.

More eyes appeared in the darkness in front of me, glowing orbs of various sizes. A shriek rose in the distance too, part howl, part scream. And then another howl came. And another.

Pulse thrumming wildly, I turned every which way, trying to determine what those howls meant and where they'd come from. And more importantly, if it was from a couple of creatures or a herd. Or even worse . . . from the *thing* Kole had battled outside of Inisville.

My magic hummed and stretched out. Dozens of creatures surrounded me. Above. Below. To my sides. All around.

Animals were *everywhere.*

"Shite." In a near panic, I commanded the carpet to propel forward at its max speed. Simultaneously, I sent a blast of mental magic out, unleashing my power upon the Wood. And at the last second, I released my hidden magic too. My forbidden one.

It'd become entirely apparent to me that if I was going to survive this Wood, all bets were off. I would need to use everything I had, and I wasn't going to second-guess the wisdom of that, especially since I had yet to encounter any siltenite consciousnesses here.

Power welled up inside me. Immense, beautiful, and sparkling *power.* As had happened when I'd been following Kole in the village, my magic breathed a sigh of relief. *This*, it seemed to whisper, *this is what you're made to do.*

Dozens of foreign consciousnesses hummed back at me, and that was only in my initial surroundings. I tethered my magic to them, penetrating their minds and grasping hold of their essences.

The sound of a stampede came from my left, and more

howls and screams rose. Whatever they were, they were coming, but they weren't in my vicinity yet. They were still far off.

Stop whatever is hunting me, I commanded the creatures I'd taken control of.

All of the animals rose from the Wood's floor like sentries coming to life. Creatures of various sizes with a range of intelligences and magical capabilities marched toward the rumbling ground.

Hisses came next as slithering snakes appeared on the Wood's floor, wiggling from underground burrows to answer my call.

Sweat beaded on my upper lip as magic cascaded out of me. Yet even though I had to concentrate, I didn't feel any hint of fatigue. The opposite happened. Power surged through me, as though multiplying as I used my forbidden magic. It was as if my magic was rewarding me for commanding it as it'd always sought.

Howls and screams tore through the air just as a herd of horrifying-looking animals burst through the foliage—not like the creature Kole had fought but still just as terrifying. They ran on two legs, backs hunched over, arms short and stubby but talons on their ends. They were hairless and eyeless, yet they seemed to know exactly where I was.

I zoomed ahead on my carpet and commanded my sentries to attack.

A clash of hairless bodies and fur came from my left just as my controlled creatures formed a wall at my side. More screams rose, and I dared a look to see what was happening.

My jaw dropped. *Hundreds* of animals were fighting, more sentries appearing as they answered my magic's call.

Teeth gnashed. Claws tore. Maws ripped.

Blood began to soak into the Silventine Wood's soil, bathing the ground scarlet as I took more control of those around me, and then I pushed my magic to extend farther until it ensnared the hairless creatures too.

The fighting instantly stopped, and sheer magic pounded out of me.

Hundreds. I had hundreds of animals under my command. Yet I felt like I could control more. Thousands, perhaps tens of thousands. Power soaked through my essence, intoxicating in a way. My magic was even stronger than I'd ever imagined it could be, but my uncle's teachings from my childhood came back to me just as fast.

"You must never control others, Prim."

But I knew here in this deadly Wood, even my uncle would understand. It was either kill or be killed, and I had no plans to die today.

I zoomed forward even faster, watching the seekerill's needle to ensure I was still going the right way.

Directly in my path, the heads of two larpanoons appeared, lifting from where they'd been smelling something on the ground. They were only five paces away.

My magic surged toward them, and when I pierced their

minds, they roared in anger. The shock of it nearly made me tip off the carpet.

More sweat poured from me, but I pushed my magic to its max. Worming my way through the magic encasing the larpanoons, I forcefully took control of them too.

Limply, the feared predators fell to the ground, growing entirely docile, and I flew right over them.

Breathing a sigh of relief, I looked at the seekerill again. It vibrated more sharply than it ever had before. I was so close to the Stone. *So* close.

But then I felt it.

An ancient presence.

A magic unlike *anything* I'd ever felt before.

A slumbering entity seemed to rise up all around me, brimming with power and might, anger and hatred, and a terrible wrath and vengeance like I'd never felt before.

Ancient magic *exploded* in a shockwave through the trees.

It was the only warning I got before chaos unleashed.

CHAPTER TWENTY-SIX

The trees thrashed, their branches suddenly swinging violently. All at once, *everything* attacked me.

I cried out in terror as a vine ensnared me around the neck, wrapping around my windpipe. The seekerill made a high-pitched whining noise, alerting me to the fact that I'd almost reached the Stone, but before I could search for it, a foreign consciousness entered my mind.

Who are you, daring female of Mistvale Kingdom?

I jolted upright, and my fire element flamed from my hands, burning through the vine that was choking me. Gasping, I coughed and sputtered, then ripped the vine off me and gripped my throat. The plant fluttered away into nothing but ash.

I continued coughing violently, but before I could answer whatever being had mentally projected to me, another tree swung for me, and then a new creature launched itself from a branch, barreling right toward me.

I commanded my carpet to veer right at the last second and zoom away, but pounding footsteps came in my wake. Animals were chasing me. Pursuing me. I no longer had control of them.

The seekerill whined even higher, and I looked every which way. Magic cascaded out of me, and I managed to grab hold of some animals near me, ensnaring their minds and commanding them to protect me, but the entire forest was *attacking* me.

Those are my *creatures you toy with*, the ancient voice hissed.

"Who are you?" I called, so breathless I barely got the words out.

Another ear-piercing whine came from the seekerill, and then I saw it.

A glowing, shimmering light rose from the black Wood's floor, only fifty paces away. It sparkled with magic, pulsing rays of starlight emitting from its core. Its beauty and exotic power called to me. Begging. Demanding. Coaxing.

The Wishing Stone.

Stars Above, I was nearly upon it. I was so close. I'd actually *found* it!

I pushed the carpet to move faster, not to stop, and flooded the air around me with more fire, anything to stop the trees and plants from reaching me.

Answer me, you insolent girl! That ancient, primal all-seeing presence clouded my thoughts again.

"I'm sorry," I said aloud. "I'm so sorry. My name is Primelle Hollaran, and I'm only here to take the Wishing Stone. I mean you, the creatures of this land, and this forest no harm or disrespect."

Yet you kill my children. You toy with them as though you own them.

"I'm sorry," I sobbed as the Stone loomed. "Please forgive me."

I do not forgive. I only punish.

A crashing wave of magic rose like a tidal wave around me.

The glow from the Stone plunged into darkness, and all sense of where I was cut off.

Magic pushed me down, down, down.

And in that moment, I knew that the rumors had been right. It was the only thing that could explain any of this. A god's soul indeed slumbered within Silventine Wood. Its terrible power and might cascaded all around me. Through me. In me. Everywhere I felt, a galaxy of power responded.

I screamed. Terror exploded inside me. *Oh Gods. He's going to kill me.*

The feel of the carpet disappeared from beneath me, and the sentries I'd once commanded vanished entirely. I knew that I was seconds away from death. The ancient force, perhaps a god thought long extinct, had awoken in the forest, and he wouldn't stop until I was dead. Until I was nothing but ash, just like the dead plant life I'd scattered on the wind.

I'd failed. Failed Timith. Failed Gwenery. Failed myself. It'd all been for naught.

I clutched the lock of hair from Goddess Nuleef even harder, then grabbed Kole's charm too. The warrior would never know what'd happened to me. Neither would my family. Or Ree. I would just be another fairy who'd ventured into Silventine Wood and was never heard from again.

"I'm sorry," I whispered. "I'm so sorry, Gwen and Timith. I'm sorry that I failed you."

The pressure upon me built.

You deserve to be punished. My vengeance is all you'll get in this Wood.

The ancient god layered primal magic upon me, stacking and stacking it, burying me alive in its suffocating wrathful punishment.

Vengeance. Power. Death.

I was seconds away from crossing to the afterlife, and I could do nothing to stop him. My magic was immense, but it would never rival a true god's.

Punish. Punish. I shall punish you, female.

It suddenly struck me who had likely died here. Diredan, the God of Vengeance, was rumored to have once walked this land. But the ancient tomes said that he'd faded away, having not returned to the stars in time to reclaim his godly place. But he hadn't. He'd gone into hibernation here. A land he had apparently never left.

I curled inward, wishing so desperately that I could have told my aunt, uncle, and Ree goodbye, told them that I loved them, and apologized for leaving them when they needed me most. But I couldn't. My magic wasn't working. I couldn't even connect mentally one last time with them to tell them a fleeting goodbye. Worst of all, they would never know what became of me.

But just as I was about to succumb to Diredan's vengeance, a memory tingled in the back of my mind.

My studies. The texts I'd read. Who the God of Vengeance had once been mated to.

I sucked in a lungful of air, hoping against hope.

Hands shaking, I uncurled my fingers to reveal the lock of golden hair and beseeched the God of Vengeance.

"Please! Please hear my call, God Diredan!" I begged. "Even if you won't allow me to take the Stone, please at least let me live so my family doesn't die wondering what happened to me! I beg of you!"

I fought against his power with everything I had and held the lock of Goddess Nuleef's hair above my head. I didn't know if the hair was genuine, but the feeling of being squashed into oblivion abruptly halted.

The pressure lifted, just enough that I could suck in another breath.

But that terrible, awful presence hissed into my thoughts again, *What do you have there?*

My hand still shook, and it took me a moment to understand what Diredan was asking. I released my death grip on the hair. Darkness still loomed around me. Utter blackness. It was as if my soul had been suspended in nothingness.

Yet I could still speak. Still *feel*. "A gift. For you," I said haltingly. "I have a lock of Goddess Nuleef's hair. Please, it's yours. Just please grant me safe passage in return. I beg of you."

Everything stopped.

Time stilled.

The feel of impending death and that horrible pressure lifted even more.

Her hair? You have her hair?

"Yes." I opened my palm completely, my fingers shaking so violently that I nearly dropped it into the void.

A brush of wind stroked the hair. Tears fell in rivers down my cheeks. I hadn't even realized I was crying.

The goddess's hair was lifted from my hand as though phantom fingers had taken it.

Nuleef. My love.

I could barely breathe as I watched the lock of shining metallic hair rise before me, and then it hit me—the metallic border that had shone silver. It'd shone as brightly as the goddess's gold hair, as though her mate had never stopped calling her, beckoning her, and wishing their souls didn't part.

The ancient tomes spoke of the gods and goddesses who once walked the realm. It was rumored that some had bred with fae before they left our realm to venture back to the stars.

But some gods had stayed, either dying out from not returning to their celestial realm or choosing to morph into new beings.

And I knew, knew to my *bones*, that God Diredan had fallen here when his godly power had faded too much to return to the stars.

All at once, the horrible crushing sensation around me lifted completely.

The Wood returned around me. Darkness was still everywhere, but I could see once more.

I hovered on my carpet, the seekerill in front of me, and I was shaking so violently my teeth rattled. I had no idea if I'd gone anywhere at all or if the void the god had created had been an illusion and entirely in my mind. Regardless, I blinked rapidly, trying to clear my tears away.

Out of nowhere, Diredan spoke again. *You may pass, female of Mistvale Kingdom.*

Sagging, I nearly fell off my carpet, but just as fast, my eyesight sharpened.

Straight ahead of me, the Stone waited.

"Thank you," I whispered. Cautiously, still breathing so quickly I felt lightheaded, I began to move my carpet forward, fearful that at any moment the labile god would punish me again.

But as each second ticked by, his promise held.

The forest remained calm.

No creatures came for me again.

And right in front of me, the Wishing Stone waited.

Magic surged around the magical gem, and it washed over me as I approached it.

Disbelief filled me that my uncle's device had truly led me here. The irony that *his* invention would save him nearly made me weep anew, especially when the Stone fully appeared before me.

Laying upon the Wood's floor, in a small crater devoid of any plant life, the Stone sat. It was so beautiful, so blinding, that for a moment, all I could do was stare at it.

Its magic sang an ancient song of beauty and grace. Power vibrated around it so poignantly that it called to me as I reached for the shimmering gem.

It was a million colors all at once, oscillating and shifting from shade to shade, as though it were alive and breathing all on its own. Its magical essence vibrated the air around it, and I extended my hand to clasp it.

The second I touched the Stone, a brush of wind graced my cheeks. Tingles shot up my arms, and the urge to claim it as *mine* grew like a lifeforce inside me.

Yes, the Stone seemed to say as I lifted it. *You are worthy.*

A shout rose in the distance, a male calling and cursing.

Your warrior is looking for you. Diredan's ancient, primal voice again entered my mind. He chuckled. *So many have tried to enter my domain today, but entry has been barred. I do not like how you all want to play with my creatures.*

I held the Stone firmly, and it glowed and heated inside my hands. "Kole? He's here?"

He's been here since you entered, trying to find his way inside to follow you.

My eyes widened. *And Nym, Jessip, and Felix?* I cringed, waiting for the worst news, to hear that my friends had all been killed in their quest for the Stone.

The god laughed in my mind. *They turned back around the second they stepped foot past my perimeter. They were no match for me. Not like you.*

I sagged, breathing a sigh of relief that my Faewood friends still lived and that Kole remained outside, unharmed. "Thank you for letting me pass."

But the god disappeared, his interest in me forgotten. I was only a fleeting second in his slumbering eternal existence, and I knew he no longer felt me worthy of his time.

Not wanting to press my luck further, I held the Stone tightly and turned my carpet around, then zoomed back the way I'd come as fast as I could go.

The creatures of the Wood watched me pass, their magic brimming and their curiosity flowing, but they let me fly by, no longer trying to maim and kill me.

Increasing my speed, I barreled back to the forest's edge.

Ahead of me, the barrier loomed, the silvery essence calling to me.

I burst through the Wood's perimeter and gulped in a lungful of fresh air on the other side. Behind me, the Wood's energy pulsed, and above, the first few stars began to appear.

"Primelle!" Kole's roar came from farther away, and then a surge of magic billowed in front of me, and the warrior was there.

Wild eyes filled with terror gazed down at me. He grabbed my shoulders, his grip like steel. "I thought you were dead."

I shook my head rapidly. Tears formed in my eyes. Shaking and still processing the craziness of what had just happened in Silventine Wood, I gazed up at Kole's shining cerulean irises.

A grin bloomed across my face. "I got it, Kole. I found the Stone." Tears of happiness cascaded down my cheeks, and I held the glimmering gem up to him, revealing the coveted relic as it glowed as brightly as a sun from within and bathed the realm in a plethora of starlight colors. "I can save my uncle!"

CHAPTER TWENTY-SEVEN

Kole's face entirely closed off, his telltale mask falling into place. "You found it. You actually found it."

"Yes!" I jumped in excitement, and magic from the Stone hummed in my grasp. "Now, all I need to do is return to Whiteolf. *Legends of Our Realm* says I must be in close proximity to a fairy if my wish is to affect another. But I can save my uncle, Kole. He's not going to die!"

Kole's throat bobbed, and a crack in his mask appeared, but instead of the joy I expected to see, he looked . . . *devastated.*

My smile dimmed. "Aren't you happy for me?"

He abruptly tore a hand through his hair. "Prim, I'm so sorry, but—"

"Is this her?" another male said.

I jolted and peeked over Kole's shoulder.

Behind Kole and walking toward us was a male who was just as large and just as broad as Kole, but instead of also seeming surprised by this stranger approaching us, Kole nodded and replied stiffly, "Yes, this is Primelle Hollaran."

The second the male came to stand beside Kole, he gazed down at me with sparkling brown eyes. Blond hair, similar in shade to Opalin's, covered his head, and his light-brown skin shone in the twilight.

Instinctively, I shielded the Stone from him, slipping it beneath my cloak so he couldn't see it. But that was pointless. The brightness of the Stone and its constant emittance of starlight made it impossible to hide. It glowed right through the material.

"Who are you?" I demanded, all manners leaving me in my shock. I surveyed our surroundings. Snow glittered in the glowing moonlight, and I wondered if there were more than Kole and this male about.

But a quick check of the area confirmed that it was only the two of them. *But where did he come from?* Kole obviously knew him, making me think this new male had traveled here with him.

The male bowed at me but chuckled, apparently finding my bluntness amusing. "Jamie Axthrower at your service. A pleasure to meet you."

Axthrower. Sure enough, a huge ax was strapped to Jamie's back. "You're an Imperial Warrior as well?"

"Indeed," Jamie replied.

I supposed that made sense if he and Kole knew each

other, and I deduced that Kole must have mistphased Jamie back here with him.

I looked at Kole for confirmation, but he stood rigidly, not making eye contact, and I wondered if he was allowed to tell me anything about why Jamie accompanied him. Maybe his orders forbade it, and it briefly occurred to me that something had to be going on because Kole had just started to apologize to me.

But apologize for what?

I cocked my head at him. "Is Jamie here to do Imperial Council business with you?" My eyes went wide as it suddenly occurred to me *why* that might be. I whipped around, and magic surged out of me automatically, searching for a threat in the area. "Are there more of those *things* here? Did you need Jamie as backup?"

"No, Prim, that's not why." Kole sounded resigned. Apologetic. And again . . . *devastated.*

Unease grew in me anew, strengthening with each second that passed. Frowning, I peered up at the warrior, but Jamie cut in. "How much have you told her, Kole?"

Kole snarled in his direction. "I've told her nothing. She saw it with her own eyes in Inisville."

Jamie crossed his arms but didn't say anything further.

"What's going on?" I suddenly felt entirely discombobulated. Kole's somnolent energy wasn't helping, but whatever had caused two Imperial Warriors to venture here today didn't matter. I needed to save my uncle, and I needed to begin the long journey home on my carpet. Or rather, *Kole's* carpet. It didn't matter why Jamie had joined Kole, or what they'd been assigned to do in this Wood, or why Kole had even bothered returning here if he had other business to tend to. Essentially, it had nothing to do with me, but just like I'd predicted, the time had come where the warrior and I would have to say our goodbyes.

"I need to go back to Whiteolf." I glanced down at the carpet, and a thought struck me. It would take me days to venture back to the capital upon it, but maybe, just maybe, Kole would mistphase me there before he had to return to work. I bit my lip, hating to ask that of him, but I was desperate to return. I had no idea how much time my uncle had left. "Would you be able to transport me there? Please?"

Jamie scoffed. "Of course, he'll transport you there. He'll mistphase both of us to Whiteolf."

My eyebrows shot to my hairline. I tried to swallow my trepidation, and I gripped the Stone harder. "*Both* of us?"

"Indeed, upon our commander's orders," Jamie replied readily, then smiled as if his remark was to be expected.

Frowning again, I looked to Kole for an explanation. "What's he talking about?"

Kole dipped his head but didn't speak. His behavior again reminded me of when we'd first met, when he'd been a male of few words. Something was *definitely* going on, but Kole's Shield had locked down tight, and he obviously had no intentions of sharing anything with me. And since I refused to use my forbidden magic to read his mind, I was out of answers.

Stomach tumbling, I gripped the Stone tighter beneath my cloak. "Can we please leave? My uncle is waiting."

———————★

THE FACT that Jamie couldn't mistphase told me that Kole had never informed his fellow Warrior that such a feat was possible for any siltenite with enough magic to learn, or Jamie didn't possess enough magic.

I didn't ask which one it was.

Thankfully, before we left, the warriors let me collect my pack with my smutty novel and the precious book from the Isle of Song. They also let me extract the seekerill from the carpet's magic.

Everything else, though, we were leaving behind, including Kole's brand-new carpet.

I briefly wondered if anyone would ever return to collect Kole's carpet and my boxes. Most of my stuff was food and camping supplies. It was wasteful to leave it, and it would likely scatter and litter the land and sea. On impulse, I burned everything in a flash of elemental fire. Once everything had turned to ash, all that remained was Kole's carpet. But he didn't seem to care. He didn't even look at it twice or try to retrieve it, and since it was heavy enough, it wouldn't fly away and it would stay there until someone retrieved it.

"Ready?" Kole said.

I nodded, and the warrior grabbed ahold of both me and Jamie. He held our hands, not touching either of us more than what was needed for his mistphase.

Another bolt of trepidation jolted through me, and it occurred to me just as the realm fell out from beneath us that Kole had enough magic to mistphase *two* fae with him at once.

But that thought was there and then gone in the flurry of mist and shadows, air and wind.

The mistphase was over in a blink, and we landed back on solid ground, rematerializing in Whiteolf. The second I had my wits about me, my jaw dropped at how precisely Kole had transferred us.

Kole had mistphased us *exactly* to where my family lived, right at the bottom of the stairs leading up to my aunt and uncle's house and out of the busy street. It suddenly struck me that I'd never given him the address, yet he'd known where to go. But I didn't give it another thought.

My uncle was waiting.

I squeezed Kole's hand tightly in gratitude. "Thank you."

Before he had a chance to reply, I sprinted up the stairs.

Heart tripping anew, I burst through the front door. Verin shrieked. The servant was in the adjacent chamber to the entryway, using charms to clean the sitting room.

"Primelle, you're back already?" Her gaze dipped to the shining Stone within my cloak, and her eyes grew as wide as saucers. "You *found it?*"

"I did." I grinned.

She took a step forward, but then Kole and Jamie crossed the threshold behind me, and she froze. I glanced over my shoulder, then remembered that for whatever reason, the warriors had been ordered to accompany me back to Whiteolf. But I hadn't realized that meant they'd stay.

I didn't bother to ask what they were up to now.

"Is Timith in his chambers?" I asked the servant.

Verin's head bobbed, and her gaze glued to the floor. "Yes, Miss Hollaran."

I made a beeline for the stairs and bounded up them, not bothering to introduce the warriors. Kole followed me, his aura pounding at my back, but I didn't feel Jamie's energy and figured he'd stayed downstairs.

It didn't matter. I just needed to get to my uncle.

"Aunt Gwen?" I called. "Aunt Gwen, where are you?"

The door opened to my aunt and uncle's bedchambers, and she stepped into the hall. I nearly collided with her since I was moving so fast.

"Prim!" Gwen's eyes widened, even more so when she saw Kole behind me.

"Look! I found the Stone. I actually found it!" I thrust it toward her, pride beaming through me. "I can save Timith!"

Her jaw dropped as she beheld the sparkling gem that shone with radiant starlight, but instead of throwing the door open and ushering me inside, she stayed in front of the door and said, "Gods and Goddesses, you did it!"

"Yes!"

She appraised Kole again, and I frowned. "Aunt Gwen, what are you waiting for? Don't you understand what this means? I can save Timith. I just need to be near him when I cast my wish."

Jaw clenching, she gave Kole a barely concealed sneer, then addressed me. "He's not well, Prim. Not well at all."

"Of course, he's not. That's why I got the Stone." I again tried to move past her, but she blocked me once more.

"He's taken a turn for the worse." She eyed Kole again, her look hard, and I glanced between the two of them.

Kole's chin was dipped, and his jaw was clenched so hard the muscle jutted out. It suddenly struck me that he hadn't said a word, and my aunt didn't seem confused by his presence.

Bafflement strummed through me. "Do you two know each other?"

Kole's throat bobbed, and my aunt's lips pursed. Her nostrils flared, and barely concealed hatred flowed from her toward Kole. "Let's go downstairs."

She made to clasp my arm, but I jerked away. "Go downstairs? Are you kidding me? I have the *Stone*, Gwen. I can *save Timith!*"

I pushed past her, not letting her deter me a third time, and hurried into their bedchambers. The second I did, I stopped short.

Pitch blackness surrounded me, and the feeling of imminent death followed.

"Oh Gods, I got here just in time." Stale air filled my nose, and my magic activated. My sensory eyesight made everything come into focus just as my mental magic reached out on its own accord. A heartbeat responded, slow, but still beating, and a body lay in the bed under the covers. My magic recognized the fairy as my uncle, but . . .

I cocked my head. "Uncle Timith?" I couldn't see much of him since he was mostly covered, but when I stepped closer, and his face appeared, everything in me grew cold.

He looked like my uncle but *different*.

Pale skin, hollowed cheeks, and the tips of fangs appeared between his lips. Despite still looking fae, he reminded me of . . .

"Stars Above." I launched myself toward the bed, but Kole was suddenly behind me, holding me back.

"Stop, Prim. We should go downstairs."

I struggled against him. "What in the realm are you talking about? I need to save my uncle! He's—" I gasped, barely able to breathe. "He looks kind of like . . ." Tears clouded my eyes, and I nearly gagged. "Oh Gods, Kole, is he becoming one of those *things*?"

"Yes, he is, or at least a different version of one. You can't save him."

I turned in his arms, my jaw dropping. "Of course, I can

save him. I have the *Stone*! I will be granted *any* wish with it. Let me go."

Regret filled his eyes, but he shook his head. "No."

"No? Did you really just say *no*? I have the Wishing Stone, Kole. *Anything* is possible with it, even curing him. I can save him. I *can*."

From the doorway, Aunt Gwen gave Kole another scathing look, but when she addressed me, her voice was thick with unshed tears. "It's not safe anymore to be near him, Prim. They're saying it's advanced enough that he can infect us."

"Infect us? But we've been around him ever since he fell ill, and neither of us have gotten sick. Stars and galaxies, I'm going to pull my hair out! Don't you *understand*? I have the *Stone*. I can *save him* right now, even if he can make us sick."

Gwen sucked in a breath, and tears shimmered in her eyes. "I know you can, you beautiful, brilliant, and brave girl. But they won't let you save him, Prim. The Imperial Warriors have orders to take the Stone from you once you arrived safely back in Whiteolf. They're not going to let you keep it or cast your wish." A low growl came from Kole, but my aunt shot him a reproachful look. "Well, it's true, isn't it? That's what you and the other warrior said earlier today."

Earlier today?

Numb shock bolted my feet to the floor. I glanced at Kole, my stomach falling . . .

Falling.

Falling.

"You were *here* today? That's why it took you so long to get back?" Of course. That was why he hadn't needed the address. He'd been here before.

Shaking, I could barely get my voice to work. I was going to be sick. I was going to vomit.

"You're . . . you're going to take the Stone from me, Kole? You're going to *steal* it?"

Kole's face was the portrait of steel. Hard. Smooth. And entirely unbreakable. But beneath his Shield, guilt burned. Heavy, hot, and unrelenting *guilt*.

And that was when it hit me.

He'd truly received orders when he'd left me.

His job had changed. It was no longer to track and kill the *things* in the Wood but instead to find me and steal the Wishing Stone that was rightfully *mine*.

"Kole?" The word came out choked, disbelieving. I thought back to our previous week together, the random encounters, the joy I'd felt in our budding friendship, the crazy attraction I felt toward him that I knew he felt too, and the fact that I'd so easily believed that I could trust him.

I'd trusted him completely. I'd even told him things I'd only told Ree before.

"No, *no*." I shook my head rapidly. "Please tell me you wouldn't do that, even if your commander told you to. Please don't. I *trusted* you."

Not one line on his face moved.

Not one breath lifted his chest.

"Oh my Gods. You're truly going to take it from me," I finally whispered. "I trusted you to help me, but you're just following orders, no matter what those orders are. You don't care if it's *me* you're stealing from."

Before I could comprehend what was happening, the warrior took the Stone out of my hands. Kole pried it away from me so easily, taking it from me in a moment of weakness when I was still reeling over his betrayal.

As soon as the Stone left me, I gasped, realizing what he'd done. I reached for it, tried to take it back, tried to reclaim what was *mine*, but he held it out of reach.

"Give that back to me!" I snarled. "I need to save Timith!"

"We're going downstairs, Primelle." Kole's voice was hard. Detached. As though it came from eons away. Guilt still burned beneath his Shield, yet he didn't return the Stone.

And then he said something that would ring through my memories until the end of time.

"Your uncle can't be saved."

CHAPTER TWENTY-EIGHT

I was numb. Broken. Destroyed. Dying inside.

All of my efforts that I'd done to save my uncle hadn't worked. All of it had been for *nothing*.

Gwen's arm was around my shoulders. She was leading me down the hallway, as though I was a toddler all over again, and she had to guide me. Care for me. Hold me.

I walked woodenly at her side, yet instead of numbness in her aura, rage filled it.

"We can't fight them," she whispered in my ear. "I tried. Trust me, I *tried*, but the Council has made its decision. The warriors told me that if you found the Stone, they were going to take it so the Council could cast its single wish. Not you."

We walked down the stairs, one foot moving in front of the other.

One step.

Two steps.

Three steps.

Somehow, I got from the second floor to the first.

All the while, Kole walked behind me, his Shield locked down tighter than I'd ever felt it before.

"Look what I found," Jamie called to Kole, then inclined his head toward Verin. "This appears to be an elixir of some kind that was hidden in her quarters."

I halted in the entryway.

Somehow, I was in the entryway, and Jamie was in front of me.

I'd completely forgotten about him.

The second Imperial Warrior stood with Verin beside him. But instead of the servant offering him tea or refreshments or ushering the warrior to a place to sit and wait, she stood next to him, *shackled*.

Blue cuffs encircled her wrists.

"Why have you arrested her?" my aunt demanded.

"We have reason to suspect she may be involved in what happened to your husband," Jamie replied, then inclined his head toward me. "Although, we're starting to wonder if Primelle was actually her intended victim."

Me?

Me?

"What?" I said dumbly.

Jamie widened his stance, standing casually, *easily*, as if what he was saying and doing was just another normal day's work as an Imperial Warrior. As if *any* of this was normal. As if the realm wasn't falling down around us.

Jamie pulled a glass box from his pocket. Inside the box lay a small vial with liquid in it, although there was barely any liquid left. Only drops remained.

Gwen's mouth dropped. "What is that?"

"That's a good question, but considering the magic that comes off of it if you remove it from this box, I would guess to say that it's an incredibly powerful potion. I've never felt power like it before."

"And you found that in Verin's room?" Gwen demanded, her tone hard, and her aura ratcheting up even higher.

Jamie nodded toward Verin. "Indeed. I found it in her quarters, exactly where you said things can be hidden in that room."

Aunt Gwen's eyes narrowed, and she hissed at the servant, "What is that potion?"

Verin's gaze stayed on the floor, her shoulders folded inward.

Fog filled my mind. I still didn't understand what was happening or why Jamie was saying these things. All I could think about was that Kole had the Stone. *My* Stone.

And Kole had said Uncle Timith couldn't be saved.

Kole's silence continued to fill the room behind me, but his pounding aura leaked through his Shield, as though he could no longer fully contain it. Yet he still kept the Stone. Still kept what was mine.

I wanted to crumple to the floor. I'd been so foolish to trust him.

So foolish.

Jamie inspected what was inside the glass box again, not even seeming to notice that I could barely keep from collapsing. "What happens if somebody swallows this, Verin? Does it turn them into what Timith is becoming?"

But Verin's eyes stayed downcast, her lips sealed.

He *tsked.* "The king and queen won't be happy to hear it if that's the case, especially since Primelle has been living in this home."

The king and queen? For the briefest moment, my mind turned. "The king and queen know about me?" I mumbled, then looked to Gwen for an answer.

But Gwen's attention was on Verin again, her eyes hard, her mouth a tight line. "Did *you* do this to my husband? Are you responsible for my sweet Timith's state?"

Verin's silence continued, and she remained with her head down. Always so submissive. So meek.

"Cut the act," my aunt sneered. "We all know you're not subservient if you truly intended to use whatever that potion is against us."

Verin's head lifted, but instead of looking fearful or contrite, or like she was about to plead her innocence, her expression *burned* with rage. So much so that I lurched back.

Verin's lips curved, and something truly evil stirred in her expression. "You're all pawns in the game of night. I am merely a servant, but my liege will get to her eventually. Now that we know for certain who she is." Her gaze shifted to me.

Gwen gasped, and Kole snarled so violently that I jumped, but Verin ignored them all and continued looking at *me* with a look of triumph.

"So we were right to suspect her," Jamie said quietly.

My heart pounded so hard it felt as if it would beat out of my chest. I gripped my aunt's hand. "Gwen, what's going on? Why is Verin saying these things? Why do the king and queen know of me?"

Jamie moved Verin away from me, and Kole shifted to my side. "Prim, come with me. Please," he said, his voice hoarse. But when his hand touched my lower back, I jolted away from him as though burned.

"*Don't* touch me."

Kole's eyes widened, and his throat bobbed.

I had no idea what was going on. What was happening. But I'd had one goal and one goal only since my uncle had fallen ill.

I eyed the Stone again, still held within Kole's grip. Magic crackled inside me. Deadly magic. All-*consuming* magic. I could take the Stone from him. Command him to give it to me, turn him into a puppet just for a moment, then I could save my uncle.

Something primal reared up in me, scorching my insides as though burned.

No.

That *thing* in my chest begged. Pleaded.

Not him.

I shoved that instinctual reaction down just as Kole stiffened.

"Don't do anything stupid, Miss Hollaran," Jamie warned, his voice low and deadly. Eyes narrowing in my direction, he added, "This is all for the best."

Aunt Gwen's hand encircled my wrist. The feel of her stopped the flash of impulsiveness that'd reared up in me.

"Not like this, Prim. *Not* like this," Gwen whispered.

I turned entirely rigid, disbelief coursing through me.

What am I doing?

This wasn't me. I didn't lash out at fae. I didn't hurt others, even if the fairy responsible for my fury had torn my heart open and had watched it bleed before him. That still didn't warrant me becoming just as cruel as him. *Have my aunt and uncle taught me nothing?*

My shoulders sagged, and my rage evaporated as quickly as it'd started.

Shame coursed through me. Absolute *shame.* My uncle would be so disappointed if he knew what I'd almost just done. Even if I'd been motivated by intentions to save him, he would be appalled. He'd spent *full seasons* teaching me how to control myself so I would never inflict my forbidden magic on anyone, and if he were well and whole right now, he would be looking at me with utter devastation.

"I'm sorry," I sobbed.

My aunt gripped me harder. "Please, Prim. I know how you're feeling. I've been feeling it too, ever since they arrived today and demanded to see Timith, but come with me. *Please*." My aunt's desperate plea broke through my grief. She tugged me toward the sitting room. "Please, Primelle. Let's all sit down."

———✦

SOMEHOW, all of us ended up in the sitting room that smelled of lemons and gleamed from the cleaning charms Verin had just used on it. Still in the entryway, still shackled, Verin waited for whatever the warriors had in store for her.

I sat as rigid as a board on the sofa, my aunt beside me while Kole and Jamie sat in the chairs across from us. The warriors looked entirely out of place in their fighting tunics with their giant weapons strapped to their backs. If it'd been a normal day, I would have made light of it, but at the moment, I couldn't imagine ever being joyful again.

"There's something I need to tell you," Gwen said.

I could feel Kole watching me. Always watching me.

I was *certain* that something genuine had sizzled between us during our time together, yet whatever that'd been, it'd now fizzled into non-existence, and even if a part of him did truly care for me, his allegiance was to the Imperial Council.

Not me.

I felt so betrayed, even though a part of me realized that

was naïve and stupid. After all, I'd been telling myself all along that he owed me nothing.

So foolish.

Gwen took a deep breath. "Primelle?" I started at the sound of my name and realized Aunt Gwenery was trying to talk to me. Tears burned her eyes.

"Yes?" I rasped.

She took my hands, both of them, and held them tightly. "I'm not your aunt, and Timith isn't your uncle."

For a moment, I just stared at her. Blinked at her. *"What?"*

"We're not your relatives."

It felt as though the realm tipped from beneath me. I shook my head. "Why would you say that? Of course, you are. Timith is my father's brother."

"No, he's not." Her grip tightened. "He's not related to your parents in any way. The crown commissioned us to raise you since Timith and I were childless, and they knew your uncle quite well from his service to them. They knew he and I could be trusted and that we'd provide a loving, safe home for you. They knew we'd keep you safe. That we would provide you with a chance at a life you otherwise would have never had. That we would teach you to find a place in our kingdom."

Blood rushed through my ears, drowning out her words, but she continued even though I could barely hear her.

"Until today, my lips were sealed by a fairy bargain. I couldn't speak of it, couldn't tell you, but when these two showed up"—she glanced at Jamie and Kole—"Timith and I were released from our bargain with the crown."

My head began to pound. What she was saying couldn't possibly be true. To be told my uncle would die, then to lose the Stone, then to be told that Gwenery and Timith weren't my relatives and never had been, that they'd been lying to me for my entire life . . .

I shook my head rapidly, my movements so fast I could barely see. "No. No. No."

My aunt gripped my hands harder, her faint Nolus lineage strength holding me in a death grip. "I'm so sorry, Prim. We never wanted to lie to you. I swear on all the gods and goddesses that was the last thing we ever wanted, but we could never tell you." Tears burned in her eyes. "But it doesn't change the fact that we *love* you. We love you so much. You're our darling girl, and you always will be, no matter what."

My breaths grew so short I could barely breathe.

Kole growled across from me. "This is too much." His words grew low and filled with tension. "This is too much for her in one day."

"She deserves to know!" my aunt snapped.

Gwenery's grip loosened, and she ran her hands soothingly over mine. Soft yet strong. Capable yet firm. She'd always been that to me, a comforting hug. Yet she'd also taught me resilience and had believed that I could always figure out a way to accomplish things on my own, like I'd done with the Stone. She'd taught me that I had strength within me. Kindness. Compassion. That I would always choose to do the right thing. That I would choose light over dark.

She and my uncle had intrinsically instilled that in me.

They'd taught me so much. Loved me unconditionally. I'd found the Stone because I'd believed in myself, and that belief had stemmed from her and from Timith's endless love, patience, encouragement, and teaching. He'd raised me to be who I was today. They *both* had.

Yet, my entire childhood had been a lie.

"Who are my parents, if we're not related?" I asked, my voice barely above a whisper.

Gwen's lips downturned, and slowly, she shook her head.

"You can't tell me?"

"No." She huffed out a breath, her words forlorn. "They've asked us not to. In time, they will tell you on their own. There's so much more to your story, Primelle, but I'm not allowed to share it."

"My parents are *alive*?"

Her lips pursed, so I looked to Jamie, even though I felt Kole watching me, his gaze so intense it burned as brightly as the Stone in his grasp.

"Do you know who my parents are?" I asked the warrior.

Jamie shrugged. "I do, but I can't release that information either."

He knew, which likely meant Kole knew too.

I glanced at the dark-haired warrior. Kole's focus on me intensified, and his knuckles turned white around the Stone.

"You know who they are?"

His jaw locked, his mask slipping, but he didn't reply.

"Did you know the entire time?"

He looked down, and the guilt in his aura *exploded*.

I sucked in a breath. Fresh tears blurred my sight. Just when I thought my heart couldn't break any more, it ruptured anew in a gushing wound. And to think I'd told him the story of how my parents had died. And all along, he'd known that story was a lie.

Betrayal cut into me so deeply it felt as though I'd been stabbed.

"You need to come with us, Prim," Kole said hoarsely, his aura like a rising tidal wave. "You're not safe here anymore, not if your true identity has been leaked. Whoever Verin's working for, they know where you are."

My true identity. Whatever that was. And whoever *they* were.

Tears shone so thickly in my eyes when I finally met his gaze that I could barely see him. But I locked down my emotions. Locked them down as tight as they would go. "Were you following me the entire time I was hunting the Stone?"

Kole's attention dropped to his feet, but not before another flash of devastation filtered through his mask.

My breath rushed out of me. "And when we met for the first time in Whiteolf, when you stopped Abel, was that a coincidence, or did you plan that too?"

His throat bobbed in a swallow, the only evidence that he'd

even heard me. "I was already following you by that point and saw that you needed me to intervene."

Silence filled the room, so thick I could cut it. I finally licked my lips and managed to get out, "I see, so *everything* was fabricated."

"Not everything." His voice shook. "Not everything, Prim."

Jamie's eyes narrowed in his direction, but I no longer knew if I could believe Kole or not. I didn't know who or what was real anymore. Least of all Kole.

Aunt Gwenery reached for me, but I fell back in my seat. Numbness crept through me as it sank in that nothing with Kole had been by chance, and all of our encounters along the road had likely been planned.

Memories flashed back to me rapid fire of every single crossing we'd had. Kole hadn't been patrolling the Wood or tasked with stopping creatures like the one he'd killed outside of Inisville. He'd been assigned to me. For what reason, I still didn't know.

Regardless, in all of the time we'd spent together, he'd let me believe that he was merely along for the ride, and that our encounters were entirely coincidental, and that I could join him if I wanted to for the last leg of my journey—

My breath sucked in, and I narrowed my gaze at him. "Did *you* steal my carpet in Inisville?"

He shifted in his seat and finally met my eye. All luster left his expression. He looked resigned. Dead. And in that unspoken response, I knew. I *felt* it.

"You did," I said stiffly. "You stole it so I would be forced to return home or join you. Everything you ever said or did with me was a lie."

"Prim . . ." Kole's voice was rough. Hoarse.

Jamie stood. "It's time to go, Primelle. For your safety, you need to come with us."

"Now?" My aunt shot to her feet. "But her uncle—"

"He's not her uncle," Jamie replied.

Kole growled quietly. "Jamie, watch it."

Despite Kole's warning, Jamie just shrugged. But hearing that . . .

Pain exploded in my chest, so much so that I grabbed my collar. I could barely breathe. Everything in me broke.

Not my uncle.

But he was. To me, Timith still was my beloved family member, even if we weren't related.

But Jamie *was* right in one aspect. Apparently, Timith wasn't my blood uncle. He never had been, but he still felt like a father to me, and I still loved him. Loved him fiercely no matter what he and Gwen had done. He might have raised me under false pretenses, but he'd genuinely loved me just as I loved him, and now, because of whatever was going on, of who I truly was, Timith was going to die.

Gwen pulled me to my feet, and I knew that if I *wasn't* going to use my magic to command anyone, that I couldn't fight this. It was either that I turned into the fairy that I swore to myself and my aunt and uncle that I would *never* become, or I accepted whatever they had in store for me.

I looked toward the stairwell, toward where my uncle lay.

"I'm sorry I failed you, Timith," I whispered. "I'm so sorry." My legs once again felt like they could give out at any second, and a surge of magic shimmered inside me at the thought of Uncle Timith's death being so imminent.

If death was even what waited for him.

Jamie blurred to my side, and it wasn't until something cold clasped over one of my wrists and a huge rush of magic coasted over me that I realized what he'd done.

My jaw dropped as I gazed down at the single blue glowing cuff encircling my left wrist. Jamie had *shackled* me with one of their magic-suppressing restraints.

My heart abruptly thundered, and Kole took a step toward me, but I stared at Jamie. "Why?"

It was the only word I could get out.

"This is for your protection, believe it or not," he said.

Gwen hissed. "Take that off her right now. Primelle isn't like that. She would never hurt other fae."

But Jamie shook his head. "Perhaps not, but I'm following orders. The cuff stays."

Gwen's aura rose fiercely, and her fingers curled into her palms until her hands had balled tightly at her sides. "You never said you would arrest her."

"She's not being arrested." Kole's voice was wooden. "We're only taking her to protect her."

"That cuff speaks otherwise," my aunt shot back.

My lips parted, and my stomach again fell down, down, down. But I didn't enlighten the warriors to the fact that their cuff didn't work on me. Didn't enlighten them to the fact that my magic could still be called forth in a second's notice.

But it wasn't like it mattered anyway. I wouldn't use my magic to command them. I *wouldn't* become the fairy that I promised my uncle I would never be.

If I were to do anything to honor his memory, I would honor *that*.

I gazed upward at the warrior whom I'd stupidly been smitten with. But that was before, before I knew everything was a lie. "Where are you taking me?"

Kole's throat bobbed, and his eyes blazed. "Somewhere safe."

And even though I had no idea where that was, something in his words rang true, which meant I had a feeling Kole would continue being my assigned Imperial Warrior, but I had no idea what was to come.

Bindings of Lore, book two, in *Fae of Legends & Lore*

Taken by the Imperial Council and guarded by Kole, Primelle is thrust into a life she never wanted.

Secrets are revealed, duties are demanded, and a dark force rises.

Now, if Prim and Kole fail to uncover and stop the force that's been hunting Prim since she was born, the entire kingdom will fall.

Krista Street is a Minnesota native but has lived throughout the U.S. and in another country or two. She loves to travel, read, and spend time in the great outdoors. When not writing, Krista is either chasing her children, spending time with her husband and friends, sipping a cup of tea, or enjoying the hidden gems of beauty that Minnesota has to offer.

THANK YOU

Thank you for reading *Stone of Legends*, book one, in the *Fae of Legends & Lore* trilogy.

To learn more about Krista's other books and series, visit her website. Links to all of her books, along with links to her social media platforms, are available on every page.

www.kristastreet.com